FIVE   COUPLES

Shirley Mason

Disclaimer

Five Couples is fiction. Names, characters, places, and incidents either are the product of the author's imagination or are used fictitiously. Any resemblance to actual persons, living or dead, events, or locales is entirely coincidental.

ISBN-13: 978-0692900345
ISBN-10: 0692900349

Published by Mason Publishing
Green Valley, AZ 85622-3212
www.shirleymason.com

Other works by Shirley Mason

The Hand at the Top of the Stairs
(detective dtories)

Chasing Neutrinos
(poetry collection)

The Cav Neumont series

The Strength of Water	(Vol. 1)
The Strength of Time	(Vol. 2)
The Strength of Love	(Vol. 3)
The Strength of Mercy	(Vol. 4)

FIVE COUPLES

Shirley Mason

For Marian

I

The Clarks

As Melody tried to button one of the twin's pajama top, and kept getting it wrong, she thought about what Cass, her husband and father of their twins, had just said. Instead of seeing buttons, she saw words. What Cass had said repeated in her head, swelling it with—it felt like—sludge, making it impossible for sense to come through. She would try again with the buttons, undoing them, re-doing. Focus. The child, looking down at the crookedness of the pajama said, "You're silly, mom," and Melody would try again. But she still couldn't see the buttons, because Cass's words had fractured her space like light through a prism. He had said he didn't love her.

"Oh." Her porcelain face had been about to fall, but she pulled it back and stacked it up into a stoic wall. Cassian Clarke had asked her for a divorce a few times before, but he had never said he didn't love her. Now, this was something new to get used to. Something different from just his falling in love with his secretary. (They were all so understanding; understood him so well.) But always, in time, Cass would grow tired of Miss Priss (the latest is Jocelyn), fire her (too uncomfortable in the office), come home to Melody, bare his soul, apologize and promise her he would be faithful from now on. So now, she had learned to wait out each of his secretaries. Yet, even though she had her own affairs occasionally—and she did not confess and did not apologize—Cass's betrayal still hurt. Now even more so with this latest declaration.

This night Cass had slipped in the door, set down his briefcase, loosened his tie, hugged the twins, and poured wine for Melody and for himself. So as not to weaken his resolve he would begin by not giving Melody her usual peck on the cheek. The twins had settled down in the family room to wait for dinner. And as soon as Cass and Melody were seated to relax out of earshot of the twins—dinner keeping warm in the oven—he had started.

"Melody, I want a divorce. It's been a dry two years for me, and I do not love you. For two years I have not been happy. I love Jocelyn and what she and I have between us is rare and special, like no other." He raced on before something could block him. "And I don't want to spend the rest of my life without her." His sentences came out edgy and plain, emotion held in check. He had more to say from the little speech he'd practiced, but somehow his breath ran out. Not a man given to say much anyway in personal situations, his voice had been green and awkward. The look on Melody's face hadn't been exactly grief, he thought. Didn't she give a fig? Couldn't she say something? Instead, he later recalled when he became able to hear, that she had merely said, "Oh," and sipped her wine. The balloon of denial he pictured her throwing up had never held air.

She had already heard about Jocelyn and had figured that it was only time until she would hear more, something more serious; that was always the way it went. But this time, the ringing in her head caused by Cass's announcement was tempered by the charge of electricity that had passed between her and the man she met during that day at the New York Boat Show. He had been demonstrating the large yacht that was across the aisle from the much smaller cruiser she represented. They had worked in view of each other for much of the day, which was the first day of the show, open only to the marine trade and lightly attended. Melody had had time to practice her sales routine, and to review the cruiser's specifications. Attendees could ask the strangest questions and one had to be prepared—know it all. She had gossiped with other models, laughed a lot, and looked around for customers to attract. That was when she saw him, a beacon of silver hair, standing on the deck of that huge yacht across the aisle. She watched his movements, his commanding presence. He looked tempered and toned, and his smile riveted her. Even from where she stood across the aisle, she could catch a flash of blue eyes. He seemed special. She had to make an effort to avoid staring, although it was not unknown for her to explore options outside of marriage, and Cass never concerned himself with her activities.

That was good, for during the day the yachtsman came over, introduce himself, and give her his card. His name was Robert Randall. She had spent the remainder of the day thinking about him, and therefore, Cass's speech hadn't hurt too much. Melody could only think about one man at a time.

Minimal dinner conversation served only to entertain the twins, and with dinner over Cass helped Melody with cleanup, their cold shoulders careful not to touch. Then Melody went to pack her tiny white shorts—be ready in the morning to leave for the convention center. She tried to put Cass's latest secretary out of mind, and as she brushed her teeth and hair and got ready for bed, she managed to overlay Miss Pris with Robert Randall.

The twins had had their bath and wanted Cass to read to them. He was good at that, mindless work gave him twenty minutes to keep out the world. Cass opened the book, *Sam Bangs and Moonshine*, a story of love, betrayal, and rescue, the twins' favorite. He had read it to them already so many times they could recite the words along with him. Baxter, their cat, must know it by heart as well; he listens. Cass's mind wandered while he read: he would rescue Jocelyn (although he didn't think of it that way); she needed him. Such a beautiful gal, and what a beautiful heart, and those rich brown curls that drew his hand to touch. And Jocelyn understood him so well. She was well worth the jolt he had delivered to Melody, and well worth the changes he wanted to make.

"Go on Dad, we want to hear about Bangs getting rescued."

Cass gazed off into space as he pictured Melody's reaction. She didn't understand—this one was for real. He would never again find a love like Jocelyn's. Some in the office called her Josey; some called her Jo, but he wouldn't shorten that lovely soft name, so

3

feminine—just like Jocelyn herself yielding the charm and confidence of Cleopatra.

One of the twins gave the book a shake and Cass continued to read. Then he felt that familiar buzz in his pocket. He reached down for it, scanned his phone's display, and saw that the call was from Jocelyn. She's as excited as he is about what they have between them, he thought. And judging by her calls, maybe more so. If only she didn't call so much. However, today she was particularly jazzed because he had promised her he would tell Melody this evening, and ask her for a divorce. The power of feeling loved, feeling Jocelyn's desire. Seeing that ardent gaze in the morning when he arrived at the office. However, he would have to ask her to be more guarded at work. The company had a liberal atmosphere, but not to the point where it interfered with office functioning. He had before sent secretaries home crying when they had become clingy. The knowing glances and envy of his colleagues were another benefit. So secretaries —

"Dad. Get on with the story!" So Cass read and, to the twins' satisfaction, finished the book.

His phone buzzed again. He checked the display and turned off the phone. He didn't want it to buzz itself off the dresser during the night; though it shouldn't matter now whether Melody knew. He had told her. Now he didn't have to hide his calls.

2

The Randalls

As he selected his clothes, Robert Randall thought about the next day, the first show day for the public, the best opportunity for showing his yacht to the most people with the most money. Tycoons who ordered one of his creations gave no thought to the expense, and Robert's ocean-ready yachts were expensive. His exhibit was displaying the largest vessel in the show and more than a year's work had gone into its manufacture. Few attendees were buyers, but that was all right; part of the process. Boat shows were diversions and he could use a diversion. All he had to do now was lay out his clothing, try to sleep, and get to the convention center early.

Obsessive about order and neatness, he wanted everything ready before he turned in, and he set out deck shoes, khaki trousers, white shirt, and a navy blue blazer with his company's insignia. As he did this, he pictured himself working at the show and thought of the impression he would make. Despite his white hair, he was youthful and fortified with determined blue eyes. People noticed him. He was proud, and rightly so; instead of becoming a jet setter when he received a large inheritance, he had studied for a degree in marine architecture, hired top-notch marine designers and craftspeople, and built world class yachts. He deserved accolades, deserved to be admired, even envied.

He imagined smiling at the pretty women who would board with their husbands or boyfriends for a tour through his ship. And he had not been able to put out of mind the fascinating model who demonstrated the cruiser across the aisle. Ahead were six more days of opportunities for him to bathe in her admiration. She had said her name was Melody Clarke. He had felt waves of electric current from her meant just for him.

At this moment, Anna was organizing their children for bed, maybe reading to them. Anna, after ten years of marriage to Robert, no longer showered him with admiration. He put aside this thought and replaced it with a mental image of long-legged Melody. But before he could enjoy the image, their two young daughters bounded into the bedroom.

"Daddy," two voices exclaimed, "Mom said you would read to us."

Robert's laughter rang out as he swung them up, one on each arm. "Not tonight. Out, guys. And take Carter with you. I guess mom forgot that I have to turn in early to get lots of sleep for a long day at the show tomorrow. I'll be staying in Manhattan for the next week, but I'll call you guys every day."

After the girls shut themselves and Carter, their cat, on the other side of the door, Robert settled into bed. Anna would probably work late on a painting, and come to bed after he was asleep.

3

Lunch deepens a Connection

In the morning, Melody showered and dried her lustrous pale hair. Then she dressed and applied light makeup—her porcelain skin required so little. While Cass dished the twins' cereal, Melody finished packing for the show. She wanted the public to think of a summer breeze, though through the frosted pane of her walk-in closet, she could see lightly falling snow. She put topsiders into a drawstring bag and then into her valise where she had already placed white shorts, a turquoise shirt, and a bright and sunny yellow sweater. After she boarded the cruiser, she would change from winter clothes into these.

When boat show attendees saw Melody's perfect long, smooth legs swinging from her tiny white shorts, they had to come aboard and follow those legs through the thirty-five-foot cruiser and gazed at her legs while she demonstrated the cruiser's features. Then some attendees—forgetting the deep-water pit into which yachting expenses were said to flow—would put in an order for a boat. That was the effect Melody had.

Melody would smile constantly and flirt with the public as they slowly moved up the stairs and through the boat from stern to bow. For some of the morning, her position in the cruiser's cockpit provided opportunities, busy though she was, for keeping a lustful eye on Robert across the way on his yacht. She wondered about him. He looked young despite the white hair. A few times their eyes locked together.

At lunchtime, taking a book, she angled through the crowds and headed down to the cafeteria. She wondered if Robert broke for lunch and if so when and where did he go? Several places in the center would be good choices. It would be unusual to meet up with him. He could be anywhere. While she moved along the cafeteria line, thinking about him, she hardly noticed someone bumping her arm. Turning, she flushed, for looking down at her were Robert's searching eyes. Blue! My God, they were blue, she thought.

"I feared you weren't going to wake up." His smile spread a flush of warmth over her.

"Oh! I was looking for Tournedos a la Béarnaise." *Help me — this man is no ordinary human being.*

"Right." A soft chuckle animated his face. "I was as well, and also looking for caviar."

They laughed over this; though to hard working and hungry people the pans of hot food before them looked good. Robert chose a plate of flounder with green beans. Melody, jolted by his touch, couldn't have said which dish she selected; it sat there on a plate, something brown and solid, and presumably was edible. She searched for something to say next: something smart, not addled. She had known another meeting was inevitable. She had longed for it. They had a connection; even so, she was surprised. She didn't know that Robert had watched when she left for lunch, stopped his demonstration and sales-pitch in mid-sentence, and followed her.

"I made an extreme effort to have lunch with you," he said. "I told the customer to whom I was speaking. that suddenly, among the crowd, I saw someone I knew who had renal failure, and for whom I had to recommend a good kidney specialist. My customer looked at me in shock and said 'Go. Go.' And I fled after you. So, after I've defamed myself and perhaps lost a sale...several probably...you must eat with me." He stretched a wide smile down to her.

"Well, you are creative! Stories as well as boats. I hope your boats are more reliable than your stories."

"Madam," he said, pretending to be serious, "they are *not boats*. They are *yachts*. And much, much more reliable than my stories. Watch out for my stories."

8

"I think your *boat* must be the longest in the show, but certainly not as tall as your stories." She laughed.

"Ah, yes. *Victory* is absolutely the longest *boat*, if you will... ninety-three feet. Come over when you get a break and I'll give you a tour through my *boat*. It's far more interesting than looking at etchings...don't you agree? If you aren't joining someone why don't we share a table?" he asked as he looked out across the dining room. Now the line had moved forward such that they were at the cashier. "And this is on me," he said and he stepped around Melody to pay.

"Thank you," Melody said and she led them to an empty table.

Both feeling a bit awkward, they arranged their dishes before them. Melody nervously picked at her food, while Robert worked over his like a logger. She liked his eagerness, his easy grin. He spoke with a confident flow. He looked terrific in his navy blazer. Slender. Firm jaw that Melody's eyes clung to as he discussed the show's good attendance, and that he should sell a yacht or two. He went on in an excited manner, asked about her modeling assignments, learned that she lived in Manhattan with her husband and two children—twin boys.

Then there was a nervous pause with only the clicking of forks.

"Let me have your card. I might hire you to model for brochures," Robert said finally, "or to work for me at exhibitions. My plants are in Connecticut, but my literature and brochures are published by a Manhattan company."

Thrilled and not wanting it to show, Melody hesitated, tried to hold back an excited flush. She wanted to appear pleased, but not too eager. Then, after a pause, she dug into her purse for her card and handed it to him. Her little boat had just sailed into wonderful waters! This must be the most exciting man ever.

When she arrived home that evening, Louise, the sitter, had already served dinner to the twins, and for Melody had left dinner, keeping warm in the oven.

"Mr. Clarke called to say he was working late. I've fed Baxter and cleaned his box, and I've started the twins' bath. If you don't need me for anything else tonight I'll let myself out and see you in the morning at the same time."

"Thank you, Louise. You run along. I'll have a glass of wine while I watch the boys."

At times, Melody's back ached at the end of a long day modeling, and now she wanted to sit back, kick up her feet, relax, and listen to the twins' tub play. She thought about the day's work; it had been tiring. On this type of assignment, you could not let up. You had to be your best all day, look fresh and perky and, while constantly pointing out the boat's features, be cheerful down to the last customer. Talk yourself to death. Today, that had not been as hard as it might have been due to Robert's presence across the aisle. She knew he watched her when he could. Several times during the day, she sensed his eyes on her, and this had kept her in a state of tension, excited and bubbly. She reached for a towel and dried the twins, then helped them into their pajamas. They squeezed her with big hugs until she bounced them on their beds, pulled their covers up, and showered them with kisses.

"I don't like for daddy to work late," said a twin as he grabbed Melody's hand.

"I know, dear. And I'll be working late at the boat show this week. I'll ask daddy to try to be home early." She switched off the lamp, said goodnight, and gently closed their door behind her. She then stood a minute thinking, went to the phone and dialed Cass's office. No answer. She nibbled at her dinner, then cleaned up the dishes and sat before the T.V. without turning it on. As it were, two shows were competing for space in her thoughts: Robert's commanding image, and Cass did not love her.

The next days were long, tiring, and serious selling days for show exhibitors. Robert was constantly in demand. His knowledge and attention to detail had won worldwide interest in his yachts. Customers and future customers from around the globe looked for him at the show, and people who had no hope of owning one of his yachts, still wanted to see one, board it and walk around if possible. He reveled in his success but he needed to see its reflection on an intimate level. He had provided the best for himself and his family

—expensive sports cars, and a beautiful large estate—and, though happy with their style of living, it no longer impressed his wife, Anna, if it had ever. She hardly acted as if it mattered. In his opinion, she thought only about painting and the children. Despite the silver hair, he was only thirty-eight, and a little extra attention from pretty women kept him feeling like a stallion at the gate. So it was perhaps inevitable that Melody's appreciation would radiate through him, and for the next three show days, they continued to have lunch together. And each night as he lay in the hotel bed he thought not about sales, or yachts, or profit, or Anna and their children, but about Melody.

And each night, after Melody attended to the twins, and had dinner, as she lay in bed, she thought not about the twins, nor about Cass's declaration, nor his obsession with Joselyn, nor boat shows —she thought about and filled her head with Robert, his image.

4

Melody and Robert Entangle

On the fourth day Robert climbed up the stairs onto the cruiser where Melody worked, and waited until she was alone.

"I can't make lunch today," he said.

Her spirits hit bottom like an anchor. Each day she had looked forward to their lunch together. Without Robert's admiration and flirtation, she would feel as cold and damp as the day outside. There was a pause during which it seemed that he waited to see the effect his statement had, but she kept a chipper face—not wise to show too much disappointment.

"Because I'll be tied up with a buyer most of the day," he continued, "I'm staying in the city though tonight, and wonder if you will have dinner with me. We can discuss future photo ops."

With renewed buoyancy, Melody's spirit pulled up anchor; dinner with him was even better than lunch. "I'd love that," she said. "I'll have to check with Louise, my sitter, to be sure she can stay." It was more than likely that Cass would not be home for dinner, which pleased Melody further, as she would not have to feel guilty about not going straight home. And for the rest of the day she rode on such waves of excitement that her enthusiasm resulted in two sales. When the show closed for the day, she changed from summer clothes into street clothes that she had worn in the morning. Luckily, the black skirt with white silk blouse and long black coat with black boots would be suitable for a Manhattan dinner for which she had not prepared in advance.

As she and Robert left the convention center the cold from the blanket of snow covering the city caused them to pull together, her arm in his. They took slippery, cautious steps to the taxi that was to whisk them to the Top of the Sixes. He gripped her arm more than necessary. She eagerly held his arm more than necessary, and allowed her feet to slide more than necessary.

At the Sixes he fixed her with his smile and said, "Let me order for you, Melody. I eat here occasionally and know the dishes that the chef does best." He ordered a special wine, and while they waited, they talked about the snow and about how it had cleaned up the city. Their table gave on to a long view across snow-iced skyscrapers, and Manhattan appeared in magical black-and-white relief with millions of sparkling lights. They enthused about the boat show and the good attendance and laughed together at the "be-backers"—those who looked at a boat and said they would "be back." Melody's high continued; this was the best of all days: sales and dinner with Robert, the first time they could relax, not have to rush back to demonstrate boats.

"Considering the size of your yacht, I doubt you would have a lot of 'be-backers,' " she said.

"No. I usually know before the show exactly who will order. Much negotiating and planning has already taken place by then, and I guarantee those buyers a special show price. The rest are merely curious. Rarely does the public get to see inside yachts such as I build."

With appetites amplified by the cold and snowy January weather, their lively conversation was willingly halted by the arrival to their table of Filet de Boeuf a la Gourmandine, and eating began in earnest. But soon, Robert found moments between forkfuls to ask Melody about her husband. It seemed natural to be close and exchange deeper confidences for which previous quick lunches had not allowed time.

"He's a salesman in a non-IBM, but like IBM, company. You know...dress like IBM, work harder than at IBM, fewer benefits, paid a lot less, but essentially do the same work."

"Actually...," she paused to touch a napkin to her mouth, and to think whether what she wanted to say next was okay, or would seem snarky. She plunged in, "He's more central to his various secretaries than to the company. He goes through many secretaries...not because they don't like working for him, but because they like him too much. And he has fallen for a few of them. He tells me this after it's all over. He has a need to confess and he always vows it's the last time. He never has the slightest serious intention with them, and sometimes they cause work interruptions, become childish, and so they have to go. He's been through three or four secretaries." Her head found the exact tilt to convey frustration and she gave Robert an innocent smile. Roiling around those words were those she omitted: that Cass had just recently said he did not love her.

"Have you ever wanted to leave him?"

Melody pushed her food around, taking time to answer. "It's not so easy. It would be financial suicide. And in between these escapades he's a good husband. He's attentive to the twins... and up until now I've met no one to leave him for. Has to be just the right person." She failed to mention her own culpable practices; the much older man who once yearly paid her way to St. Thomas to join him for a week.

"Cass and I don't argue; he's relaxed about what I do," she said. "In fact, he doesn't care what I do. For example, some years I go alone to St. Thomas for a week and he never quizzes me about it. Nor does he ask how I pay for it."

"Well, I'll quiz you now," Robert said. "How do you pay for it and what do you do there?"

"I do nothing there except swim and relax...and I earn the money," she fibbed. She cocked her chin up and flashed him a teasing glance. Used to being on display, Melody had become so conscious of how she chewed, that she actually tried to eat without working her mouth; tried to keep her perfect mouth from moving. She had read about a super-model who had lost the ability to chew in public, and she could understand that. She almost had done so herself.

Robert, however, ate with authority. He leaned on the table and shoved down the food, unconscious of the act. And anyway, imperfection in a man—something little-boy like—could be appealing to a woman. He liked Melody's hesitancy, the iciness evident in her restrained manner. She belonged on a throne and he'd like to put her there.

"No doubt you enjoy your work," he said. "It's a perfect way for you to get around. Also, it makes you interesting...not that you weren't already interesting," said with a sheepish grin, "but it just adds to it. These days any woman with half a brain is out doing something in the real world. I believe your children will respect you more for having a career. My wife, Anna, does nothing but manage the house and children and work her hobbies. She paints and makes jewelry. And she has a fulltime, live-in housekeeper." He failed to mention that the size of their home *required* a housekeeper, and buying it had been *his* dream. Anna had never pushed for a large, grand home. He paused to think about that, but Melody didn't need to know all those details.

"Except for chauffeuring the children around, and painting on site, her activities rarely get Anna out of the house. Therefore, she leans on me to be home and forces me to admire her paintings that are not even of a style I like." He had found a comfortable level of exaggeration. "We were mere kids, you know, when we married and now here I am with two children and a wife who is barely a friend." He paused to think about that: Anna was quite friendly and warm toward him—he was the one to throw up the cold shoulder. What was it about the requirement to acknowledge Anna as a good mate that was so off-putting? Actually, up until now, he hadn't really known how much unrest he felt in his marriage.

Melody was quietly glad that Robert's wife was not competition. "That must be a drain on you with all the demands of your company," she said. While she waited for his affirmation, she pulled a strand of flaxen hair forward over one shoulder and toyed with it. Then she repositioned food around her plate while she waited and watched him.

Robert mulled over exactly what he wanted her to hear. "I like a painting with some high drama," he said. "You know ... mountains and sunsets, an ocean roaring in, but Anna paints apples, pears, flowers, local landscapes, and things we see daily. They don't interest me. Aside from that, being surrounded with architectural work, especially marine, inspires me. I have to keep thinking, planning, and designing. Each year buyers want to see my company's new ideas, and we compete with top European manufacturers. I can't let up." He paused to set the importance of those words; let them drift out and settle on Melody with proper force. "There are those with money to burn, who swap out their ship for something new every few years. Many of them pay cash. It's crazy." He delivered this with a nod and hand gestures.

Melody issued sounds of understanding, encouraging him to keep talking.

He backed a wedge of lettuce into his mouth and sawed at it while forming his next comment. "Anna is a cute shorty, not statuesque like you." He paused to admire Melody and let the compliment air. "Rather timid, Anna fades away into the background. Brown curly hair;" he gestured with his hands forming the shape of a full head of hair. "Worlds apart from your spun gold."

Melody fingered her hair and gave Robert an expectant look to assure him that she wanted to hear more.

"I think her manner of raising our children has alienated them from me." He absolved himself. "They never want to do things with me. I can't carry them on demonstration trips and sometimes I go with yacht deliveries...can't take the children on those." Exaggeration flowed like high tide.

Cupping his hand, he arranged the crumbs that had fallen from his roll, into a tidy pile on the side of the table. He then set one of the crystal candlesticks on top of the pile, and with a devilish grin, he looked up to Melody for her reaction.

She laughed at his antics. He was relaxed and self-assured. He could get away with a lot. Melody liked that.

He shifted around in his seat, arranging a new stance from which to launch another speech, momentum building behind his lips. "The effort of breathing life into my company takes nearly one-hundred percent of my time. Anna complains about that. She doesn't see what my company provides for us." Not true at all, he thought, but what are you going to do?

Melody's approving nod and slight frown, one of the rare ones she allowed across her brow, conveyed the concern she felt—that he should have to be bothered with such considerations.

Propping his fork in air, Robert stopped releasing words when he caught himself talking too much. He lowered his fork and sighed. "But I want to know about you, Melody. Are you the loveliest woman to come into my life, or what?"

Under the floodlight of his admiration, Melody warmed up to tell more of her own frustrations. "My marriage...is half on the rocks," she said. While this was a true statement, it was also misleading. Melody and Cass's marriage had reached a certain plateau of understanding. An arrangement where you do your thing and I'll do mine had worked itself out years ago, and by now was status quo. And there was her dependence on Cass and a certain mild attraction to him—she liked his face and he had tall, erect posture; she liked his blonde hair, they made a glamorous couple. She wished he would be home at night. But when it came to her own freedom, she wanted to be away at times. Nor did she want to explain herself to Cass. Occasionally, riding this two-headed train was unsettling—especially now that he had just again asked her for a divorce. Still, she wouldn't take that seriously, and wasn't about to mention it to Robert.

"Recently Cass was on a business trip," she said, "and I called his phone, and then his room, up until 3:00 a.m. He never answered. Should I ask him why...he would say he was in a deep sleep, didn't hear the phone, usually turns it off, and sometimes puts a pillow over the house phone. His reasons vary." Melody pulled a wounded look as she opened a silver case and selected a cigarette. "He's indifferent to what I do."

For Robert, If there were any blemish to be found in Melody, it was her smoking habit. He avoided people who smoked, and he

17

deplored the constant fumes around smokers. Indeed, he would not allow smoking in his boatyards, automobile, home, or on any of his yachts. Of course, after a yacht was delivered, whether to allow smoking was the new owner's decision, but Robert always warned them that cigarette smoke and burning candles would foul furnishings and finishing. However, he pushed this problem with Melody ahead into the future. Melody would not be the first woman he had convinced to quit smoking. Reluctantly, with a frown and with a candle from the table, he lit her cigarette. She took a long draw from it and channeled the exhaled smoke upward with a tilt of her head. As he watched, he thought her gesture was so beautiful that he could learn to put up with her habit. He studied her while her eyes studied his face.

For a while they said nothing—aware that they were comfortable with the silence, and that they were the most dazzling couple in the dining room. His silver hair and her pale hair sparkled along with the glitter of surrounding crystal. The clinking of coffee cups seemed to peck at a surreal awareness of what was to come. Their thoughts were entwined. He wanted to reach over and take her hand, but instead he closed his legs around hers. Melody's hands trembled ever so slightly.

"A beautiful...and also special, I might add...woman all to myself for a brief moment. I can't allow you to get away so soon. Let's go over to *The Plaza*. We could sit in the lounge downstairs," he offered for propriety's sake, "but then the college kids have not yet all fled the city, and the lounges will be packed and noisy. So, I recommend we go up to my room there, and have a nightcap sent up."

"Indeed, I could use a nightcap before I make the trip home in this weather," Melody agreed. And while Robert signed the tab, she watched his assertiveness. He commanded the waiter's attention with the positive authority that was always missing in Cass's passive manner. He helped her into her coat, and as they walked over to the Plaza, Melody sliding in the snow, Robert kept a steadying arm around her.

When they slipped into his room, he quietly closed the door

behind them, shutting out all others and all other concerns. Then he stepped to the window and closed the curtains. She watched him with longing that she thought had been long buried. She watched the toned muscles shaping his slacks. He turned Melody toward him, fumbled with buttons on her coat, and then dropped it behind her. He folded her into his arms. His slight trembling revealed his expectation. His hands moved into her hair, caressing its softness, then down her sides, learning her firmness. She clung to him, hands moving all over. They were not surprised with their mutual conquest, but Melody had fallen—fallen for his attention and his power. He picked her up and carried her into the bedroom.

Before he took her down to find a taxi, they showered together.

When Melody arrived home, Louise wondered why Melody's hair looked different. Looked strangely damp.

5

A Dark Scheme

Melody wanted the boat show to last forever. Why wouldn't she? Even with the exhaustion of spending all day wearing a constant smile, giving eager little talks about what the attendees would see as they moved through the thirty-five-foot cruiser, never letting up, enough to wrinkle one's cheeks inside of a week, she wanted it to last. She could see no future beyond the show and her trysts with Robert. As for arriving home late and what Cass would think, she would explain that some of the show people had gotten together afterward for drinks. Besides, Cass was busy with his own thing and rarely knew when she came in.

On the last day of the show, Melody felt a chill for the downside of this astounding high that had lifted her for the past seven days. But Robert had asked her to have dinner with him after the show closed, and at least she could look forward to that. He had said that he didn't have to help break down the exhibit, because his staff would take over, and the large yacht would not be hauled out of the building until the next day.

When the show closed, he went to get the old and slightly battered blue Volkswagen he used when he stayed in the city. With no radio, the car was hardly tempting to thieves. Melody waited for him in front of the convention center. She had changed into January, New York City clothing. This was their last easy night to meet, and wanting to make it special, Robert drove them to the Drake to dine at the French restaurant. If they were meant to be, future trysts would have to be arranged. With his living and working in Connecticut and having but few occasions to come into the city, and Melody's living and working in Manhattan, something clever had to be worked out. He dropped a hint that he had given much thought to a long-range plan to bring them together regularly and he had reached a conclusion.

For a while, avoiding the topic foremost in each of their thoughts, they passed the dinner by talking in general about work. The cuisine was refined and decorative, and large gaps in this evasive communication were given over to savoring each morsel. Though it was apparent that Melody was mostly rearranging the bits on her plate, she attempted to be cheerful and hopeful, but she looked pensive, even solemn; if she would have allowed it to, her mouth would have turned downward. After the waiter cleared away their plates, Robert ordered two coffees, and then, while they waited, he pushed back his chair, crossed one knee over the other, and focused an intense gaze at Melody. He was about to announce a plan. But first he relaxed his arms on the chair arms, studied Melody a few seconds, and corralled his rangy thoughts.

"Is something bothering you tonight, Melody?" he started, knowing full well what it was.

"Well...yes." Her fine eyebrows raised as perfectly as he saw them when he pictured her in his dreams. "I won't be seeing you now and that'll be hard to take. I can't put you behind me." She didn't think he was indifferent either, or that he could end it, but she knew that seeing him infrequently would leave her with loose, unknotted ends. She wanted him to be available on a steady basis. Surprising how that feeling had sprung up suddenly, like a flower opening in fast-forward time.

"Melody...I want to keep seeing you," he said. It was time to get down to his plan. "Of course, if you are available, I can always hire you for modeling, but such assignments would not necessarily bring us together and not often." He paced his words rhythmically,

21

playing for the right effect. "But I have a plan." Pausing to impose the weight of his plan, he stared hard at her. "It will take a little time to put in place and you can help me shape it. I believe we can make it work."

While thoughts exploded within their souls, they waited silently while the waiter poured coffee from a silver pot. Robert offered Melody the cream and then splashed some into his cup, stirred it, and gazed across the room at nothing while he structured his next thought. His pause, the gap, stretched time for Melody so that she wanted to urge, Go on. Go on.

"I have a plan...a way for us to be together more." He ran his fingers under his collar and worked his neck as though to get more breathing room. "And that is...for you and my wife, Anna, to become good friends. Then we could easily invite you and Cass to the house for weekend fun."

The gap sprang shut.

Melody's cup clinked loudly against the saucer.

And in case he needed to persuade, he went on. "We have plenty of room. And of course your children will also be welcome. Anna loves children. We have a housekeeper...you won't have to worry about a sitter. It will be easy. We entertain often; the house is arranged quite nicely for entertaining." He rushed through his plan before something could stop him. He had been thinking about this for several days, unable to imagine a fall from this passion. And in case Melody was uncertain, he added, "Anna often goes off painting."

During his little speech, Melody hung in suspension. Before she could believe their meaning, she had to back out his words to replay. Her face froze in disbelief until, finally, what he had said found purchase. She stared at him. How easy and perfect he made it sound: a simple solution for two people who couldn't bear to be apart. She brightened. "Robert...how thoughtful." Her voice rose and rounded up in ripples. "A brilliant idea. We'll be thrown together for breakfast, lunch, and dinner, and from what you've told me, Anna makes friends easily. I probably have something to offer her. We must be alike in many ways, and with Cass so easygoing, you and he are apt to get along well. I'm certain the two of you have many topics of mutual interest...computers and business and so on." She had to try not to sound so effusive.

The cunning device was set. Robert would subtly pave the way by first inviting Melody and Cass to a small dinner party at his and Anna's home. Just the two couples. Melody would have plenty of opportunity to chat up Anna, invite her into the city for lunch and perhaps a fashion show. After that, while Robert would convinced Anna that for business reasons he needed to know Cass better, Robert and Melody would work out the rest, one week at a time.

"Now that the boat show is over," Robert said, "I'll head on up to Connecticut early tomorrow, but I'll arrange a way to see you soon."

She reached across and laid her hand on his arm. Her look implied, "You won't be sorry."

After finishing the evening with a nightcap at The Plaza, Robert put Melody into a taxi, kissed her goodnight, paid the driver, and waved goodbye. The city had never looked as beautiful to Melody as it did that night. Covering all surfaces, the new snow seemed to her to be vanilla frosting, a sweet life. There was a way forward.

When she entered her apartment, she found that Cass was home and had made dinner and fed the twins.

"I've kept dinner warm in the oven for you," he said. "The twins are already asleep. When I remembered that the show ended early today, I came home to cook my secret recipe of tomatoes, peppers, zucchini, garlic, and basil over linguini. But Louise said you had called to say you wouldn't be in until probably ten or so." Cass, good husband, good father, seemed already to have forgotten Jocelyn. He was good to do this sometimes; why Melody didn't get too excited about Jocelyn.

"Yes, dear," she said. "And thank you. Some of the exhibitors met afterward to celebrate the show's end. I thought you would still be trying to meet your deadline for tomorrow's sales' figures and wouldn't be home for dinner. So, I took my time...sorry." What she did, she would keep to herself, as did he.

Cass took her coat and hung it in the coat closet, then headed back to the kitchen to finish the cleanup. Melody trailed along behind him.

"Incidentally, dear...I've met an exhibitor whom I think you should meet. He manufactures huge yachts. His yacht, the largest in the show, was across the aisle from the cruiser where I worked... that's how I met him. And when I told him you sold computer systems, he said he wanted to upgrade the systems in his two boat-building facilities in Connecticut." Melody puttered around the kitchen helping with dishes. "I named some of the companies where you've installed software, and he wants to discuss his requirements with you. It could mean future contracts; you never know. Anyway, he's going to invite us to his home in Westport for dinner and you can discuss it with him then."

"It's always worth the effort," Cass replied, as he wiped off the counter. "I've been eager to break into the marine industry. We have a new software system built for tracking marine construction. However, the competition is tough, and it's hard to convince companies how much time and errors our system will save them. But you know that."

Though Melody listened and nodded her understanding, she was soaring with her new sense of need and passion. Let them have their systems; she had found something core, a renewed reason for living. In bed that evening Melody's thoughts were scenes of breakfast with Robert, of walking with Robert, of taking a drive with Robert, cocktails with him in the evening, reading in his library, stolen kisses. She could help Anna; actually be good for Anna. Take her to showrooms where she could buy designer fashions at discounted prices. Numerous such ideas swarmed Melody's imagination and sleep took its time finding her.

6

A Bead Give Away

W obbling and weaving its way to Westport, the old train rattled its soporific dialog. Even so, for the entire hour, Melody sat upright, not dozing or reading, too expectant over the prospect of seeing Robert's town. Seeing it; being in close proximity to his home. Because Anna and the children were down with colds, he had not been able to invite Melody and Cass for dinner. The boat show ended the middle of January, but now it was the end of February, and with his work mainly in Connecticut, Melody had seen Robert but a couple of times. Tension and desire kept her strung out; strung out all the way from Manhattan to Westport. The train ride somewhat soothed her edginess, and during the trip she fantasized about him. In her inner eye were scenes with him; one-act plays in which they were solidly bonded together.

With the pretense of seeing Westport and looking at properties for sale, she hired a taxi and directed it to pass by Robert's house. Well, it wasn't simply a matter of passing by because, by cracky, Robert lived on a circle. Right at the end. If he came out, he would wonder why a cab was circling and might notice her. He had said his house backed up to a fairway, but hadn't mention a circle. Her first clue was a sign at the front of Stanton Road that read, "No Exit." Moreover, all the property on Stanton Road had acreage. Few houses. You wouldn't drive down it accidentally. The thrill of seeing where Robert lived was tempered by the dread of his coming out right then. When she saw his house number coming up, she dropped her bag to the floor and leaned over to retrieve it so she couldn't be seen.

"This can't be the street the broker told me about," she said to the driver. "Please take me to the shopping center."

He took her to the river's side of The Market Place and explained how she could make the short walk from there to the train back to Manhattan. She paid him, and thanked him for a pleasant ride. He had let her off alongside the river at a covered walkway where she could pass through to Main Street. The river appeared purposely to slug its way to somewhere mysterious and unknown, seemed to carry along secret messages, perhaps one for her, if she could divine it, or maybe it chased something as she did — a dream. For a while, she walked along the river admiring the old New England houses that lined the opposite side; at least two old houses had been razed for a new structure recently started. She turned around and headed through the covered walkway to Main Street. Robert's town.

In both directions and across Main, shops jostled for her attention, but in particular, a window display of hand-made jewelry looked interesting. Draped around and hanging from white-painted branches were various beaded necklaces. She was fond of beads, both exotic and glittery, and sometimes her modeling assignments requested that she provide the jewelry for the shoot. Melody entered the shop and asked to see several of the necklaces in the front window.

"All our jewelry is handmade by local artisans," the salesperson said. She spread three necklaces on the counter. "They use only 14-karat gold or sterling combined with precious and semi-precious stones and lampwork beads. Each piece we carry will last for generations. And we ask that our artisans make only one of each style."

"I'll take this rather simple choker," Melody said. The necklace was made of large translucent-blue twisted-glass beads, strung between silver beads and finished with a sterling clasp. It certainly looked to be one-of-a-kind. It would go perfectly with her white-silk cocktail dress that had a twisted splash of blue lilies spiraling diagonally upward and across the front. "It will be my Westport souvenir." She paid and took her package, a pale-blue satin pouch tied with a silver ribbon. After discussing places to have lunch, she left the shop and continued browsing Main. She wanted something to eat before she walked to the train station. At the Pizza place, she ordered one slice and water, and while she waited she carefully opened the satin package and fingered the beads. She could see herself wearing them for Robert, dressing for Robert. Such things as a new piece of jewelry conferred a sweet reality. She closed up the satin pouch and buried it in her purse.

The pizza came hot and dripping with fresh tomatoes, basil, and mozzarella; exactly the way she liked it. A rare treat. She looked around at the Westport citizens. If she should see Robert, she would act as if she hadn't and rush on. If the worst happened, and he saw her, she would say a friend of hers had invited her up and she was waiting while her friend looked next door at furniture. Actually, she did have a friend, Eva, a fashion model, who lived here. It would be amusing to hang around and call her to meet for dinner. But no, she'd had enough of Robert's town for the day, as well as the stress of possibly bumping into him. She left money on the table, and then walked down to the train. Riding back was peaceful and not crowded. She had the seat all to herself; she would spend the hour watching the passing scenery. However, the express train flashed by towns quicker than she could study them. All was dull. She was going to her dull home. If it didn't include Robert, it was of no value or interest. Well, at least she had *Vogue*, bought at the station, and could see fashions; maybe she would find herself in there. She knew she would be in an ad, but she didn't remember whether this was the issue. Well, it didn't matter. Nothing mattered.

By now her self-esteem was totally dependent on Robert's attention, even to the point of leaving the twins for an unreal Connecticut excursion. The daughter of beautiful, vain parents, her mother had been offered a movie contract, but turned it down because it would have inconvenienced her controlling husband.

Melody's outer self knew that she was beautiful and admired by all men; her inner self could not be convinced. Her mother and father had always filled their own needs, to the exclusion of Melody's. She had been a kind of appendage—an appendage that you have, but can live without. She had grown up feeling excluded; neediness kept cropping up.

7

The Randalls Entertain the Clarkes

With Cass behind the wheel, the old Rover heroically tried to warm its occupants as it lunged and swayed, spraying slush up the Merritt Parkway, toward the Randalls' home. Normally a calm, steady person, Melody's heart thumped and bumped keeping time with the windshield wipers in their struggle to beat back rain. The Rover didn't heat well and she sat in her Aquascutum, rigidly wrapped against the cold. One multifaceted topic, and only one, riveted her thoughts: seeing Robert in his home; meeting his wife, Anna; trying to be at ease; not smoking (which she knew Robert would detest, and would probably make her smoke outside); being close to him without touching; averting her eyes from his; and acting as though she hardly knew him. Not slipping up. Not reaching out and grabbing him. Not saying something embarrassing. It was going to be a challenge.

Belle, the housekeeper, greeted the Clarkes at the door and took their coats. The entry hall led to stairs that generously curved outward at the bottom, then gracefully rose up to a landing. A six-foot-tall grandfather's clock that stood in a curve of the entry echoed the pounding of Melody's heart. Belle led them through double doors opening off to the left into a drawing room where Robert and Anna Randall waited before a fire. In contrast to the dreary evening outside, the Randalls' home radiated warmth with soft colors braced against traditional, well-oiled furniture, and sparkling light from a crystal chandelier, under which a two-foot-diameter repoussé silver bowl adorned an ebony grand piano. And here and there similar pieces of sterling decorated antique tables; the collection of several generations of casual collectors, or perhaps one generation of anxious collectors. Melody stopped thinking about Robert for a minute in order to take in the splendor; she had a particular fondness for silver.

Robert and Anna came forward to greet them. Melody hoped Anna hadn't noticed how eagerly Robert shook her hand and held it, but in all the initial introductions and talk about weather, it appeared as though his attention went unnoticed. Anna urged Melody and Cass to warm before the fire while Robert, after asking for their choices, made their drinks. Melody, torn between wearing something sexy to excite Robert, or something demure not to arouse suspicion in Anna, had decided on the white silk dress with the swirl of blue lilies. This dinner was her first opportunity to wear the blue-glass and silver beads bought on her train trip to Westport.

"So good to see you, Melody," said Robert, trying to keep some distance from her. He felt that he was seeing her cream-like skin and pale hair for the first time. The affect would have captured the heart of any normal man. Reluctantly he turned his eyes to Cass. "Did you have any trouble with my directions?"

Little did they guess that Melody knew exactly where to find the house.

"I had some confusion at the last intersection," Cass said. "Melody said we should take a right, but I saw two possible rights and I thought she might be wrong about which one you meant. But she was right on."

"You're wearing my beads!" Anna exclaimed. "You had to have bought them at the little jewelry shop on Main. I *made* that necklace. How exciting to see it on the buyer. I never get to do that."

Melody flustered. *Oops*! This came as a shock springing in from nowhere. What could she say? She fingered the beads. Cass, Robert, and Anna stared at her. She hadn't mentioned being in Westport before. Didn't want to mention it now. Both Cass and

Robert would be puzzled that she had not told them about her Westport trip. True, Cass didn't much concern himself about her activities, but one couldn't let too many secrets pile up. "Oh, what a ...uh...coincidence." Melody recovered. "No...I didn't buy them. A friend who lives in Westport gave them to me. They were a gift to celebrate a special modeling contract." She was safe. Cass would never bother to ask what that was all about.

But—drat! he did.

"You didn't mention that, Melody, how nice," Cass said. "Who was it?"

"Eva...you know...I worked the Sax show with her. Short dark hair. And we modeled hats together at Bergdorf's."

Anna's happy smile showed her excitement, like having children come back home after a long absence. "Well, this is a good one," she said. "To make the necklace here in Westport, leave it with a jeweler, have it sell and make its way to Manhattan and then back to my house. All accidentally. And so soon. I just took that necklace to Katie four days ago."

"Yes. That *is* amazing," Melody looked for some diversion and stooped to pet the cat that, deciding for himself whether her presence was okay, circled her feet. "Well, hello. Who are you?"

"That's Carter," Robert said. "Leave it to Carter to appreciate attractive guests. He's no fool."

Whew—she had managed to end the conversation about the unfortunate necklace purchase. She put on a smile and tried to relax.

Robert had paid no attention to the discussion about the necklace. He concentrated on how to get Melody off alone. It had been too long since he had had a chance to hold her, and he needed a shot of her loving energy to reinforce his substance. Meanwhile, he began to reminisce with her about the boat show, as though they hadn't seen each other since, and had scarcely seen each other then. When he could, privately, he gave her a wink. They were working the plan.

"You two must be thankful you don't have to do that boat show more than once a year," Anna said. "All those long days and late nights. It was tiring for Robert. He stayed over all week, and he *hates* the city." Anna, trusting her marriage—while knowing that it could be better, that Robert and she could be closer, spend more time with each other—nevertheless felt that their marriage would stand the test of time. Even though his interest in her was clearly not what it used to be, she was not an envious wife, not apt to worry about another pretty woman attracting Robert. He had been associating with beautiful women ever since she first met him.

"Um...yes, nasty, the city," Robert said. Only the most perceptive would have noticed that he sounded vague and uncommitted. As he sipped wine, his eyes met Melody's for the briefest second.

She couldn't look at him for longer than that second; her desire would circle around his face like bees around honey. She didn't feel discomfort, rather she had settled in and enjoyed her place in Robert's heart, but her revealing look would have alerted anyone around who was the slightest bit aware.

"It was a drudge," he added.

"I even offered to come into the city with him and help," Anna continued. "But he said no that with all his salespeople and customers on board, one more person would be in the way."

"But, I did sell *Victory*, Melody," Robert said. "No surprise there. That was arranged before the show. And, I had another order as well, and several future prospects. A profitable show. Our plants will have solid work for the next year."

"Oh, good, Robert." Though she had known this all along Melody feigned surprise.

Cass, always comfortable to quietly fade into the background, roused sufficiently to say, "We must drink a toast to your success. Those were seven long days!" They raised their glasses. "The show was hard on Melody," he added; although most nights he had arrived home later than she had. Truthfully, he had not observed whether those days had been hard for Melody, so he thought he'd better say no more. Mainly, he remembered his mild relief that Melody would be in late and would not be concerned about his activities.

Before dinner was announced the children were invited down to meet the guests and say goodnight. Even Carter seemed to enjoy the fuss, as he pranced about, around all those shoes, reading their recent history, switching his tail to show his opinion.

Soon, Belle announced dinner, and they moved into the dining room. She had arranged an array of lighted candles that flickered off white china and glittering crystal. Supplying an abundance of color for the centerpiece was an array of large Zinnias, straight from a florist, Melody decided, for it was too early for them in the garden. How nice she thought to have the option to be so spendy. Robert helped Melody to her seat, and then poured a fine Bordeaux around. Belle moved in and out of the dining room, serving and removing the various dishes: consommé with a dash of sherry, followed by beef bourguignon, served with fire-roasted potatoes and a steamed vegetable assortment, glazed with a touch of green olive oil. Belle looked to be relaxed and to be enjoying the dinner equally as much as were the guests. As she was housekeeper, occasional babysitter, and top chef for the Randalls, Anna respected the work Belle did and was cautious not to overload her. She had thoughtfully hired an assistant to help Belle in the kitchen, and the dinner went smoothly.

After desert, while Robert and Cass remained at the table for a brief discussion about computer systems, Anna and Melody moved into the drawing room for coffee. Melody found that she could not relax until Robert and Cass joined them; the seriousness of the plan that Robert had started with her, left her tongue-tied around Anna. Her face fought between calculation and guilt. Robert's plan, for her to become friends with Anna, to serve his and Melody's needs, almost caused beads of perspiration to form on Melody's perfect brow.

"Katie, what a kick! You've already sold my necklace. That was fast. Almost overnight!"

"Yes, proof of your good taste. A tall, striking well-dressed blonde snapped them up. I had scarcely hung them in the window.

Someone not from around here, judging from the questions she asked."

"Are you sure she was a tall blonde? You didn't mix her up with another customer?"

"I'm quite sure. It was a slow day and she and I talked about Westport for a few minutes, and where she could get a quick bite. I wouldn't have forgotten *her*...a beautiful woman. Poised."

A puzzled Anna said goodbye. She would bring in more jewelry soon she said. And driving home, she wondered about the tall blonde who Katie said had bought her beaded necklace. She distinctly remembered Melody's saying the necklace was a gift from a friend who lived in Westport, a woman with short dark hair. And how would the friend have had time to give it to Melody? Buy it a day or two after Anna took it to the shop? Go into Manhattan that day and give it to Melody the next? And Melody wear it the next night to their dinner party in Westport?

8

The Painting Day Bribe

The sleek red Porsche oiled its way left and right up Route 9 through the hollow hills along the Hudson River. Hollowed out for trap rock, these hills seemed to Robert to symbolize his marriage to Anna—beautiful on the outside, lush, but empty under the crust. Robert had calculated that a day's outing with Anna would provide an opportunity to advance his plan, and so he had sweetly offered to drive her up to Rensselaerville, New York, an historic village chock full of painting sites; he remembered that it was a favorite painting destination for Anna. He wanted time to discuss involving the Clarkes more in their social lives; wanted to impress on Anna that importance. Cass might give his company a significant discount for a new computer system and training. His company needed a network and that was not small change. And, if Anna would take Melody around and show her the Westport area, become good friends, he could easily find quality time alone with Melody. An added benefit.

Not the best buggy for a painting trip, Robert chose anyway to take the Porsche; he needed to baby himself to make the trip. After all, he had taken a driving course at Lime Rock Park, and wanted to practice his skills. He had lined the Porsche's hold with plastic sheets against wet canvases.

Pleased with Robert's inviting attitude, his pleasantness that morning, Anna was eager to spend personal time with him, a rare event—and she enjoyed cruising in the Porsche as much as he did.

"I sold a painting at the John Slade Ely show in New Haven," Anna said. "A twenty by twenty-four oil of the marshes and River, at the Duck River Cemetery in Old Lyme. Plenty of blue and gold. Gold grasses, blue sky, and across the river a white Victorian house peeking through the trees. It's a haul up there, but worth the trip. One of my favorite sites."

Robert said nothing. He seemed to find it hard now to lend his goodwill to the occasion.

"Sold for two thousand."

Robert was not listening.

"That's dollars."

"Uh huh." He felt that his heart hurt, and his defenses began to swell. He needed to build a fence to protect his heart. "Oh, by the way, I'll be gone Wednesday through Saturday. Back Saturday around noon. I have to see a boat builder in Rhode Island. If I like the quality of the dinghies he builds—and I think I will, for I've seen them around, I'm thinking of ordering three for yacht tenders. I have to be there on weekdays because his plant isn't open weekends, and I want to see his process." (Melody was going with him.)

Anna nodded understanding.

"Otherwise, I'd ask you and the children to go along. Besides, we'll probably get down to business...pricing and specs."

Anna said nothing. She was used to Robert's being away—lately more often.

Robert had turned the Porsche east to the Taconic State Parkway—not as direct, but more serene and scantily populated. They watched the soft green hills roll by, dotted with a few traces of snow. Winter tried to hold on, but with warm fingertips, Spring pushed back.

"I love this ride," Robert said. Now he was making a new effort to tune in and be sociable; though these days, that was his last instinct with Anna.

"I keep thinking about the coincidence of Melody's wearing the beaded necklace that I placed for sale but a few days ago," Anna said. "And yet it was bought and made its way to Manhattan where it was given as a gift to Melody, and made its way back to our house."

"Uh huh."

"Is that weird, or what?"

"It couldn't have been another necklace? A look alike?"

"Not a chance."

For a few years now, Anna thought, Robert had expressed only mild interest in her doings. He seemed to have no ability to appreciate her life, her side of the marriage. Too often she had the aloneness of talking to herself, for he found her too banal for his need for continual change and excitement. He should have had a wife who had no interests of her own; made his interests her interests. Early in their marriage, he had told Anna that he loved her for her enthusiasm. But his own enthusiasm, it turned out, was directed toward hot spots: hot models, hot cars, hot ships, keep his enthusiasm level at a high pitch. It took time for Anna to realized this. Hadn't recognized this side of his character. No woman would hold Robert's interest for long, she thought. He was perhaps the only sailor in America who would put down *Yachting* and pick up *Vogue*. Anna hadn't subscribed to *Vogue*—Robert had, ever since *Vogue* had featured one of his yachts with models wearing skimpy clothes, thongs—that kind of thing. So during this rather rare opportunity to have him to herself, she wanted to strengthen their bond, get him to communicate with her. And throughout the long drive, she punctured the air with statements about the wonderful Greek Revival houses they would see in Rensselaerville, and about the landscapes she had painted there and sold.

Each of her comments jabbed Robert more sharply than the preceding one. He just wanted her to be quiet. He drove in silence, studying the landfall, looking from side to side to show his mind was elsewhere. Anna drained him; although he saw that the problem was within himself. His efforts to tune in were tuning out. He consoled himself that his kind of person was impossible to live with.

He lived in his mind on a detailed level. He didn't seek the latest styles, he created them. He strove to find new ways to enclose space in a boat, to describe new shapes, or to search for the true and simple color harmonies for staterooms. Then, if Anna spoke to him, he was annoyed, irritated at the interruption. She was incapable of grasping this, whereas Melody, he thought, with her acute sensitivities, never spoke at the wrong moment; left him quiet space.

He would get to the point now, and taking control of the air, he complemented Anna on their recent dinner party. It had provided him with an opportunity to introduce her to Melody and Cass, part of his cunning plan with long-range consequences. Baby steps. By bringing the Clarkes into his family circle, he could see Melody more frequently. It was hard to see her now, with their working in different directions, different states even. True, he could hire her on occasion to work a boat show out of town with him, and he would, but long gaps would occur in between when she worked in Manhattan and he in Connecticut. He could see Melody in his future and needed to secure her there. The best solution, he schemed, would be to talk the Clarkes into making a move to Westport. It made sense anyway with two little kids close to school age.

"The Clarkes are an interesting couple," he said. "I was eager to meet Cass and hear which computer configuration he recommended. And, Melody is the sort of model I need for brochures that feature the round bar that we just designed for *Olympus*. Plus, she's a talented demonstrator, excellent with customers. I've watched her work. She also models in fashion shows and sometimes organizes and moderates them. Moving up in her career. I should hire her before her rate becomes too expensive."

Anna was used to Robert's hiring many people for many different situations: models for brochures, sales people, show organizers. And, if she thought at all about the Clarkes, it was that they were a glamorous, pleasant couple. Melody's last words had been a suggestion that she and Anna meet for lunch in Manhattan sometime soon. It would be good, Anna thought, to have such an easy-going friend who enjoyed day trips into the city.

There was silence now between them as Robert concentrated on the Porsche. Arms and legs stretched out in front of him, both hands evenly spaced on the wheel, he drove the machine as though he were wearing it, smoothly, at one piece with the curving road. Soon he said, "Cass's background in systems can help keep the installation simple when I am ready to install software. He has already given me practical suggestions. We'll have to see more of them," he urged. "That way I'll be sure to get the best value with the least complications. I want us to invite them up again."

"Oh, of course, I look forward to seeing them again," said Anna.

Then he turned off at Route 90, pointed the Porsche west, and crossed over the Hudson River toward Rensselaerville. They rode the rest of the way in silence.

At Rensselaerville, Robert tried to be patient while he waited for Anna to paint. First he investigated the library, and then he had coffee and Danish in the café, and then back to the library, and then to the car for a nap. Not a good car for napping, and too cold. Then back to the café. There, in the café's cozy back corner, he spent a half-hour on the phone talking to Melody. He had to talk to her, couldn't wait another minute.

"How can I endure this? I'm so bored," he said to her. He had the phone pressed hard to his ear so he could hear her over the music coming from somewhere in the café. "It's such a long day. I brought blueprints to study, thinking about some new directions, but I can't concentrate. And we won't get home until late tonight, and it's cold here. And I can't get to you soon enough." His voice carried a whine.

"I know. Poor thing. So unreasonable of Anna to ask that of you. Too cold for painting outdoors."

"Nah. Anna's used to it. She's often painted with outdoor classes in winter weather. But, I'm long suffering, sitting around waiting." He didn't mention that the painting trip had been his idea. "I had to listen to a violin quintet for part of the drive up, because Anna liked it. Just so much groaning over catgut. Truly phenomenal what they can do with catgut. Is it catgut? Anyway, don't tell Carter. That cat is temperamental enough, as it is."

"I promise I won't breathe a word to Carter." She giggled.

Robert winced. He hated to hear women giggle.

"And Anna's paintings sell for paltry sums," he continued. "She's all excited today because one went for two thousand. 'Dollars,' she said. Pffft! Talk twenty thousand and I'll pay attention." He sniffed. "She isn't even painting houses. She said she had captured two houses here months ago, and wanted to do a different subject matter today...a weathered barn...and I thought we drove all the way up here for Greek Revival. We have barns in Westport, if you know where to look. And some have been *revived*, as in Westport Revival." He laughed.

Again, Melody's giggle vibrated over the phone line. Then she said, "A waste of your time, certainly."

"Indeed. But not a waste for Anna; her landscapes have occasionally taken a First or Best in Show."

This was not something Melody wanted to hear. She had never put to use her own art school years.

"Oh, if I could reach you right now," he said. "That would revive me; get some of your 'Robert Revival.' Let me try some heavy breathing into the phone. See if you get the message." Then, more seriously, he said, "I can't imagine that you would spend my valuable time keeping me waiting while you painted." He forgot that Anna usually painted alone, finding time when the children were in pre-school and he was at work. It was convenient to forget everything that was inconvenient to remember.

Anna's painting took three hours to complete. The subject was a barn behind one of the houses on Main Street. In the painting, a long low roof supplied a slash of deep shadow underneath, and overhead were bare limbed Maple trees. Sharp blue sky and shafts of sunlight worked through puffy clouds, while spots of snow carpeted about. Robert could see, though he was reluctant to admit it, that the design was good; several opposing angles, colors were good. If Melody had painted it, it would be perfect.

*

The next day Robert slept past his usual time. He managed to get one eye open enough to see the clock, then shot out of bed and showered, leaving a trail of pajamas and towels. Belle had breakfast spread for him in the morning room. When he saw that, he slowed enough to eat and start the day with coffee. Just as he chomped on half an English muffin smeared over with butter and strawberry preserves, the phone rang. Belle answered and handed the phone to Robert.

"Yes?"

A few seconds of quiet.

"He doesn't have what!" Robert yelled excitedly into the phone. "No steering! Bloody Hell! The plant should have tightened *Victory's* cables before he was allowed to try her out! Why in Christ's name does he have Dr. Bauter on board? My instructions were to leave him entirely to me! Bloody Hell! Get the helicopter with a mechanic out there *NOW*!" Just then through the window he saw the trees bending over in response to the wind. "This wind will cause the waves to pick up and complicate the situation!" he yelled.

Projectiles of anger hammered the air while Robert ground his jaw. "Oh, Shit! I'll take care of it! You guys really screwed up! Radio and tell them I am on my way. Now! Tell Compo to let go the dock lines on the inflatable when they see me coming."

Throttle-banging the Porsche, he cut off State Street before an on-coming truck, barely missing it, making the sports car dance around the VFW building and up Compo Beach Road toward Long Island Sound. Christ! he swore to himself, they managed to stall Dr. Emil Bauter out in the middle of the Sound, adrift with no steering. And in this wind he won't be able to steer with the engines! Bauter's damned cautious anyway. Robert uttered non-stop oaths as he and the red auto jimmied the pavement. He might never get Bauter sold now. And, furthermore, he's stuck out there with his chicken-hearted, cackling, tart of a wife! Only possible chance of recovery is to get out there fast and find the right diplomacy.

Careening onto the club dock at Longchamp's he tossed his car key to the guard, jumped into the Hypalon dinghy, ignited the motor, pivoted the twenty-horse outboard, and pointed the bow out of the harbor. The bow, with no weight forward, rode high on incoming waves. The dinghy moved at an hysterical speed. He was before planing her up to skim the surface, when he half stood in order to see better over the bow—a fatal decision—for a micro second later a determined wave knocked him aft, slamming his elbow back onto the throttle. The throttle reacted with vengeance twisting forward, pumping its fuel, gunning boat and man into projectiles up in the air and over. He had three interminable seconds to realize that he was in the frigid water looking up at an eleven-foot boat suspended in air for a moment, twenty-horse motor running. Over his head.

Up to that moment, each instance he had ever followed of precise and carefully planned actions couldn't mitigate the effects of the one he had omitted: that of connecting to his belt, the emergency release cable on the throttle shut-off. The twenty-horse motor, still running—over his head—was tearing the air and anything in its path into elementary particles. Robert dove down as deep and as fast as he could, but not before the mass charged and caught him across the legs. What—exactly what—*was* the problem? Where was he? What was closing in? The pressure: he felt himself exploding; thoughts lost within dark roiling plasma. He passed out.

9

Having Legs in Casts Isn't all that Bad

"Ah! It was your sweet face, Melody, that inspired me to get home fast. And heal." Robert spoke to Melody over the phone. "And, thank you for the visit and the card...especially your insightful comments about my doctors whom I'm sure I saw working behind the meat counter at the butcher's. I'm certain that I saw one of them grinding meat, probably of suspicious origin. I must remember to tell Belle never to buy meat there again."

"Sounds like some doctors I've heard about. Probably their second job," Melody's laugh rippled over the telephone. "So, they operate in Connecticut, also?"

The dock crew at Compo had seen Robert's accident and immediately called for an ambulance, jumped into an inflatable, and raced out to find Robert a bloody mess. They were able to pull him from the water. Even with multiple contusions and fractures, a week in the hospital was all Robert needed to feel put-upon, and out-of-sorts. Happy to get rid of him, doctors and nurses patched him up with stitches, bandages, and casts; supplied him with crutches and sent him home with good wishes, and admonitions to stay off his feet. Let his wife deal with him.

He now sat in his library, propped up at a table in a sunny window. "I have to tell you this is most annoying." Robert spoke with his dignified smoking-jacket voice. "Anna has brought in a nurse! We had a bloody row about it." He complained over the phone to Melody as he idly moved the queen around on a marble chess set. He twisted to the side to catch his reflection in a nearby mirror and to smooth back his hair. "What a nuisance. This nurse is bossy, strict, and unsmiling."

He feigned exasperation in response to Melody's pushing laughter over the phone. He explained that until all the stitches were out and the casts were off, he needed help fetching things. If his boat plans or financial sheets were in the library, then chances were he would want to work with them in the morning room to catch the sun. And if the papers were in the morning room, he wanted them in the library before the fire. Or he needed the copier in the den, or sometimes in the library. Belle had all she could handle with the house and meals, and Anna had all she could handle with the children, painting, and attending classes.

"I try to keep Noel, my nurse, out of my way as much as I can. She has possibly never comprehended a joke in her life. She's stiff; you know...white cap perched up like a sail...I didn't think nurses used those things anymore. Anyway, I like it, makes her look official." He pulled in a long sigh to let that sink in. But, he had second thoughts about those statements—where did they come from? Noel didn't wear a cap. And the truth was, as long as he did what Noel said, she kept him laughing. She was good medicine, but he couldn't win Melody's sympathy if she thought his convalescence was actually amusing.

"You know you love being fussed over," Melody teased. Their mutual laughter at this temporary halt to Robert's freedom, soothed a little of the ragged stress spreading through these sandpaper days when Melody could not get to him. Somehow, she had to deal with his convalescence. He told her he would soon be walking more, though with crutches, and when he could get out and about, make it back to work—another few weeks at the most—they would have a day together. No, he could not use any help. He was as sorry as he could be. Missing her, a vital part of himself—more than he could say.

Noel Tasker entered the library carrying a large silver tray covered with homemade minestrone soup and salad. She wore a sort of blue uniform that pinched in her small waist and stopped an inch above her finely chiseled knees and well-turned calf muscles.

"Incidentally," Robert quickly changed the subject, but turned to watch Noel's legs as she removed the chess set and placed the lunch tray on the table where he sat at the window, "since I lost the Bauter contracts, I'm thinking of consolidating my two plants into one location. My staff has been doing some preliminary research into buildings, and has a few sites for me to see when I'm mobile. I hope you can come with me. If you can, I'll show you around Westport. I'll pick you up at the train." He whispered, "It would be wonderful, though, if you could move out of the city. I need you closer."

From the other end of the line, beginning to feel the sun turning its life-giving warmth upon her face again, Melody brightened a little, and hope wove through her words with her reply. "I'd love to go with you, darling. I can hardly wait to see your face and touch you!"

For a moment Robert did not respond. He watched Noel arrange the food before him and draw up a chair to join him. Finally he said over the phone, "Still, things are going along smoothly here, all things considered." He thought he was soothing Melody, unable to witness her sour frown. "Goodbye, dear. Lunch is waiting for me." He hung up.

Melody set down the phone. She sat still, staring ahead at nothing. Should she be relieved? She couldn't see him now, but he *had* called and he *had* made plans with her. And yet she thought she had distinctly heard his nurse more or less order him to hang up the phone and eat while it was still hot. And he had.

Nurse Noel Tasker, had not been hired as cook, but when Robert heard that cooking was one of her hobbies, he said he could spare her a couple hours a day if she would shop for and prepare something special for his lunch. And, he said, please eat with him. Belle was an excellent cook, and cooked breakfast and dinner, but not lunch. And with the children, and such a large house, it would relieve Belle if Noel cooked lunch for him—at least some days. Anna was busy painting and taking a class, he said, and she had the children to chauffeur back and forth to pre-school and what all, and, as well, he often asked her to drop by the plant for something he needed.

Noel viewed that as a winning opportunity, so before her day began at the Randalls, she shopped at Trader Joe's. She loved the clean, smart efficiency of the place, and the endless variety of produce and prepared dinners. On occasion, she might select two prime-rib steaks, small for her, large for Robert, or sometimes a pork tenderloin which she would stuff, and at other times maybe salmon steaks. And while the butcher wrapped them, she would browsed the store for something else—possibly something exotic to surprise her client, Robert (she avoided the term "patient"). Sometimes it would be a box of chocolate-covered Brazil nuts, or walnuts, or Kalamata olives, or slivered almonds, with which she would bake a chicken and rice dish for him.

Today she would also buy dinners for her freezer at home and perhaps a lemon tart to take to her fiancé, Peter. Peter was feeling neglected and had complained that he was eating too many frozen dinners to have a fiancé who was a good cook. After she had cooked a meal for Robert, she wanted only to nuke a frozen something for Peter and herself.

"Couldn't you control your hours more?" Peter had asked. "You work late too many evenings."

"It isn't easy. Robert is in a lot of discomfort, and as a result, demanding." She had to help him move around, she said. She had to supervise his pain medications to assure he didn't overdose. And Anna, his wife, was never home.

"Well, they have a housekeeper. Didn't you say?"

"She's useless," Noel said. Not a bit of it true, but she couldn't tell Peter how much she enjoyed her time with Robert. She loved Peter, but next to Robert, she was finding Peter to be, well—sorry to say—dull. Robert was brilliant. She loved to watch his mind work, overhear his telephone conversations, and hear the power of his commands. And his zaniness amused her, whereas Peter had relaxed into his more mature years with no need to be dashing; too much at peace, and so settled. She would take a tart to Peter to pump him up a bit. Show him she was thinking of him.

10

Noel Does What for Robert?

Though Robert often took time to assure Melody of his need for her, more than a week had elapsed with only phone conversations, and Melody's tension would not abate. Life was flat without Robert, or without knowing that some hour soon they would be together, and now he couldn't come into the city. She had various modeling assignments and the twins to feed and to read to at night, but after they were in bed she was lonely — her head filled with Robert, his face, his arms around her. Had Cass been home more, Melody's tension wouldn't have been quite so great, but Cass was still attached to Jocelyn and usually came in late, or not at all. However, he had stopped mentioning divorce, so maybe he was on the winding-down stage of that fling. Powerless as Melody was to control her connection to Robert, and feeling especially gloomy, she decided that "the plan" needed furtherance in any way that she might affect. She called Anna.

"I finally have a break in my schedule so let's meet in the city for lunch as we discussed."

"Let's do." Anna reached for her calendar. "Since Robert's accident, I haven't been out much...too many errands to do for him. He's running the business from home and often needs something fetched when his secretary is too busy to leave the office. By the way, the latest brochures have arrived, those that show you in the lounge of *Olympus,* and you *are* striking. I'll bring you some. Robert is quite pleased with them."

"Oh, good." Anna didn't need to know that Robert had called her to tell her how beautifully she enhanced his brochure, or that he had put some in the mail to her.

"Could we meet at the Metropolitan?" Anna asked. "It's time I made another duty trip there. I enjoy the French and 20th-century American Impressionists and enjoy soaking up their energy. Perhaps I'll buy some slides to add to my collection. We can have lunch there." Remembering Melody's pleasant manner, Anna welcomed her idea of escaping to the city for a day, especially since Robert had expressed a desire to know the Clarkes better.

Melody searched among her demure dresses for one suitable for a day with Anna at the Metropolitan Museum, something plain that would understate her sexuality. She had several different images, sultry and sexy, innocent and empty slate, hale and hardy. Today it should be something simple and loose for comfort, with flats for moving around easily. She chose a plain beige dress and a single strand of pearls. She would top these off with her Aquascutum and blue scarf. Her Italian flats with wooden scrolled heels, would be perfect; they were comfortable and warm. After washing and blowing out her hair, she dressed and applied the slightest touch of makeup. Then she studied herself in a mirror; the look was as simple as she could make it. She arranged for Louise to take the twins around the park before bringing them in for lunch and naps, and then she went down to find a taxi. She looked forward to the leisurely day. She hoped to hear from Anna's lips, sounds of marital discontent. If Anna were not forthcoming, Melody would find a way to move her onto the "Robert" subject. Surely Anna found her marriage to Robert to be less than perfect. Way less. Perhaps even empty. Perhaps even a frustrating emptiness. There were moments when Melody felt on the brink of issuing a little speech claiming Robert for herself.

After finding their way through the African exhibit into the

American wing, Anna showed Melody some of the painters she liked best. "Here, thankfully, we can see Benton, Hopper, Hassam, Homer, and...Actually, the Met is rather stingy with the American painters of note, compared with the French. Well, here are a couple of de Koonings," Anna continued, as they walked on toward the end of the room. "At least they show one of his more workable pieces." Anna's chirping commentary supplied a few good laughs.

Melody had no opinions of her own, and was soon exhausted from paying attention to Anna's prattle and from agreeing with each of her points. She just wanted to hear about Robert. She pictured Robert with this woman as his wife. No wonder he's discontented. Anna's opinionated—she's not good for him—too smart. Up until now Melody had thought of Anna as shy and submissive, but when you got to know her a bit more, she was assertive, maybe officious. However, Melody admired Anna's way of slowly opening up. This friendship could advance in different worthwhile directions than those she had with her modeling friends. It would be easy to be with Anna and thus, of course, around Robert more—which was their plan. Moving to Westport would further the plan. Still, she needed to find something right now to calm this helpless feeling. But, so far, she could find no opening to casually ask about Robert.

They found the dining room and chose a table near the pool. Graceful bronze statues, each one representing a different muse, cavorted through the water.

"I've heard a rumor that the pool has to come out in order to feed more people," Anna said. "It's a shame, really. There are too many of us. However, there has to be a certain quantity of us or there would be no museum." Her hands waved with a gesture of hopelessness.

When the waiter placed menus before them, they ordered wine, and settled into a long pause while they pondered the selections. Melody's concentration was split between the menu and anxiety over news of Robert. Surely Anna would soon mention Robert. She didn't want to herself—on guard to show no special interest in that topic. After all, he had been in a serious accident, and, Anna had said that he needed a full-time nurse. But, other than saying that his heartiness was contributing to a quick recovery, she seemed uninterested in further discussion about Robert and his mending. Obviously the topic of Robert was not foremost in Anna's thoughts.

Soon, the waiter arrived with hot plates of poached chicken in lemon sauce, and poached salmon with caper sauce. Eating began in earnest, and the conversation turned to different ways to prepare salmon.

"Wild caught salmon is a favorite at our house," Anna said. "Noel, Robert's nurse, is poaching it for him today, and she makes a savory mustard sauce to go with it—delicious! I've sampled the sauce. He will love it."

At last. The "Robert" subject was on the table, and Melody began to prod it. "Is it much of an aggravation to have a stranger in the house every day?" she asked, remembering Robert's sourness when he mentioned his nurse.

"Oh my word no. Noel is devoted to Robert. Works her tush off for him. She often cooks lunch for him. Relieves Belle, you know; Belle has enough to do with such a large house. And Noel's always on hand to carry things for Robert. He can't get around easily with his casts, so this is a full time problem. He verily dotes on Noel. He needs the massages and stretching she puts him through...you know ...to keep his hips flexible."

A chill swept through Melody's cells, and she stopped her fork in midair. She could barely disguise the stunned look that slammed her face on hearing these words. Slowly she lowered her fork.

"I don't know what we would do without her," Anna continued, not noticing Melody's distress. "I could never keep up with that. I would love to put Noel on the staff permanently and Robert would probably agree. And, he's so finicky. Not much I do completely pleases him. I prefer simple foods put together quickly, fresh but unadorned. I like to cook, but Robert wants elaborate concoctions... dishes that require a lot of time. I could never just give him a sandwich or salad, and he's completely unaware of the amount of time I spend on his errands, and on driving the children around. It's a good thing we have Belle. But generally we haven't asked Belle to make our lunch. She takes classes at Quinnipiac.

While she passed the silver bread tray to Melody, Anna paused with her story. Melody, who without a thought for what she was doing, moved a mound of butter onto her plate, selected a roll, spread butter on half, and sank her teeth into it. Comfort food. Keep her hands busy; distract her mind. The agony of waiting for what she was afraid to hear. She didn't care a fig for what Belle did, she needed to know what Noel did. She took a sip of wine.

"Noel has nothing else to do but cater to Robert and *she does*. She's there most all day, and busy as can be." There was a pause while Anna broke her roll apart and applied a tiny dot of butter to it. "And, she plays chess with him. I can't distract him that way...he's too impatient waiting while I consider my move. He's patient with *her* moves I've noticed...waits eons for her. Anna paused in her diatribe about Noel's worth, and nodded her assurance. "We couldn't do without her help at this time. Also, before Robert's accident, we had started renovations in two rooms, built-ins, and you know," she gestured with a hand, "and decided to continue and get the work finished. So we have more than the normal amount of disorder. Workers all over, coming and going."

Picturing to herself a well-appointed home of her own with Robert in it as her husband, Melody knew that catering to Robert would be no problem for her. She didn't paint and she wouldn't have to work; he would not want her to work, and they would, of course, have a maid and childcare. She would have plenty of time to cook the most involved dishes. But the pain in her solar plexus that had started two minutes ago, when Anna used the words "dotes on her," was sapping her happiness. She had to seek opportunities quickly to strengthen the bond that Robert and she had started.

11

Robert adds Spice to the Scheme

"Dr. Emil Bauter is no ordinary doctor. He's a European phony doctor." Robert stormed across the room, pressing shoe prints into the plush of the hotel's carpet. "You *know* how those Europeans are about titles." Robert had come into the city to go over photographs and layouts for new brochures, and had taken a suite at The Plaza. He had asked Melody to meet him there for cocktails and dinner. Discuss their future.

Melody *didn't* know, but with a worried look, she managed to nod an affirmative. She said nothing. Her heart hammered and her glass shook just ever so slightly. For weeks she had worried about not being able to see him. Was he still getting therapy from Noel? Now that he asked to see her, was it to give bad news? He hadn't yielded a clue. He had asked Melody to have a seat, and in silence, she watched him pace. For a change his eyes weren't sweeping over her; he had something serious to relate, and appeared to want to stay focused. He used a cane and walked with a slight limp. As he talked, he emphasized his points with the cane sometimes hooking it on his arm to adjust his collar, or to freshen their drinks.

"They attach an unearned doctorate to their name and thrall stupid Americans." He paused, cocking his head at an angle while he thought that over. "At least they *think* Americans are stupid. Well, Emil...*Dr*. Emil Bauter...let me not forget the 'doctor' is actually a chemist, but a lower level chemist. A bathtub chemist. Not a doctor in any country. However, he is something many doctors aren't: he's creative. He's developed two famous perfumes and did a sensational job of marketing them. And...he spends! Crap he spends!" Robert jabbed the cane into the carpet as he spoke. He paused to let that sink in while he stared out the penthouse window at the long dark Manhattan skyline. Today it was moonless, and looked to him like an out-of-control garden of sharp, contrary weeds. On the horizon, he could see just a thin sliver of silver lining.

Melody tried to nod at appropriate places. She kept quiet; sensed his timing. He hadn't reached his point and did not want to be interrupted.

"He was about to buy a yacht for each of two different ports and I, of course, geared up production for that." Robert spun around, faced into the room and stared hard at Melody. "Now both deals are off...at least for the time being." He slumped into himself. "At first, Emil said he was putting off buying until I was back on my feet and could oversee production. Now...though he's still my good buddy ...he's taking a longer look around. He's burned about *Victory's* loose steering cables, and my spies say he's been looking at German yachts. And, he has to contend with that nagging harpy of a wife. Says she has her eye on some futuristic piece of crap like a Russian oligarch's. He brought her to the plant a few times; she's hard to take. Never shuts up. I suspect he wants to throw her overboard somewhere in the middle of the *Roaring 40's*." Robert's scowl deepened.

Melody began to fear the worst. All along, by hinting about a divorce coming up, he had kept her hanging on, expecting and hoping. But now—

"Hell! I can't afford a divorce now," he erupted.

He shrugged his shoulders and put on a mournful face. He shook his drink, and listened for a moment to the tinny sound of rattling ice. He hooked the cane over a chair arm, and stretched himself up with a deep sigh. He loosened his tie, picked up the cane, and wrapped another turn around the room. While he stopped to light the cigarette Melody had placed in a silver holder, he glanced at her, and was satisfied with her worried look, what he could see of it with her head cast down so. He turned to see her reflection in a mirror, and saw that she despaired.

Often, on other, easier days, Melody would draw a silver powder case from her purse, and touch up her face. But now the room was still. She said nothing; did not move. Soon, she thought better of showing discouragement and used her fingers to smooth out her frown and force up the corners of her mouth—not too much, just enough to appear understanding, not clingy. She waited for Robert to speak. He was the first man for whom she knew she could, and would, end her convenient marriage to Cass.

He continued cruising. At the end of the room, he turned and placed his glass on a table. He hooked the cane over his arm and rubbed his hands together. He nervously twisted his wedding ring while he watched Melody. "I have given this a great deal of thought lately," he said. "That should...considering my tight schedule...show you how necessary it has become for me to be with you." He pounded each syllable.

Melody's spirit lifted.

There were a few quiet minutes.

He picked up his drink and paced back across the room. "And the only way a divorce can be affordable, my dear, is if my seemingly innocent wife could be shown not to be so innocent." As he walked, he watched Melody in the mirror. He reached into the ice bucket and plunked ice cubes into their drinks. Then he opened his hand toward Melody, and added without explanation, "Besides, she's not so innocent!" His agitated manner eased while he drew a deep breath and waited to let Melody assimilate this information.

Melody wondered how Anna could have earned that soubriquet.

"Let us catch her screwing around or shacking up with some guy and then we have a case. That's what I need...a case against her. Then no court will award her more than what is reasonable, considering the kids and all. Otherwise, I stand to be cleaned out."

Now Melody had such a worried look that Robert almost felt

guilt. But he was just building up; hadn't yet called on her real attention.

"This is where you come in, Melody. You have developed a friendship with her. She trusts you. You can convince her that there is no future in being faithful to me. Get her out to some singles' scenes or parties where those great Westport studs hold forth. Help me get evidence. You will be doing that for us. Meanwhile...move to Westport. That'll make our plan easier to execute." It sounded like an order. He knocked back a long swallow of scotch and then, while his speech rang in Melody's head, he refreshed their drinks.

"I'll have a detective waiting in the wings with a camera." He smirked, "Then our future together will be a sure thing. We'll have plenty of money. We'll move north of Westport, maybe to Weston, or Westbrook, where housing is cheaper, to have a little more breathing room. Acreage. We'll have the world by its ass!" He rocked on his heels, one hand thumping the cane, the other around his glass. The lights in his eyes flared; his face glowed with enthusiasm. A gorgeous man, cocksure of himself now that he had released the words, had outlined his plan. He grinned at Melody as if they had already accomplished this silly little trifle.

Looking around the room as though Robert had listed ways it should be redecorated, Melody began to see the possibilities, in fact, the absolute requirement. Her initial surprise subsided, and her courage grew. The more she thought about what he had said, the more practical it sounded. She could take heart—Robert was intent on their future together. This man had emphatic intentions.

"I see the potential," she said finally. "Each of us could be happier. I'll try. Certainly, Anna and I are friends now and she does listen to me, seems to like my ideas. And she admires my freedom, that I get around a lot, so she is probably already susceptible. But, I don't know how much I can accomplish."

"You don't have to do any more than point out what a bastard of a husband I am, and get her interested in someone else," he said, moving his head from side to side in a compassionate appeal to her. "Get her out." He paused to think of more reasons why this was a good idea. "A divorce will make it easier for me to spend more time with you and," he paused and added, "with my children. Anna would want me to take them from time to time." He had found an acceptable tack. "But enough about that now, I just want to be with you, feel the excitement of you and know we'll be able to plan for ourselves. I could never be a bastard to you."

As she watched him move around the room, Melody felt passionately drawn to him. He was a forceful planner. She felt encapsulated in the mystique of their togetherness. This plan was for them; he had referred to it as "our plan."

12

The Clarkes Discuss Moving

Occasionally, with Cass's version of a jovial family evening centered on a special meal, Melody and he patched the rifts they had carved in their marriage. He would cook, with Melody assisting on the sidelines, twins heckling from their stools at the kitchen counter. The twins loved to watch their father skillfully dice the onions and mushrooms that seemed to start each dish. They would wait expectantly for his inevitable jokes; they could always count on him for some corny act. Sometimes he would pretend to be a Japanese chef flipping up a bit of food to catch—his mouth agape —or flip it toward a twin's mouth, usually missing, until the floor was a mess, and the twins were doubled over with laughter.

Melody would watch and marvel at how he could be relaxed and playful while preparing a creative, meal that was always delicious. Tonight she had something serious to discuss and was pleased to see that Cass was in an expanded mood. She started, "This apartment is too cramped for these clowns. Why don't we go up to Connecticut and find a house with a yard and play-area?"

"Yea!" the twins agreed. "A yard to play in! We want a yard! Baxter wants a yard."

Aside from saying, "Yeah, and fleas," Cass did not immediately reply. He moved more slowly. Melody's suggestion had the effect of subduing him as he crushed peppercorns for sauce Béarnaise. He thought about the commute from Connecticut into

Manhattan, and the loss of freedom due to an hour spent on the train when he might instead be at dinner with his secretary. (Those young, lithe, single girls never had enough to eat.) Finally, his thinking momentum built up enough to expel into language.

"You've said on numerous occasions, Melody, that it was crucial for you to be in Manhattan near your modeling contacts."

"That's true, dear." She minced shallots for the Béarnaise while she searched her brain for reasons to make the move to Connecticut. She chopped with great care as if each morsel were a fine diamond. "But I have discussed it with Eva and Kim, who both commute in on the train, and they rather enjoy it. They say they relax and read, and that it's good down-time. I've even been thinking of organizing fashion shows in Connecticut. You know...all those country clubs and women who lunch...that's what they need. Moreover, Anna told me that Westport schools were so good that we wouldn't have to send the twins to private school. Think of the saving. And guaranteed, they would have a play area." She had no need to reveal that Robert had shown her around Westport.

"I'll have to think it over," Cass said.

"Who is Eva?" asked one of the twins.

"A friend at the modeling agency where I work," Melody said.

The twins thought about this for a few seconds. "Dad, did you have a girlfriend before you met mom?" one asked.

"Yup."

"What was her name?"

"Spinish."

"Spinach! That's a dumb name."

"Not spinach...Spinish. Her father was Finnish, and her mother was Spanish, so we called her 'Spinish.' "

"Arrg! That's horrible!" Groans and banging on the counter. "Who's gonna believe that!"

"She probably called you 'Finished,' " Melody said.

Cass gave her a look.

"Everyone had to have a nickname," he said. "You couldn't use their real name."

Silence for a moment while the twins watched Cass chop.

"Do you have a nickname, Dad?"

"Don Juan," Melody said, before Cass could answer.

Cass's mouth gaped open. He stared at Melody, but continued silently chopping.

"Don Juan!" a twin exclaimed. "Who wants that for a nickname?"

"You two are silly," Cass poked at the twins with a carrot.

One of the twins picked up a celery stalk and pointed it at Cass, "You're *sillery*, Dad!"

"Did mom have a nickname?"

"Oh, yeah." Cass thought about what he would say next.

"Come on, dad, tell us mom's nickname."

" 'Looney Tunes.' "

13

The Randalls Entertain Again

S oon, without help from anyone, Spring took a better grip. Seeds and plants sent down determined roots, and sent up exploratory shoots. Greens asserted themselves with deeper color and tentative leaves grew larger, fully intent on providing shade. Evenings were warmer. On such a night, the Randalls' home, brightly lighted from all pores—including lamps that circled the driveway—exuded a warm invitation to enter and dine. They were entertaining again.

Among the guests were Melody and Cass and Noel Tasker, the nurse who had attended Robert after his accident. Also invited was a sleek and slightly mysterious widow, Stella Wilson, the Randall's landscape gardener. She came alone. While she was building an arbor off the Randall's rear terrace, she had been invited in for iced tea so many times, that she had become a good friend, and felt at home with them. Her latest coup was in winning the bid to install landscaping around the new office complex about to be finished on the riverside in Westport.

Last, there was a tall, refined, scrubbed-looking man, Benjamin Powers, a physician and old friend of the Randalls. He also came alone. About forty, appealing, and still single (for reasons of his own), he was chased by many women who just knew in their bones that he wanted to get married. He was presently drifting into

Melody's gravity.

She in turn wired him with the full effects of her highly practiced seduction techniques, disguised, as they were, to include a combination of large searching eyes, and sultry mouth. If that was not enough, her graceful black dress, tissue like, dividing at the most interesting cleavage, provided the perfect backdrop for her pale hair. A lone pearl hung alluringly at the perfect place amid that cleavage. Moreover, her satiny shoulders, showing just so much, would stun even the most unsusceptible man. Ben, beholding Melody, seasoned though he was, found a new susceptibility in himself. He was rooted to her spot, and intended to speak to no one else for the remainder of the evening, if it were up to him. Though enjoying his attention, Melody found the doctor to be—not exciting—but useful. Since someone always had Robert cornered, Melody permitted Ben to manufacture conversation. More like an undulating black light rather than a solid person, she oiled the air between them with frequent soft utterances, the cooing of pigeons. Ben was fascinated in a way that hadn't happened to him in years. Even so, his training and good sense, the feelings he pulled down deep for, told him *see, but don't savor*. However, no harm in exploring why that might be so.

Across the room, leaning on a walking stick to ease the weight on his legs, Robert leaned over for close conversation with an attractive woman whom Melody had not seen before. The stance of the couple suggested familiarity. The woman was young and confident.

"Who is that with Robert?" Melody asked Ben. She finger-curled a strand of hair, and looked in the opposite direction as though to study a painting on a nearby wall. (Ben shouldn't think she cared. Shouldn't think she was all that interested in the woman.)

"That's Noel Tasker. Noel was Robert's nurse after his accident."

"Oh. I understand she's quite capable."

"She is indeed...sought after. She does it all, nurse, cook, play chess. Energetic. Anna says Noel has spoiled Robert beyond help."

With her hair piled-up like that, Melody thought, she's more suited to be a dancehall hostess in Queens. Managing to excuse herself and disengage from Ben, Melody wove through the group and opened the circle around Robert.

"Melody," he said, putting his arm around her waist, "I haven't yet had a chance to introduce you to Noel Tasker. Noel is the long-suffering saint who tended my broken bones and me."

Melody offered a stiff smile and a limp hand to Noel.

"We were congratulating her on her engagement. I hope to meet her fiancé, Peter Lytton, and assure him that he is lucky to have acquired such a caring nurse, without having to first break his legs." Robert waved his cane around. "Noel is joining a fascinating culture, Peter is a film producer, and Noel has been regaling us with anecdotes about movie stars."

Welcome news for Melody: that Noel's relationship to Robert was purely professional. And just incidentally—perhaps friendly. She quickly summoned up a big smile of approval.

"I've been selling Melody and Cass on the fine idea of moving from Manhattan to Westport," he said to Noel. "They have two preschoolers who need a lawn to play on, and good schools that don't cost a year's income."

Turning to new arrivals, Robert introduced them around, then took Melody by the arm and pulled her aside. "Damn, have I missed you! I haven't been able to get away from the business that piled up during my convalescence. Meet me in the library in about ten minutes." He pointed the way with his cane. "I need to have a tight hug from you in private, but first I want to move our guests out of here and onto the terrace to dance. We've brought in a combo from a local night spot. Good dance music, and they're starting up now. I think it's warm enough, and I have two heaters out there."

But before he could take his hug, Noel took his hand and pulled him out on to the terrace to dance. Protective of his legs, he merely bobbed around, barely moving. Noel, however, used the beat as an opportunity to move her body in a graceful, but suggestive, manner. The other guests stood to the side unable to take their eyes off Noel's legs and gyrating torso, showing just so under her short skirt with a thigh-high slit. Noel owned the dance floor. As Melody moved up behind the group to watch the display, an acute observer would have noticed that Melody's smile was frozen into place. Someone should ask her to dance, she thought. She would show them. But no one did. Ben wanted only to stand by her and deeply inhale.

"We thoroughly enjoyed your beautiful party, Anna," Melody assured her over the phone the next day. "How brave of you to entertain us while you must still be in the middle of restoring order after your renovations." *Not to mention that you have a cook.*

"True, two rooms still have to be put back to order, but Robert becomes restless if we don't entertain regularly. The plumber is still here, but at least the carpenters and painters are finished. Yet, I'm quite annoyed this afternoon. I had to miss a painting class because Robert wanted me to supervise moving the furniture back. Today!"

"That Guy! He has wonderful qualities, but making you a priority is not one of them." *Drive a little wedge.* Really, when you consider it, Melody thought, Anna was always drifting; not focusing on the inconsiderate, cold treatment Robert gave her. She *would* be happier without him.

"You know, you're right," Anna agreed. "But he always has excessive demands on him to propel the business forward. It doesn't let up. He has little spare time." Anna's loyalties were undivided. "And, I'm sure his thinking is, that I have a housekeeper to help. What else would I need?"

The wedge needed pounding. What else indeed, thought Melody—but maybe something you haven't thought of—an exciting affair; a lover to fill your heart with desire.

14

Stella and Tess

While growing up in Japan, Stella talked a landscape gardener into letting her help him after school hours. She explained that she would use his ideas and techniques back in the States when she returned there for college; his ideas were too effective not to spread further afield. So, when Stella arrived back in the States, she continued her interest and worked part-time at landscaping to help pay her way through college. Her clients thought her to be a green-thumb genius; she would change a dull lot into a magical garden. And in Connecticut, a green and colorful state with homeowners who cared about appearances, her wand spun winter gardens and summer gardens into magic. She understood what they needed to thrive and life throve under her green thumb. Eventually, she earned a decent income

She met Wally Wilson in a Master's class and a year after that they married. Two years after that, Tess was born, making those good years complete, and Stella stopped her business to stay home and raise the baby. Five years after that, when Tess was starting school, Wally fell ill. Stella had had to start up her landscape business again; medical expenses were taking the bulk of their financial worth. Five years after that Wally succumbed to his illness. But now, Stella was able to provide quite well for Tess and herself. On occasion when Tess's homework load was light, Tess worked with Stella. They enjoyed working together and Tess was slowly learning the art and tricks of landscaping. For the time, giving love to the land, seeing it flourish was romance enough for Stella. That, and her daughter, Tess, and a few friends, were all she needed for a while. But she sometimes found herself looking forward to the next dinner at Anna's, that Ben would no doubt attend, and though he never really looked her way, she regarded him with more than casual interest. Even so, his thoughts were clearly on Melody's assets. Stella imagined having her own brand of magic dust to throw on Ben; maybe some of her fertilizer. She could laugh about it.

15

Who....Recommended the Wallpaper?

A s the delicate sun ambled on its westerly trip across the arc, one cottage, lighted by its trip, fairly burst with activity. Inside an open window, Melody was scraping paint off a window jam. As Anna drove the Miata over the graveled driveway, she saw Melody in the window and waved to her. She saw her sleek hair tied back out of the way with a red scarf, and saw the red-flowered smock she wore. Even scraping a windowsill, Melody managed to look striking. Anna had arrived for her first look at the Clarkes' new Westport home, the Clarkes' first house, and not a new house at all —a rickety one. It needed endless amounts of paint and spackle, and even lumber. With prices of housing in Fairfield County being inordinately high, if young couples wanted a fenced-in lawn for the children, they had to start with the market's worst—and work almost daily to combat termites and carpenter ants to convert a derelict, or barely acceptable house, into a comfortable, and even beautiful, home. And the Clarkes, undaunted by these prospects, had begun home improvement in earnest. Despite their romantic ventures outside the marriage, when their home needed work, they pulled together.

"Hello, Anna. Let yourself in," Melody intoned from the window. "I'm glad you've come by. You're in good time...I need to take a break." She would have preferred visitors to come after Cass and she had finished remodeling, but that would be a year from now with the amount of work there was to do, thus she had issued an open invitation for friends to drop by. Melody put down her scraper, opened a silver box that sat on a nearby end table, and removed a cigarette. With a silver lighter that sat next to the box, she sparked a flame, lit the cigarette, and drew a long breath through it. Then she looked up at Anna coming in the front door.

Anna placed a gift-wrapped box on the coffee table. "A little new-home gift," she said.

Melody laid her cigarette on an ashtray, untied the gift's ribbon, and opened the box. "How lovely, Anna. I recognize this porcelain company. From Denmark, right?"

"Yes. And you can use it as an ivy holder with water, or as an ash tray, or simply as a beautiful thing to admire."

Melody set the porcelain down and picked up her cigarette. She pulled air through it and, tilting her chin up away from Anna, she slowly blew it out. "Have a seat and tell me what's new."

"What's new?" Anna said, as she collapsed onto the sofa, "I have nearly finished carrying all of my canvases...about a dozen counting varnished and unvarnished paintings...up to my new studio over the garage."

"But I thought your studio would stay in that side room on the first floor. You mentioned painting by the steady north light there."

"I did. And that would be ideal; however, Robert wants that room now and has had built-ins installed for him. He's allergic to fumes, and even though when I'm painting, I vent the room by drawing the air outside, he wants my paints moved upstairs out of the way, over the garage. Real sensitive. You know how he's barked at you a few times about smoking." She took a sidewise glance toward Melody. "After listening to his reasoning, I decided to have peace and quiet, and make the move."

She picked at paint spots on her pants while she thought of ways to soften this information; she didn't often complain about Robert. "He has wanted that room for an office all along anyway. The upper room is fine for me; it's heated, you know, you can't let oil paintings freeze. Plumbers have installed a sink and there's plenty of light. It's quite spacey. But I have to go up and down, up and down so much."

Melody aimed smoke toward the ceiling, and bobbed her head. Robert probably wants to get a little space from Anna, she thought. Here's a gal with a housekeeper and a perfect house, and all she has to worry about is moving stuff upstairs. She could ask her housekeeper to do that; whereas, I must slave in between modeling assignments, to paint and repair an entire six-room cottage.

"He's demanding, all right," Melody agreed.

"And I still have all the paints, brushes, taboret, and easels to move. An afternoon's work ahead of me." Anna looked fatigued at the thought.

"Oh, poor thing! Can't you get your housekeeper to help?"

"No. Belle's off today; she has classes. I can't expect her to do more."

"You have a live-in housekeeper that you let go to school. That's admirable. I'm surprised her homework time doesn't take away from your needs."

"No, not at all. She cooks and keeps the house and often watches the children. But, they're easy. Robert and I have encouraged her to get an education. We won't always need her contribution. I help, of course, but it's a far larger house than we should have bought." She was keeping Melody from her work; she had delivered the gift and could think of no more news. "Well, I must get going and complete the move so I can finish a painting that has to dry and be signed and varnished for a juried show coming up."

"That sounds like fun," Melody offered.

"It's fun. It's disappointing. It's rewarding. But it's mainly hard work. You have to have a tough skin. My paintings are rejected from many shows. You can't get discouraged though; you have to go right on painting and submitting and remembering the sales and awards you've won. Many of the entry decisions are political anyway. It would be foolish to take it personally."

Melody, thinking about wedges, decided to fashion a wedge,

"Robert must support your art though...even if he does want to chase you out of the downstairs room."

"Not really, Robert has little patience with my painting, though I've had many sales and awards and have almost completed a Fine Arts degree. I could say to him, 'I had a great time today painting with Van Gogh. He gave me some important tips.' And Robert would probably glance around the room, bob his chin up and down a couple times and say, 'That's wonderful. I'm glad you had that opportunity.' He wouldn't have heard me."

"Still, whatever you do, don't quit painting," Melody stressed. "I love the painting you had over the mantle...the winter woods scene. That large size was commanding, and with your beautiful colors, perfect in that place. However, it was gone, I noticed, the other night. Where is it now?"

Anna sighed, "It's also been moved upstairs. Robert needs all the space he can get for his marine prints and ship models. They're all over the main rooms. I'm sure you've noticed. Keeps him in the right spirit for his work, he says, and provides history and examples to show clients whom we occasionally entertain. He praises my work now and then, but in an off-handed way." Anna laughed and intended to sound cheerful, but a flicker of sadness that only the most attuned would have caught, crossed her brow.

"Have you thought of painting boat portraits for him?"

"I would have to work from photographs, and he wants photorealism. I've worked up a few and he picks them apart; he expects an architectural rendering. And the results are stiff ... not my style." Anna stood and walked over to a table piled with wallpaper books. She started flipping pages.

"Beautiful papers. You found my favorite company."

"I love them," Melody said. "Each one is a classic. It was hard to choose." She went to the table to show Anna her selections. "I haven't pick them up yet. I'm so pleased that you told me about this company. These light colors and delicate prints are precisely what I wanted for this old house. Classic without being trite. Saved me a lot of looking."

"Did I tell you about this company? Funny...I don't remember that. Shows you how busy I've been."

Whoops! Melody now remembered that Robert had told her about this wallpaper company. The last time he came over.

"Show me your house now and what you plan to do," Anna said. "I should be off, and you're busy as well."

As the house tour evolved, Melody described their plans for each room. The cottage had been a gatehouse and had managed to escape modern conveniences such as closets, showers, and dishwashers. As she looked around at work to be done, Melody thought how nice to be in Anna's position; merely engage the housekeeper, or call in a builder when you wanted to make changes.

Meanwhile, Anna thought the Clarkes' cottage and their plans for it, to be genuinely warm and delightful, and it wasn't in her nature to compare it to her own large home. If it came to it, Anna would have organized a cheerful, peaceful living in just such a cottage, and would have been surprised to find that Melody hadn't quite the same attitude.

"Invite me over to see your studio," Melody said as Anna picked up her car keys.

"I will soon. I have to have molding installed to support some paintings. Once things are back in place we'll be having another dinner. Robert has to have something social going on. I'll let you know when in plenty of time."

"That's nice, Anna. You can see I have a long way to go here before I can entertain." Melody pictured herself living with Robert — they would have a housekeeper and entertaining would be a high priority. Easy. Robert would delight in showing off his bride. Anna will be surprised to find her happiness elsewhere.

It's nice to have Melody for a new friend, Anna thought, as she headed for home. She had been somewhat reclusive, not a joiner. She had good friends in Stella and Ben, a nodding acquaintance with Robert's colleagues, and also friends in art school; however, her painting classmates were much younger and had their cliques. It was good to add Melody, a woman who gets around, to her own small circle. And yet, there was something about Melody.

Something Anna couldn't define. Something puzzling. Melody always has that knowing smile. A smirk? Anna wondered where that came from.

16

A Slow Burn

Melody saw Cass's car pull into the driveway; she wondered why he was so early. She had spent the day hemming a skirt, as well as other mending. And dinner was already in the oven.

The aroma of chicken dashed with cinnamon and nutmeg greeted Cass at the door. His favorite: *Chicken Hash a la 21*. If it weren't for the other thing, Cass would have looked forward to dinner.

"Surprise," he said. "It was hot and muggy today at the office, and the air wasn't working well on the train. A cold shower will be a good thing. What have you been up to?" He was desperate for that shower, the itch in his crotch was unrelenting.

"The phone has rung two times with hang-ups from number unknown," Melody said. "Funny that only seems to happen when you're home, or on your way home. I wonder whether you ought to call work. Maybe they're trying to reach you."

"I'll give them a call shortly," he said, "I forgot and left my phone turned off." He suspected he knew who was ringing and it wasn't the office." It had to be Jocelyn, for before leaving work, he had fought all the fires that needed attention. He had warned Jocelyn not to call him, but she was anxious; anxious to spend as much time with him as he could manage. He understood. Now he had to take a shower and let no one know the real reason for that. Though he had

had one in the morning before leaving for work, and it was quite cool at work, and the air conditioning on the train was adequate, not the sweat box he had described for Melody, he had to take another shower. Now.

"Good thing I was home today," Melody said, "for I found fleas on Baxter."

"Eeeuu!"

"Yup. And also in the carpet. So I called Shortcut Grooming and they said to buy a flea bath product and bathe him, then spray the carpet. They told me what to buy."

"I'm happy to have missed that," Cass said.

"You always miss the fun."

"True. I lead a flea-free existence." Fleas were not his problem.

He stepped into the shower. The twins had asked him for a story and he had begged off, saying he was so hot and so tired today; it had been a hell-of-a-day at the office. Hell-of-a-time scratching. Damn that Jocelyn, she had given him crabs. It had to be her, for he had been with no one else, including Melody. Another troublesome secretary. That brings up the question: where did Jocelyn pick up crabs? What's going on there? He knew that she had lunch sometimes with Roger. Did Roger have crabs? Maybe the entire office had crabs. Did everyone look with suspicion at everyone else? He would have to watch to see whether anyone else was scratching. And Jocelyn wouldn't stop calling. These dependent, possessive women! And she kept asking when was he going to leave Melody? Maybe after all, he didn't want to leave Melody. He was ashamed to go to the doctor; he would try to self medicate. Flea bath. He saw it on the bathroom counter. He would try that. If fleas couldn't survive it, probably clap couldn't either. He stood in the shower and vigorously shampooed his genitals. A little bit of the poison was left that he would use later, perhaps in the morning. Melody might wonder why so little was left. Couldn't let her know. He would have to hide that as well. Next problem: Jocelyn. At least Melody seems to have forgotten all about his asking for divorce. He and she probably get along better than most couples.

"You must be the cleanest salesman at work," Melody said

when he came in for dinner wearing a light cotton dressing gown.

Cass didn't answer, but Melody was used to that. Cass was often other-worldly. The next day his testicles had a good burn, an other-worldly burn.

17

Ben Dodges Valerie

It was not many more weeks, before Robert and Anna entertained again. Robert no longer needed the cane and enjoyed feeling lighter and freer. If that weren't enough to make a man happy, his company had scored a large sale. He was ebullient.

After the guests arrived and drinks were served before the drawing room fire, he excused himself from the group, saying he had brochures to show Melody. He directed her to his library, but there were no new brochures that Melody hadn't already seen. He directed Melody to a leather couch and sat beside her with an album on his lap.

"I had to have a chance to be *really* close to you," he said. He opened the album. "And this, darling, is me when I started kindergarten. And here I am going off to boarding school. I gave 'em hell there. I was voted the one most likely to become an anarchist." They laughed as he turned pages, and pointed to examples of his youthful antics. They sat close, thighs touching. They heard Belle announce dinner.

"There's the dinner call, but first look at this picture of me on the day I soloed. My father's pilot, Emory, had kept his instructor's rating current, and as he had a son of his own coming along, Tony, my father told Emory that if he would teach me, he could use our *Cherokee 180* to teach Tony. So one summer both Tony and I soloed. But if we don't quickly go in to dinner, someone will come looking for us."

He stood, pulled Melody up, took her in his arms, and pressed her to him. "Darling, he sighed, it's been only a week but it seems like months since we've been together for enough time so that I can touch you." Then he pressed his lips to hers. Melody clung to him, thirsty for his touch and his warmth. "Ah, you found the joy stick," he said.

Off to the side, Melody saw movement. A slight turn and she saw Belle in the doorway. Belle had come to say dinner was on the table. She spun around and left—the words unsaid. Melody was not embarrassed; instead, she thought, this could be interesting. Before leaving the library, Robert used his handkerchief to remove traces of Melody's lipstick from his mouth. He had not seen Belle.

"I had to regale Melody with my war stories," Robert said to the group as he and Melody entered the dining room together. "Poor thing, she was desperately trying to get away."

Melody, always the good actress, nodded and sprouted a look of irritation.

Rubbing his hands together, Robert surveyed the candlelit room and nodded to the others assembled there: Anna, Cass, Stella and Ben. Ben was often around when Melody was invited. Robert pulled out a chair for Melody to his right, and poured wine around before taking his seat at the head of the table. Belle and her assistant brought in the first course. Throughout dinner, soft chatter rounded the table with different animated conversations dividing the group. Robert and Cass discussed system specs and quote that Cass had brought. (Cass could speak of nothing but systems, and paid no attention to Melody.)

Melody, listening to this conversation, appeared happy to sit near Robert and to touch his knee. Although she couldn't occupy the foot of the table, she knew she was Robert's de facto queen. No one noticed the special attention Ben paid to Melody; which attention, she seemed to invite as often as she could. He was trying hard to be polite, though divided between listening to Anna's banter and observing Melody's perfect shoulders.

Occasionally, with half-closed eyes, Melody would give Ben an encouraging glance, and a Mona Lisa smile. Though Melody adored Robert, it never hurt to show him that she had attracted another. Robert paid no attention.

In between noticing Ben's appeal, and in particular wanting to hear whatever he had to say, Stella listened to whoever talked the loudest. As Belle quietly moved in and out with dishes, Melody avoided all eye contact with her. A blue wave of electricity seemed to animate the table, only Anna escaped its path.

When all had praised the last bite of dessert, *Tuile d'amandes* wrapped around a homemade raspberry sorbet, chairs were pushed back and the party moved to the drawing room for coffee. Ben attended to Melody by pulling up a chair for her close to the coffee table where Belle had set up coffee and liqueurs.

"Thank you," Melody said. "However, tonight my back is bothering me from standing for hours at a fashion show today. I have to find a straight-backed chair, or else I might not be able to get out of it."

Ben now had ever more reason to subject Melody to his admiration and to show off his professionalism. He found a straight chair and brought it over for her. She seemed so alone, he wanted to find a way to connect with her.

"What have you been doing for your back?"

"Nothing...except using a heat pad."

"Is it moist heat?"

"No."

Hearing that, Ben dove in with his medical prowess, more than happy to flow the tides of his doctoring experience over the lovely apparition before him. "I recommend a moist heat pad instead. You simply heat it in water. I'll pick one up for you." *Anything— anything to forge a link.* He didn't feel awkward tending to Melody; for it was clear that Cass was wrapped up in some other world and hardly knew she was there.

"Ben is always so helpful to us. We're lucky to know him," Anna added.

Melody thanked Ben. But while Robert asked Cass software

questions, and Cass displayed his technical acumen while taking notes for software requirements at Robert's plants, Melody looked as if their three-letter computer jargon was the most interesting topic to ever come her way. Tilting her head to the side in just such a way, she tried with meaningful glances to get Robert's attention, but with frustrating results: his attention to her was not equal to his attention to software.

On the sideline, Stella relaxed with coffee. She was among friends who did not push her, and in between exchanging comments with Anna, she listened to the conversations around her. She would welcome interaction with Ben, but he appeared to be firmly caught in Melody's orbit. Well, that made sense—not surprising: Melody sucked in attention in ways for which Stella had no training. Stella thought Ben was suave, someone worth knowing. And it appeared that Melody had an unobstructed prospect for knowing him.

Outside of offering her common politeness, Ben paid scant attention to Stella. Though she was certainly easy to look at with her lanky and graceful posture and wide, cheerful eyes, hers was a quiet attractiveness. She didn't put herself forward; it took time for people to see her excellence. Moreover, Anna had indicated to Ben that, she wasn't certain, but Stella was probably involved with someone. Stella kept her status private, and if she wanted to talk about it, she would. In her own time. Ben said he was happy for Stella, and he thought no more about her.

"Ben, we'll have to set our heads on finding a special friend for you," Anna teased. She knew there was a line-up for those wanting Ben's attention, but the temptation to rag him was irresistible. He was a good sport, and one whose appeal attracted commentary. People wanted to connect with him.

"Although we'll have to protect her from Valerie Llewis, lest she get her eyes scratched out. Valerie may have a private eye following you around. I'll ask Belle to check for her car...she's probably out there waiting to follow you home." Anna laughed as she said this. She waited for Ben's reaction.

He threw his head back and groaned. "I wouldn't be surprised.

She always seems to turn up wherever I am. And loud. I cringe when I hear that husky, brandy voice coming toward me."

He winked at Melody. "Valerie Llewis is on the hospital board, and she's generous with her time for fund-raising. So, I can't conscionably run when I see her coming."

"But she's after Ben," Anna said. "In more ways than one."

"She's trying to raise something, and I don't think it's only funds," Robert said, tuning in to this repartee.

"Well, she causes an inverse relationship to your point," Ben said. He rolled his eyes toward the ceiling.

"Actually, I think it's *your* point," Robert said, to the group's amusement.

"Ah...and thank you, but no thank you, Anna. No special friend," Ben said. "I am quite content to remain uninvolved. I'll join the Peace Core if I attract one more clinger." Yet he thought that he would be quite content to have Melody cling to him, if only she would, but she remained aloof, which enticed him more. He was encouraged by his sense that Cass and she were emotionally distant from each other. Who could say what would happen there? He couldn't imagine beyond picturing how splendid Melody would look arm-in-arm with himself. Anyway, he could wait and see.

"Well, just don't ever cross me," Anna said. And she pointed a large smile toward him. "I'll take revenge. I consider Valerie a weapon and I'll throw a dinner you can't resist and sneakily include Valerie."

"Ah, revenge. Served up at dinner. My dear, you might as well cook my goose."

Ben's friends knew that he had been avoiding Valerie Llewis. He had met her when he attended board meetings, and as one of the few unmarried and highly attractive doctors, the hospital core of nurses and secretaries discussed him at length. They felt a high excitement all day when he was the Attending, and for this reason—wanting no complications for his private office—he hired a Mrs. Muggs, who resembled her name and was quite myopic, and twenty years Ben's senior. Thus, it was that Valerie learned from the hospital chatter, that not only was Ben eligible, but that he was also wealthy from inherited wealth—two recommendations she could not ignore. Her bossy ways had driven off two husbands, and she was on the prowl. She decided that if she persisted, she could have Ben. She was aggressive in pursuit and found ways to corner him. She continued the entrapment with first, big parties at her house, and then increasingly smaller parties, until she had him alone to herself. Not one to avoid parties, Ben had gone right along ignoring her specificity for him until it was too late. Catering to her a bit was worth the large checks she made out to the hospital, but he wasn't going to sell himself, and being around her had become difficult. Therefore, Ben enjoyed Anna's parties where no one chased him and where he could focus on Melody. If occasionally, he thought, Melody and he were seen around town together—an innocent pleasure—maybe Valerie would cease.

Anna continued, "He has all the women chasing him, Stella."

Stella thought she could understand why. She smiled and said nothing.

"He's such a doll." Anna smiled at Ben, fully meaning her praise though couching it behind a playful countenance. She wasn't flirting; she knew him well as a good friend and had an easy manner with him.

Ben turned his attention to Melody.

18

Ben's Private Quest

Ben had had his heart broken when he was in medical school. He had fallen in love with a pretty blonde, Judy Lassiter, who lived near the hospital. He met her when she came into his dorm to use the piano in the lobby. He had grown to love her deeply and thought they had become close. But when she became pregnant, and he ask her to marry him, begged in fact, she had said no. Raised in a strict Catholic family, unable to face her parents to reveal an out-of-wedlock pregnancy, she had given up the baby boy to a doctor who black-marketed it in exchange for her medical care. Judy's decision—against Ben's wishes. She couldn't see a future with Ben, a struggling medical student, who, after finishing his residency and beginning a medical practice, would have large debts. True, he could expect a large inheritance, but he had never discussed this with anyone, and anyway, he wouldn't receive that for many years. He had repeatedly begged Judy to marry him and keep the child, but she had turned against him She said she loved a guy back in her hometown, was engaged to him, and though Ben pressed her to, she could not marry him. Even her roommates came into play, urging Judy to see the wisdom of marrying Ben, at whom they all would like to have a go. They would say things such as, "You havn't seen your fiancé in six months, and what has he been doing during that time?" Anyway, such situations have a mind of their own and sometimes take a wayward course: before she could be married to the fiancé back home, she fell ill with Lyme Disease. It had been misdiagnosed, had gone untreated for months; it didn't appear that she would fully recover. Achy joints. She was miserable and wasn't good company. After that her husband-to-be found a reason-to-be gone. Shunned more or less by her parents, who didn't want a daughter living back at home, Judy moved east to start a new life.

Each year, still carrying feelings for her, as well as a sense of responsibility, Ben had sent her money; he could do without it and she needed it. Now, after nearly fifteen years, his torch burned with only a weak flame, and until meeting Melody he had not put himself into the position of becoming too close to any woman. He wanted a life companion, saw that as the best future, but had that aspect of his future on the back burner.

He had long grieved for the lost child, and now he decided it was time to do something about it. Quietly. His secret project. He was not ready to tell anyone about the search to find his son. He would never forget the name of the physician who had black-marketed the infant, Leon Faber Sample, MD, OB/GYN. And fifteen years later, Ben was in a much better position to find the boy; he even wielded a bit of influence in the medical community. He had followed Leon Sample's career and knew that he had a thriving practice in Manhattan. He would talk to him, apply pressure, and if necessary threaten him with exposure. Obviously, Sample knew where he had sold the child. Under the guise of conferring about a relative's problem, Ben made an appointment with Sample, and on that day Ben drove to Sample's office in Manhattan.

Facing Sample across his desk, Ben quickly revealed his mission. The room was quiet while Sample absorbed the information that, years ago, he had sold Ben Powers' and Judy Lassiter's baby against Ben's wishes. Now Ben wanted to find that child. Ben waited.

Sample rocked back in his chair, legs crossed, finger tips together, alarm slowly changing to control; he would control this meeting. It took him a few seconds to remember to which woman Dr. Powers referred, and he would reveal nothing though he could see the need to be diplomatic. He stared hard at Ben. *Who did he think he was*!

Ben waited, returning Sample's stare.

"I assure you the boy is in a wonderful situation. I placed him with personal contacts...a family of professionals. And of course, I won't reveal who they are. Your friend, Judy Lassiter, wanted it that way and I was perfectly correct in my actions. In exchange for the child, I gave Judy good medical care and paid for all her bills and my time. A real bargain," he said. "You know that in those days the unwed father had no say in the matter."

Only the most observant would have seen the trace of guilt that crossed Sample's face when he remembered the vast sum he got for the boy. Back in those days, from some people, pale skin and yellow hair drew a premium. He had had a nagging thought that he could have shared some of the payment with Judy, but he had quickly abolished that thought with another: that the situation had been her responsibility, and she had been willing to give it all up.

"Dr. Sample, you may want to reconsider your position. I don't wish to interfere with the boy, his life, or the family in any way. I want to meet the parents and introduce myself. I might be some help to them. Then, if they agree, I'll meet my son. These days, as you know, many adopted children seek their biological parents. It must have crossed my son's mind."

"I guaranteed the family and Judy complete privacy, and I will not go back on my word."

"Like I said, Doctor, you may want to change your mind. Consider my viewpoint and the harm I'm prepared to do to you. I'm quite prepared I assure you. Your reputation can be sullied by the revelations that you take advantage of young women, and that you are a black-marketer of babies, especially against the biological father's wishes. I was offered no chance to raise the child."

Leon Faber Sample, M.D. toyed with the *Concord* model on his desk. He fingered it lovingly. He remembered the trips he had made on it, paid for with money he had earned delivering babies and selling them; the women he had purposely impregnated in order to sell their infant. On occasion, he had even promised them marriage.

But in the end when he confessed to them that sadly he was already married, they had to be satisfied with a generous sum of money. What would happen if that became a news item? What if they all came after him these years later? The room was awash in silence. He thought about how much stature he stood to lose with his colleagues, maybe even be barred from the medical associations he had strived to earn the privilege to join; have his medical license revoked. Already there had been questions raised about just who had paid the bills for some of the women.

"I'll give you one day to think about this," Ben said. "This is not a snap decision on my part. I've labored with this need for nearly fifteen years, and now is my time to act."

In time, Anna told Melody Ben's history, and although Melody knew she had his full attention, found him to be attractive— certainly admired his wealth and position—she didn't care one way or the other. She had a future with Robert. Still, she understood that Ben would be happy to hang around attending to her like a devoted puppy. That could be pleasant, especially when Robert and Cass weren't around. Good thing Ben didn't have the child: she wouldn't want a teenager hanging around, and the child was surely a teenager by now. Cass was not a consideration; he was down-river, or even dry riverbed.

19

How Much Does a Man Need His Shoes?

The invitation read "Lobster and Clambake and Cocktails, and all the Beer You Can Drink, at the Beach at Chez Llewis, Saturday night, 6:00." Appended was a hand scrawled note that said, "Be sure to come. All of your department will be here." It was from Valerie Llewis.

Wouldn't you know, Ben thought, my favorite food: lobster. He was determined to avoid her dinners, but this was too tempting. He would have to go to Valerie's party once more. With such commotion as a clambake, surely Valerie would be too busy to appropriate him for herself.

So on Saturday at six-thirty, Ben arrived at Valerie's house and found her long, circular driveway already choked with cars. He drove over the lawn and wedged in between a Mercedes and a Volvo with barely enough room to open his door and squeeze out. He reached over for the bottle of Moët & Chandon, climbed out and locked the Beemer. As he trod across the grass toward the brightly lighted house, waves of music, competing with aromas of roasting delights, poured out across the lawn, flavored the gentle breeze, and pulled him in.

"Ben!" Valerie said, greeting him at the door. She had been looking for him.

He handed her the champagne and gave her a slight cheek kiss. She stood close enough to touch him and arrange his collar, while gazing into his wary eyes. Her fingers caressed his neck. He backed up a step, not enough to be offensive, but enough to satisfy his discomfort.

"Ah, Ben...thank you. This champagne is too fine for this gang. I'll save it, if you don't mind, for a special dinner with you."

Ben stared ahead to the source of merriment.

"Come on back," she said, taking his hand. "The makings for cocktails are on the terrace, along with plenty of beer. Our feast has been roasting for a little over an hour now, and we can eat in half-an-hour." She wore pajamas rather like something one would see in a harem. They were dashed here and there with violets and greens, and on her feet were thong sandals covered with lavender posies, chubby toes with pink toenails showing in between. Stuck near her ear and helping to prop up her curls was a white hibiscus. A satisfied smile seemed to pull her through as she looked up at Ben and led the way.

"The caterers came this morning to get the pits and rocks ready. We're in for a feast. As you'll see, most guests are already here. You'll know most of them, but let me show you around." Her rush of words insisted that Ben just follow orders. And as they reached the back terrace, she hooked onto his arm in a proprietary manner, and proudly looked around for all to see her conquest.

He hoped coming to her party had not been a mistake.

Over to one side of the terrace, a drinks bar had been set up to which she now led Ben, overseeing that the bartender handed him a good, dry double martini. The Hawaiian motif in the bartender's shirt matched the apron on a waiter who was arranging pitchers of water and glasses on an array of picnic tables that had been set up on the sandy beach. Valerie looked around to see which guests saw her with Ben.

And when to welcome new guests, she let go of him, he used the opportunity to look around, stopping here and there, to say hello and offer toasts to the fine evening. It's always amusing, he thought, to see how different his colleagues looked outside the hospital. Then he followed the scent of lobster down to the beach where pits lined with rocks contained large cans that steamed over wood fires. Lifting a lid, he saw clams wrapped in cheesecloth and potatoes in foil and lobsters and corn and onions. He could smell rockweed beneath it all. He felt like drooling; a feast. It had been years since he had been to an old-fashioned clambake and he intended to enjoy himself. Valerie had really done it up right. Then he pushed through sand back up to the bar for another martini and, with Valerie not in sight for the moment, he enjoyed relaxing with colleagues— something he rarely had time to do during the day. But, as she mingled with her guests, Valerie kept returning to him, hooking her arm in his, or caressing his shoulder. Her possessive manner was on display for her guests, and it was impossible for Ben to push her away. He was her guest, partaking of her largess, and he would not be rude.

Soon Valerie called her hungry guests to take a seat around tables laden with food. Finger food. Buckets of shucked clams and trays of lobsters, corn, and potatoes were placed on each table. Take a lobster, a lobster cracker, and a bib, and make a mess. Down both sides of the tables were candles, sheltered in glass lamps, ready to be lit as evening folded around them, and before each guest was a bowl of drawn butter. Nothing for a grand clambake was missing, and anyone who arrived without serious hunger quickly saw his or her mistake.

Ben started to sit next to an orderly he knew from the hospital; it would be a good opportunity to praise the young man's work ethic, but Valerie had other ideas. Catching him before he could be seated, she joined her arm to Ben's, and hauled him off to sit next to her at another table where she held court. It would have been impolite for him to resist; after all, accepting her invitation meant accepting the hostess as she was: it was her domain. Besides, the picture in his mind was "lobster," and the sooner he could fork into one, the better. The caterers had found the pick of the day's lobsters and one, it turned out, was all Ben could manage. He wanted to have another —out of the question.

Finally, as the sun grew weaker, shadows grew longer and fires faded to a soft glow. Valerie lighted the candles while her cook,

Sherrie, brought out dessert. Anyone who had thoughts of leaving was drawn back to feast on homemade blueberry pie. Its aroma had preceded Sherrie onto the beach as she and a helper placed trays of pie and tubs of ice cream on each table for guests to help themselves and pass. Valerie was satisfied that hospital employees would rave for days about this successful clambake. The loud clamor tapered down to the soft groan of full bellies, until slowly—people said their goodbyes and took their leave.

By midnight, only Ben was still there, in the drawing room asleep in a wingback chair, feet propped on a hassock. Big mistake. He hadn't intended to fall asleep but when he sat for a moment to speak to colleagues on their way out, exhaustion, coupled with the sensation of being overfull, overtook him. Valerie tiptoed over to him and removed his topsiders. She knew he had had a wonderful time, a time he would remember, and she wasn't going to let him go now. She stepped up the stairs to bed. She would know when he wanted to leave—she had his shoes.

A half-hour later she heard his call.

"Valerie! Valerie, I need my shoes. Do you know what happened to them? I don't remember taking them off." He felt good. He had actually had only two drinks along with an extravagance of food, and he wanted to go home, get a good night's sleep, and be ready to be the attending staff-physician the next day.

"You'll have to come up here for your shoes." Valerie called down.

Oh, hell, we're going to play games now, he thought. He started up the stairs. "Where are they?" he called out at the top.

"Just in here."

He turned toward Valerie's voice and peered into an open door. She was sitting up in bed, draped across an orchid satin sheet, wearing only a beguiling smile. She beckoned him over. Her body was as smooth and satiny as the bed covers. But he had seen tons of smooth, satiny bodies, and was unmoved, though he had a sudden urge to quite innocently say, "Gee, Valerie, I haven't seen that much flesh since that whale washed up on shore," but hospital contributions flashed across his eyes, and he controlled the urge. He stood in the doorway and pretended she was fully dressed.

"Valerie, your party was probably the tastiest and most entertaining one I've ever attended, and now I want to go home. I want my shoes."

"You don't *really* want to go."

"I do, Valerie. I do." His face wore a determined seriousness.

"Well, Ben, you can't have your shoes until you come over here and give me a hug."

"I'm not going to do that. Now, will you please tell me where my shoes are?"

"Sorreeeee."

Ben turned with a sigh; he was in no mood to play games. What's a pair of shoes? Tomorrow he'd stop into the sport shop for another pair. She had put on a great party, but her price was too high. He walked barefoot down the stairs and out the front door, closing it loudly behind him. Making it down Valerie's front steps was easy, but crossing the grass to his car was a challenge; the short, grassy spikes pricked and pierced the soles of his feet. Her gardener must starch the lawn, Ben thought, wincing with each painful step. He wouldn't go to another of her parties. Her intentions were too clear. They always had been. He should have known.

"Ben, dear, I brought your shoes," Valerie called loudly. She came toward him down the hospital corridor, waving his shoes for all the physicians and nurses at the nurses' station to see. From an upper window, she had waited and watched, Ben's shoes in hand, for his car to pull into the staff parking lot. "You left them at my house last night...you careless man!" She brandished around an enthusiastic and public grin.

"Oh, shit!" He quickly turned into a stairwell. Let her do what she would with his shoes. He wouldn't give her the dignity of reaching to her for them. He ran down a flight of stairs onto the floor below, walked rapidly to the other end of the hallway, and took a freight elevator back up. Still, he would have to watch for her. He reached his office, quickly slipped in, and locked the door behind him. He'd have to endure the grins around him until time dulled their memories. Actually, he didn't care what they thought. If they could envision him with Valerie, that would be proof of their ineptitude. He would keep his professional stance and that would force those around him to do the same.

He had done his duty by writing her a thank-you note saying what a gracious hostess she had been to entertain so lavishly. And now he was attempting to be among the missing and unavailable as much as possible. However, Valerie continued to phone him, and she seemed to have antennae to signal her when he was at the coffee shop, or on his way in or out. On such encounters, she beamed. She knew he was happy to see her; any other thought was intolerable. She had pegged him for a shy man, simply needing help with personal relationships. She could provide that.

20

An Interfering *Porsche*

Spring rolled on, days lengthening into long twilights. Ben started visiting the Clarkes' cottage during the day when Cass was in the city. Ben's office was only about two miles from the Clarkes' street, and on days when he saw patients at his village office, he would drop in for a short visit with Melody; something to do when he took a mid-day break. He knew Melody was usually working at home, the children off to a playgroup. She enjoyed his visits and reveled in the attention he gave her. They would talk a little and then he would leave. He examined his intentions regarding Melody—he had none, he thought. He didn't see himself as a marriage breaker—not even a fragile marriage such as the Clarkes' appeared to be, but he enjoyed Melody's presence more than that of any woman he had encountered in years. He felt his power around her and he was enlivened to be in her aura. As well Melody's needs and emotions seemed to be hanging out—raw.

Clearly, Cass and she had a marriage of convenience, Ben thought. It had probably not started out that way, but over time, their personal needs had not been compatible. It was easy to see that neither Melody nor Cass felt at home around the other. Actually, Cass never looked as though anyone were at home. They didn't seem to feel hostility toward each other, and yet there was a barrier of some kind between them, keeping them spaced apart. And Melody, Ben had noticed, would sink into lethargy unless he or Robert attempted to inspire her; then she came to life.

Ben didn't prefer to live alone, but he had not been in a hurry to find a mate. He ran from women who chased him, which was most all of them. He had lived alone now for as long as he could remember. And, he had the Randalls for good friends and for low pressure dinner parties. Besides, he had something of a new challenge in mind, a secret project. That would keep his emotions occupied for a while. As for this situation with Melody, he would see how it worked itself out. He had learned that stuff was self-sorting, usually without his interference. He wouldn't step over the line and have an affair with her. Would she? Dangerous. On the one-to-ten danger scale, ten being the highest, that would be a nine or ten. As it was, he knew he was already fodder for gossip around the hospital. Still, he could envision Melody in bed, and could imagine how her long legs would feel wrapped around his own. His visits were short because it weighed on him to keep a conversation going; Melody hadn't much to say.

Today, he would see if Melody was at home. But as he approached the Clarkes' driveway, he was surprised to see Robert's *Porsche*. Ben drove on. He returned an hour later. The *Porsche* was still there. Again on another day. On these occasions Ben didn't stop. He mentioned this business to no one.

21

The Marlows

The phone call from Leon Faber Sample, M.D. couldn't have been more welcome. "Dr. Powers, there's a good reason now to give you your son's name and contact," Sample said. "I knew that, sadly, his adoptive parents were killed in a car accident about a year ago, but until now, I hadn't thought it wise to mention that to you. The young man has had to move in with his adoptive grandparents. The lad's name is David Marlow. After learning that they're having minor difficulties with the boy, I realized that they may well need your help. They live up your way in Noroton."

While sitting on hot timbers ready to pull the next punch if twenty-four hours lapsed without hearing from Sample, Ben now had the precious information for which he had been waiting. He regretted the adoptive parents' accident, but if anything, he now wanted to find out more than ever how David was doing. David—he had a name for his son. A good name. Ben immediately phoned the Marlows. He had had to stiffen his fingers to dial their number; the anxiety made him feel limp.

"Mr. Marlow, I am Ben Powers. I'm a physician in Westport. I'm on the staff at Stamford Hospital, and I've been practicing in Fairfield County now for twelve to thirteen years, and I am a respected member of the community." Ben rushed to get out all the essential words before Mr. Marlow hung up.

"Sorry," Marlow interrupted, "but I'm not interested. I have enough to concern myself with right now." He thought it was a marketing call of some kind. The heavens knew he had more of those than a body could stand, what with estate planners and insurance companies hounding him.

"Please don't hang up, Mr. Marlow. This is a personal call, regarding your grandson, David." Ben could hear Marlow's deep breath of hopelessness. "I have good news that should interest you. At least for me, it's good news. I hope you will let me come to meet you. I am your grandson's biological father." He gave Marlow time to digest this news; all the world was still as though to listen. Airwaves had stopped moving. Sound had quit. The gods were holding their breath to hear what came next.

Taking a long pause to feel this reality, Mr. Marlow said, "Mrs. Marlow and I are most interested in meeting you, doctor." And they arranged to meet the next day when David was in school.

For the next twenty-four hours, Ben thought about nothing else. He could hardly sleep. *David.*

He came prepared with several kinds of identification so the Marlows would have no reason to fear that he was not who he said he was, and his visit went well. He had prayed that they would be reasonable people, and he had found them to be so. The Marlows said that David had indeed wondered who his biological parents were; a quest they had decided to leave up to David. It took them less than ten minutes to see the blessing they had just received in the person of David's father. Especially at this time, after the loss of David's adoptive parents, the lad needed plenty of support.

"We've had a few problems with David lately," Mr. Marlow said. "Minor stuff we hope. He's trying to adjust to the accident and the loss of his parents, and having to move in with us. We all have to adjust. It isn't easy on any of us. He has skipped some school and soccer practice, and recently he was temporarily suspended from the team. We're so worried about that. Seriously, maybe you *can* help."

They agreed that Ben should slowly move into David's life; first, by watching his soccer games when he could. Marlow explained to Ben that after Coach obtained apologies and promises from David, he granted David a reprieve, and David would be playing in a game that afternoon.

"If you are free, Dr. Powers, you might attend the game."

"Nothing will keep me from going to that game," Ben said. "Even if I'm called in to excise giant worms from the President's gizzard," he laughed, "I will be there. And please call me 'Ben.' "

"Would you point out David Marlow?" Ben asked the coach.

"He's the one who just kicked."

"I understand he's the team captain," Ben said.

"Yes he is. I didn't pick him to be captain...the team did. He's popular. Been having a hard time lately though. Neglecting school work. Parents were killed in an auto accident and he's been living with his grandparents." Coach swapped his feet around, taking a different stance while he looked toward the team. "As well as having to adjust to that loss, he wasn't happy about changing schools. His grandparents are doing their best, but aren't quite up to the stress and tragedy. They always come to the games, and are probably in the crowd somewhere." He leaned around to see if he could spot the Marlows. "I've been worried about David. He functions well on the court, but he looks sad."

The Marlows and Ben had agreed that before they introduced David to Ben, they would have a talk with David and prepare him for the big news. So for this game Ben sat by himself, and said nothing to the coach about being David's father; too soon to put that forward. He hadn't even met David yet and was unsure how the lad would accept him. He watched his son move on the field, coordinated, skilled. A joy to watch. When the game ended, David and his team congratulated each other on a good game, then David walked over to give his grandparents a hug.

Reluctantly, Ben drove home. His heart was with David. He was already proud of his son. He hoped the boy would accept him. If, someday he could tell him how his heart had been broken to let him go, that would make Judy look bad. He didn't want to do that — something she no longer deserved. He couldn't blame adults for decisions made when they had barely embarked on their life's journey. He would tell Judy about David, though, and about the accident, and that he hoped he could help the lad in some way. That day he wrote to Judy, and straight away took his letter to the post office.

22

Judy Lassiter Has a Son

Alarmed, Judy Lassiter warily opened the letter from her far-away history: Ben Powers. She had not heard from him in fourteen or fifteen years. He had always sent her money; she wasn't even sure why he had sent it all these years, and how could a letter from him be anything but bad news? Maybe he couldn't send the money that she had come to rely on. She read while walking—one step, one word, in dread. Instead of bad news, though, it contained good news. Or did it? Almost anything compared to the loss of income would be good news.

Judy pushed aside beads that hung in the doorway, and went into her small sitting room to read Ben Power's letter for the third time. The man who fathered their son—*lordy,* she hardly remembered, *fifteen years ago*? —wanted to visit her. He wrote that he would drive down; he had news. Judy's hair bristled. *This could be weird.* She had briefly loved him when he was a penniless medical student, but she hadn't wanted to marry him. The pregnancy was a slip, for she had been engaged to a young man back home before the airline had moved her to New York. Now, she feared that Ben might want to tell her that he had fallen on bad times, and could no longer afford to help her. Could she manage without his generosity? She would write and say that of course he was welcome. She could hardly do otherwise.

23

Stella Meets Bad News

After Wally died, Stella had been too busy for much of a social life, but now that hers and Tess's lives were settled and quite routine, having a pleasant man with whom to share the ordinary life events, someone with whom to laugh, someone who would put her first, wasn't a bad idea at all, and it was time to exert herself in that direction. She regarded Ben with more than casual interest and yet, his thoughts were clearly not on her. So when she read in a church bulletin that on alternate Friday evenings, the building hosted a singles' wine and cheese social, followed by a lecture, she started attending.

For the first third of the meeting, people stood around sipping wine and munching cheese and crackers. They introduced themselves and looked over each other. During the second part of the meeting, a speaker gave a talk on a topic that related to the life and challenges of the unmarried. During the third part of the meeting, they broke into small discussion groups.

That's when Stella met Ryan Black, a professor at a community college in New York. Ryan had to be a nice guy, she thought. If he were not, surely the college would not have hired him. She enjoyed his laugh and he laughed often, appeared to be popular. Neatly put together, he was tall, slender, and quite presentable. He asked her to have dinner with him the following weekend. She was eager, but before she mentioned him to her friends, she would see whether he had staying power. Her first indication that he had a dark side came soon after they had had two dates. She had invited him in for dinner with Tess and herself, and afterward, while Tess was busy in the kitchen, Stella and Ryan talked over coffee.

"An old friend and I went to a disco in Westchester last night," he said. "It was good to see him and hear what he's been doing lately. I like that lounge...the *Cocoputz*. Always good music and dancing. But, I don't think you'd like it," he said, his head tilted and eyes narrowed as he tested Stella's reaction. "Dark in back and along the sides, and I could see in the shadows that some were going at it."

Stella needed a few seconds to realize what he had said, and to wonder exactly what he had meant. "And you're okay with that?" She frowned. "It's okay with you, going to a place like that?"

"What others do doesn't bother me. I do or don't do what's okay for me. Others can do what they want."

Stella gave him a look. Without another word, she rose, collected dishes, and took them into the kitchen. She stood at the sink a minute, not seeing, but staring through the window at moonlight reaching across the lawn. She turned back into the dining room.

"I have a heavy week, this week, many plantings to install. So, I'd like to say goodnight now, if you don't mind." She went to the entry closet, removed Ryan's jacket, and stood holding it at the front door, waiting for him to decide to leave. He took the jacket and said goodnight. Stella watched him leisurely negotiate the steps, then she closed and locked the door behind him. For a moment she leaned against the door to replay what had just happened. She felt relief that he was gone, but also disappointment. It was hard to relax her deep frown, although things weren't that bad, she reminded herself. She would go help Tess finish in the kitchen.

As Ryan walked to his car, he passed the canvas-wrapped saplings Stella kept damp, that were waiting beside her van. He put

his fist into one and knocked it over. So some of its branches broke
—tough! He felt a little revenge.

While Tess dried pots and Stella put them away, she noticed that
Tess seemed unusually glum.

"I think you're carrying a heavy weight tonight. Anything I can
help with?"

Tess paused for a bit, then said. "I *am* sad. About a year ago, a
classmate's parents were killed in an accident, and he had to leave
school to move to his grandparents."

"I remember your telling me about him and the accident. A
tragedy."

"He was in my shop class. He helped me with some of the
equipment when I made the little pagodas. He was so much fun and
his leaving was so sudden. Happened fast...one day he was there and
the next, he wasn't. I didn't even have a chance to tell him goodbye
and good luck."

"I hope you hear from him. If not, you could drop him a note.
I'm sure the school office has his address."

It's a night for disappointment, Stella thought as she later turned
into bed. Her brain doubled back along the path of her discussion
with Ryan. What was right? What was out of the question? People
were different. Were they expected to conform to her morality? She
had been drawn to Ryan and now did not want to admit
disappointment. In any case, she would not be in a rush to see him
again.

The second clue she had, that Ryan was not a man with whom she
would like to associate, was a conversation they had a week later.
She had acknowledged to herself that he wasn't her kind of guy, but
when he called to ask Tess and her out for barbecued ribs, taken by
surprise, instead of the big *no* she had planned, she heard herself
saying yes. She would go through with it, but it wasn't looking
good. Afterward, back at her house, Stella served coffee and ice
cream. Tess took her ice cream to her room where she was working

on a project. Over coffee, Ryan and Stella discussed news since they had last seen each other.

"Soon I'll be buying a new laptop," said Stella. "Tess needs it for homework. The one she's using now freezes too often; it's overloaded and is too old anyway. Rather than repair it, I'd rather put the money toward a new one."

"I can get you the latest and greatest," Ryan said. "Brand new. Top of the line."

"Thank you, but we'll look at Walmart; they'll have a good brand without breaking the bank...one I can afford."

"Can you afford twenty-five dollars?" he asked.

"Twenty-five dollars for a new computer?"

"Brand new in the box."

"You're not serious: brand new, in the box, top of the line, for twenty-five dollars?"

"Yup."

"It has to be stolen," Stella gave him a puzzling frown.

"Let's just say the teachers at college have a source."

"Well, that's stolen. I won't buy stolen merchandise."

"Someone's going to buy it. It might as well be you."

"No thanks. But thanks all the same." That was all Stella needed to know. She would not see Ryan again. He and she were on different planets. The next few times he called, she was busy.

24

Who Was That on the Phone?

Robert asked Melody to take a trip with him for a few days, and her heart was soaring even before the Cessna Skylane took flight. It was a clear, spring day, and they were flying out of Danbury Airport. While Robert handled the controls Melody silently studied him, enjoying his power. Men who pushed machines, she thought, that was more powerful than pushing symbols. They were flying to Rhode Island for a few days and would stay in a beautiful old inn on the shore. To parry any potential problems, Robert had registered Melody into her own suite with fireplace; it would, adjoin his with a convenient door between. Melody knew that the day would come when he could sign her in as his wife without the need for separate rooms. The purpose of the trip was to select dinghies for yacht tenders. Robert didn't have to buy them yet, for he had two waiting at the plant, but this was business he would have to do eventually, and at this time he felt like getting away with Melody.

In Rhode Island, he transacted business while Melody read and walked along the shore. At night, they read and watched TV before a fire in Melody's suite. Cass thought Melody was working a show in Newport. Anna thought Robert was in Rhode Island buying dinghies. Well—he was.

This would have worked to their satisfaction had not the phone rung right in the middle of an amorous movie scene. Of course Melody thought it might be about the twins and answered it. But those mix-ups that will occur came down hard on this night—for Anna, after trying Robert's phone with no answer, had asked the inn's switchboard to ring his room. Reception rang Melody's room, for that's where they had Robert registered.

"Hello," Melody said.

Silence. Anna needed to think this through. It was supposed to be Robert's room, but a woman with a familiar voice had answered. What to do? She thought for a moment, hung up and dialed back the reception. "That's not the right room for Mr. Randall. Please try again."

The savvy inn clerk, taking his time in the hotel's register, and noticing that a Mr. Randall was registered also in the adjacent room, decided to chance it and ring the other room. Robert heard his phone ring and jumped through the adjoining door to answer it. The first thing Anna said to him was that the inn had just rung a different room and a woman had answered. Robert assured her that it was just a mix-up and he was securely in bed, about to go to asleep.

"Why did you call?"

"I figured I might catch you before you went to sleep, to ask you how the dinghy-buying business was going, and when you expect to be home."

"Find, just fine. I'll buy two or three tomorrow. I should be back tomorrow night late. But, now, I'm really tired and want to sleep, Anna." And he hung up abruptly. He breathed a sigh of relief when he rejoined Melody in the next room. "Checking up on me," he said. "You wouldn't do that, would you?"

"How silly of her," Melody said.

Somehow that call had cooled Robert's romantic steam.

Anna went to bed feeling quite unsettled. The sense that the woman had sounded like Melody would not let her fall asleep. She tried to think of what reason Melody would have to be in that room at that time, but nothing sensible came to mind. She could call Melody to see whether she was home; nothing wrong in doing that. If she got Melody on the phone what reason would she give for calling? Anyway, it was too late to call. Maybe a call in the morning to ask Melody to lunch. But, the next morning Louise answered and said that Mrs. Clarke had left to organize a fashion show in Newport, Rhode Island. And Robert, Anna thought, had gone to Warwick, Rhode Island. Surely she was imagining things. But that had sounded just like Melody. Had she imagined that?

25

Pounding the Wedge at Le Cirque

L ast Christmas Eve," Anna said, "Robert was in Manhattan with his graphics people going over plans for promotions...you know ...ad campaigns. The children and I were waiting at home thinking he would walk in the door any minute."

While having lunch at Le Cirque, Anna and Melody discussed the pitfalls of their marriages, the negligence of their husbands. They were not at the best table, but Robert had been able to get reservations, and he said the place would be full of big names; they should go for the fun of it. Anna assured him she would not recognize anyone anyway, unless they had appeared on *Sesame Street,* then maybe it was a possibility. But Robert urged them to go for Melody's sake and there they were, neither one recognizing a soul, but being stared at by some who thought they must be famous; if they only knew why.

"Then he called me quite late to say he was having dinner with one of his publicists and wouldn't be home until near midnight... and for me to go ahead and put the children to bed. Imagine their disappointment! And there we had been waiting up for him," Anna confided. "Christmas Eve!"

"What a thoughtless tur...key," Melody sympathized. She looked around to see the new arrivals that were blowing air kisses at acquaintances, and to see if they were as curious about her as were the rest of the regulars.

Anna, totally uninterested in who was around her in the restaurant, continued to pick away at the poached salmon before her. It had arrived in the most exotic fashion possible, surrounded by waves designed out of truffles.

"At least Cass, who certainly is not the most attentive husband in the world, has never pulled that one," Melody said. Another little wedge. She wondered whether—if Anna acted a bit more interested in Robert, dolled up more dramatically on occasions, flirted some, he might *not* have felt that dinner with his publicist on Christmas Eve was a big priority. No. A glance at Anna's serious, unadorned face assured Melody that that could never be. She would be certain, she assured herself, to keep Robert interested and enveloped in her bubble—once she had him. As Robert had stressed, Melody continued to lay groundwork for their plan. She would slowly convince Anna that she could use the attention of some other masculine source; that there were thoughtful, considerate men out there.

Anna listened, not aware that they were weaving a fate she didn't intend. Didn't recognize the wedges. "That wasn't the end of it either," Anna said. Normally, she did not discuss her husband with a soul, but Melody had revealed bits and pieces of Cass's shenanigans and slowly, Anna felt free to open up about a bit of discomfort in her own marriage. "During the holidays he invited her to our house for the weekend."

Melody's eyes rounded out focusing like slide projector lenses.

"I didn't mind that, except he showed her around in the Porsche, gone for hours on end, leaving me alone to see to the festivities."

"Does he still do this?" Melody cut in.

"No. Not since then."

And therefore, not since the boat show when he met me, Melody thought.

"But he's gone so much," Anna continued. "He recently returned from a three-day trip to Rhode Island. For all I know he may have taken her with him. However, I don't dwell on that, but the strangest thing, Melody, when I called his room, just to ask how things were going, a woman answered. The motel clerk had dialed the wrong room it turned out."

Through Anna's little speech, Melody kept a blank face, although her thoughts choked in her throat, and she felt a hot flush.

"And the woman who answered sounded so much like you, Melody, that for an instant I was disoriented." If she sought a reaction from Melody she was disappointed. "The next day your sitter said you were in Newport for your fashion show. How did it go?"

"Hard work," Melody said. "It was a relief to get back home." Fortunately, Melody had organized many fashion shows, or had helped with them, and knew the drill. "You know, getting everyone up there, and the wardrobes. Rehearsing the day before."

"Sounds expensive," Anna said. "Where was the show held?"

Yeesh! She won't let up, Melody thought. She couldn't think of a place in Newport. She had been there once and toured—, "*The Breakers*," she blurted out quickly.

"How nice," Anna said. "Lovely place for your show."

Melody nodded agreement and said, "But back to your Christmas story...you ought to think more of yourself, and perhaps you shouldn't always wait around on those occasions. Actually, I've wanted to get out in the evenings sometimes when Cass is away. You know...girls' night out kind of evening."

Anna's brow perked up. She waited to hear more. An unusual idea: girls' night out.

"I've heard about a wonderful nightspot in Darien," Melody continued. "It's quite a proper place with an upper-crust group who go there to dance. Nice décor, good bands. My friends tell me there are always nice guys there to dance with. No one cares whether you are married or single, it usually doesn't come up. Why don't we cut loose a little and have some fun? Why should we sit at home while our husbands are amusing themselves without us? And you have Belle...a built-in sitter. You don't even have to worry about that like I do."

Interesting, but not an activity Anna would consider, and she dismissed it with a shrug. Melody pressed no further, and they sat making occasional side-glances at haute couture displays around them. Each person here was *somebody,* and because of Melody's striking looks and carriage, she was thought to be *somebody* also, but no one could figure out quite who. When Melody glanced around in her most casual manner, she saw that eyes were on her. Caught up in admiring the colorful decor, Anna continued to have no interest in who occupied the tables around them.

The next evening, while Anna and the children were eating the dinner that Belle had kept warming for them, the doorbell rang. It had been a long day, tiring, for Anna had taken the children to Old MacDonald's Farm for hamburgers and a tour around the little zoo followed by stop-offs at various shops. Later, after the children had finished their dinners, she would supervise their bath, read to them and tucked them into bed. Belle went to answer the doorbell, and welcomed in Melody. The yellow flower tucked over Melody's ear matched the sparkling earrings that dropped low enough to reach the shoulders of the mink jacket that hung over her black lace, roller-coaster hemmed dress that barely topped off her knees. She towered on toe-power spikes. Belle tried to avoid staring, and her impression, top down, forced her to quickly turn her back. She led Melody back to the dining room where Anna sat eating.

"Melody! A nice surprise; can you sit and have a bite?"

"Not now, thank you. I'm on my way for a few hours of dancing, and dropped by to make a last-minute plea for you to come with me." *Work on the plan.* "Ta, ta-ta. Ta, ta-ta." Melody rumbaed around. If she could get Anna out, maybe she would become interested in some guy, any guy, and start an affair, rather than sit here alone.

Anna was unsure whether to offer a comment on Melody's get-up; not sure which way to phrase one—she might blurt out the wrong thing. Safer to say nothing. "Not tonight. The kids wore me out at Old MacDonald's today."

Belle, carrying a basket of fresh rolls, came in from the kitchen in time to hear Melody's request. "I can vouch for her tiredness," interrupted Belle. "Ms. Anna doesn't need to be cavorting tonight."

Melody looked at Belle, her frown reflecting her astonishment; Belle was *way* out of line. Neither Anna nor Belle seemed to notice.

"Do stop long enough to eat something," Anna said. "Belle is a magician who always has food in the wings ready to go. No pun intended."

"No. I have eaten, thank you. I well remember Belle's tasty dishes." Melody rattled her car keys. "Okaaay," she stretched out the word. "If you change your mind, come on down. I'll be there until at least midnight; don't want to waste my sitter. You know where the Congregational Church is...well, it's the place on the short road behind that," she said, just in case.

Anna saw Melody to the door, closed it behind her, and watched as her car rolled down the drive.

On her way, Melody pondered what enemy, and what obstacle, Belle might bring to Robert's and her plan. Rats—they didn't need that. She reflected on what Belle may have seen when Robert kissed her in his library, and whether Belle had seen where she had her hand.

Anna continued to finish eating. Melody is pretty smart, she thought. She has a beautiful hunk of a husband who is a good father to his children, but who scarcely pays any attention to her. He always seems to be off in space unless he's talking about computers. But Melody hangs in there anyway and enjoys the attention of numerous other men around her, such as Ben, and goes off without guilt to have fun dancing; never worries about appearances. While she herself—what does she have? A handsome, self-absorbed husband, who isn't a particularly involved father for his children, isn't easy on her, isn't home much, and doesn't care whether she's at home. Yet, she doesn't feel free to test the waters outside of homeport. Is this how it will be from now on? She thought of the dance band and pictured herself there with the music's vitality. She hadn't danced in a long time. Would someone really ask her to dance? She sat thinking over a cup of coffee while Belle cleared dishes from around her. The conviction started rising that she should go, should go tonight and try it. Peek in for an hour, or maybe half-an-hour, and see what it was like. Belle was great with the children; she would be more than happy to give them their bath, and tuck them in; no concern about that. Stepping out seemed such a weird thing to do, so seldom had she and Robert been to a nightclub in past years. Melody would be there; it wasn't as though she wouldn't know someone. Maybe Stella would go with her. Stella was kind of a free spirit, always ready to kick up her heels.

"Belle, I do want to go out tonight. For an hour or two. I'll give Stella a call. Maybe she will go with me." She took a quick shower, pulled on a slinky dress and high heels, dabbed on lipstick, and then dialed Stella.

26

A Backward Introduction

Stella stretched her long legs out of the car. "Come on Babe," she barked. "You are about to see the great Stella knock 'em all dead on the dance floor." She had pumped herself up for this setting, a bit new for her also. Anna didn't laugh much lately, Stella thought. Music and new faces might lighten her mood.

"Uh Huh. I can see you...normally so quiet, leaping and bounding in there," Anna said.

"I saw that twisted smirk."

"Uh huh."

"I stepped out of character," Stella agreed.

"Your fertilizer's getting to you."

"You should try it. Have Belle add it to your spinach."

One rarely saw Stella out of her work uniform of hat pulled down around her face, sunglasses, jeans or shorts, and sneakers. Tonight, though, she revealed her other self: silky, straight dark hair cut an inch below her chin, and bangs that curved closely over her perfect, straight eyebrows. A blue knit top and a simple blue skirt that stopped above her knees revealed straight legs, toned muscles and good bones. Stella won't remain single for long, Anna thought.

Anna and Stella stepped into the lounge, and heard the first tantalizing beat of the band lifting them up, almost gliding them over to the coat-check attendant. Self-conscious and eager to locate Melody in the lounge, to anchor herself to something, to face the strangeness, Anna quickly thrust her coat over to the attendant. She then backed up, and, unused to high heels, lost her balance. She stumbled onto the foot of a man who had just stepped in line behind her. She started going down and braced herself for a fall when she felt a strong arm catch her around the waist. Before the stranger could right her, she caught a glimpse of his soiled and paint-splattered sneakers. Next, as his paint-spotted jeans came into view, her mind replayed Melody's assurance that she would not be bothered with any rag-tag scruffy types at Harbor House. Indeed, rag-tag and scruffy described him perfectly.

As he steadied her. he looked slightly embarrassed at having his arm around her. He helped her stand, and then stepped back. He apologized for being behind her at the wrong moment. She caught his accent. French? Though he wasn't exactly handsome, he had a pleasant face, soft, dark hair curling just slightly below his ears, and a wonderful voice. His embarrassment was appealing.

Stella looked the Frenchman over as she handed Anna her purse which had fallen to the floor. She had a fleeting hunch that he looked familiar, but she couldn't place him and she knew no house painters.

"She doesn't get out often," Stella teased. "Doesn't know how to behave in public. Can't walk in high heels. I come along to keep people out of her way. You poor unfortunate man...you came up too quickly for me to warn you."

"Yes, I see," he winked at Stella. He watched Anna smooth her dress and realized that he was not the only one who was embarrassed.

"I apologize," Anna said. "You came out of nowhere. Of course, I didn't see you. Thank you for stopping my fall. I hope I didn't hurt your foot."

"That's all right, Madam," he had seen her wedding ring. "It was nothing. I'm always looking for damsels to catch. It's my primary occupation."

He'd better watch it, Anna thought. He's getting a little too cute and cozy. Another time she would have matched his humor, but not in this strained, unusual situation. They stood without knowing what else to say; his eyes looked so directly into hers, that she felt captured. Finally, he gave her a slight nod and turned toward the lounge. Anna glanced around for a second while she thought about what had just happened. Did he work at the restaurant? But he had on a jacket and appeared to have just come in. Feeling a tug on her sleeve, she turned to see Stella beckoning her toward the music, and she soon forgot about her encounter with the stranger.

"What a surprise! I can't believe my eyes...you actually got here." Melody shouted to Anna and Stella over the music as she beckoned them to take seats near her. Richly upholstered in soft leathers, seats and loveseats were grouped in clusters around coffee tables. Low lights for the onlookers and dancers—spotlight on the pulsing band. While the band rang the last drop of emotion from a vibrating chord weaving throughout the lounge, hungry-looking men leaned with their backs to the bar at the back of the lounge and watched the dancers. Gyrating as if she could not bear not to be on the dancefloor, Melody barely paused long enough to introduced Anna and Stella to the men hovering nearby, vying for her attention, and all too soon one of them pulled her up and moved her toward the dance floor. Her tall, svelte figure and pale hair swayed rhythmically, drawing all attention her way. The remaining men stood around uneasily, bereft from the loss of their star, and a little baffled now that Melody was not on hand to admire them with her practiced flair. They gazed with blank stares, impatiently twisting their glasses and tossing back their drinks.

Soon, a moose of a guy drug Stella to the dance floor. Anna watched them bob lightly and gracefully around the crowded space, weaving in and out of other dancers as though a path had been carved out just for them. When a waiter appeared, Anna took a deep breath and ordered a drink. Her fingers were nervously twisting together, and having a glass to hold might help her to feel more natural. Despite the inspiring band, it was a mistake to have come. Her eyes wandered around, not sure where to place themselves, and then she saw the paint-splattered Frenchman leaning back at the bar, elbows planted behind him against the rail. He appeared to be assessing her situation. She didn't have long to ponder this, for she found herself looking up at a man, whose most compelling characteristic was that of being quite on the short side. He asked her to dance. Grateful to be occupied, rather than sit there and be stared at, she said yes.

Missed opportunity, thought the Frenchman. He wanted to ask the interesting woman who had stepped on him, to dance. He had hesitated. After work, he had decided to step in for a quick drink and hear the music that one of his employees had praised. It had been a long and tiring day and he hadn't gone to his hotel to change clothes first, thinking to stay at the lounge not more than half an hour. And, dressed as he was, would she want to dance with him? He did have on a jacket. Too bad—the band was rousing, and their energetic vocalist, with one leg in a cast, rocked to the music as though the cast itself were animated. The Frenchman was in no hurry. He could wait a bit and admire the woman who stepped on him. He enjoyed watching her. Exactly his size—not too tall, not too short. Her dark curls were lovely. When he stopped her fall she had fit into his arm perfectly. He could still smell her perfume on his sleeve.

The next few minutes proved that no one need apologize for Anna's dancing. The dance was swing, and Anna had learned it from her father when she was little. She could swing with the pros. Time was, she realized, when Robert had occasionally taken her dancing, to this very place. Years ago.

"Am I stiff?" asked Anna. Short man was limbering his way around, leading Anna in time to the beat. "I haven't danced much in years. My husband is either in New York, or too tired to go out."

"He must be in New York now. Else a fascinating woman like you wouldn't be stepping out."

Not his business, Anna thought, a mistake to be discussing her life with him.

When she didn't answer, he said, "You dance well. You're not stiff at all. You must have been the prom queen." And in between twists and turns he smiled continuously and fixed her with an unpleasant leer. After the dance ended, he hung on to Anna and kept her occupied for another and another dance, until she found him to be quite annoying. To anyone watching, they would have appeared to be together, an idea which Anna loathed. While they moved to a slow, quieter piece, during which it was easier to talk, short man explained that he was from Texas and was staying at a hotel while in Connecticut on business. Wouldn't she like to see his hotel room, furnished with lovely antiques. Thoroughly tired of him and weary of being held captive, she ignored his appalling suggestion and excused herself, saying that she had agreed to be home at a certain time; that time was now.

"Why not have a drink with me first? It's drizzling out, and roads will be slippery. You can stay over in my hotel room. It's close by and I have a huge king-size bed and I promise not to bother you." He managed to look innocent with his cunning, beseeching smile. He couldn't believe that he would be turned down.

At first, Anna politely demurred, assured him that was out of the question. But when he started to insist, she fixed a determined glare at him. Then making sure that Stella could get a ride home with Melody, Anna marched off the dance floor with short man following. Stern faced and impatient, she waited for her coat.

"Well, at least let me walk you to your car," he insisted.

Anna said nothing. She avoided looking at him. He was on her heels all the way to the parking lot. She unlocked and climbed into the Miata. She couldn't shut the door. He was holding it open.

"You know what you asked me back on the dance floor about whether you were stiff?" he asked, smiling sweetly into the car at her.

"Yes." She had no choice but to answer — he continued holding the door.

"Well, you *are* stiff!" he snarled, and slammed the door shut in her face.

She sat still for a minute, disbelief holding her attention, then she drove off depressed; stunned by treatment she had not invited. For the first time, she felt a little sorry for herself; felt for the first time that things weren't quite as happy in her life as she had always dreamed and expected. Her husband appeared to grow more indifferent and more wrapped up in the company. She was appreciative of the good life Robert's work had provided for them, but she would have traded much of that good life for a warmer relationship with him. Now this: this insult from a worm of a man. Never. Never would she come to this place again. She would sit home in abject loneliness for the rest of her life before exposing herself to another event like this. She had the children, and she had painting. She would be okay.

Driving out of the parking lot, she passed the main entrance of Harbor House, and saw the Frenchman standing just outside the door. He seemed purposely to be watching her drive away. That's strange, she thought. She shuddered. Probably another loony. A paint-covered French loony. She tried to leave some rubber on the road as she pealed the Miata out of there.

The next day, Melody called to ask Anna about her experience on her first night out. "You left so early."

"Horrible," said Anna. "I was appropriated by a creep, who wouldn't let go of me, and finally he slammed my car door, and said I was stiff. All because I wouldn't stay over in his room. He was offensive. Insulting. Of all the nerve! I won't try that again. Not my kind of thing. Maybe, if I could carry a ricin dart to stick to men such as he, otherwise, I'm not likely to repeat that."

Not the best news to give Robert, Melody thought.

"Our plan has hit a roadblock," Melody warned him. "I think Anna may climb into her shell, and resist going out to meet someone. I had finally gotten her out to go dancing, but she met up with a jerk so appalling to her, that she asked me to take Stella home, and then she left immediately. When I called her yesterday to ask how the evening had been for her...I had noticed that she danced a lot and so expected her to be happily excited about it...she said that she would never do that again, that she had had a horrible time. Major disappointment for me."

"Keep working at it," he said. "You may find it's not a

roadblock, but merely a detour. It's vital for you and me that we get our evidence. Time's fleeting. Keep working at it," he said again. "At least you got her out. That's a big step. I'm dying to see you.

For a few stolen minutes they sat on the wharf at Essex. Robert had asked Melody to meet him at the wharf, and he would treat her to lunch at the *Griswold*. And now they were holding hands, bodies touching, not speaking, listening to surrounding sounds. Other than the laughter of children playing on the tiny beach near the wharf, the only sound was that of gulls cawing for handouts they expected, and gentle waves lapping their way into shore, lapping at pilings. But soon the sound of a motorboat caught their attention. With two people onboard, the boat was heading straight in to the beach, and as it neared the wharf, Robert's and Melody's eyes widened to see it continue at a high speed, as though it were out of control. Then its wheels engaged, pulled it up the sand, onto the street, and down the road it went; its occupants laughing cheerfully. The children had scattered just in time.

"How about that, Melody, an amphibian. That describes you and me. We need a change; we've been all at sea for too long, and now must seek to anchor ourselves together on firm land."

For a few more minutes, they sat quietly watching clamorous gulls competing for bread that children had tossed over the rail. Robert pulled Melody close.

"I must be with you always," he said admiring the upturned tilt of her nose. She hardly responded, transfixed on movement of waves. "You seem to be quite pensive," he said, "not your usual lightness of being. What's going on in that pretty head of yours?"

"Well," Melody took her time to reply as though rounding up a rangy thought from somewhere out in the Universe. "I think our plan may have an adversary in Belle. When I went by to get Anna out to dance, Belle stepped in and firmly told me that Anna had had too long a day for any more adventures. Anna didn't say beep, just sat there agreeing. I thought Belle was quite impudent to speak up like that."

"If that happens again, maybe you'll have to tell Belle that you'd appreciate it if she stayed out of it. That is...if Anna won't speak to her. Belle's been with us many years; she runs the place, and her kind of help is hard to find. She's like a member of the family. You can expect her to be loyal to Anna. In a sense, Anna saved Belle from a life of hardship, and is helping Belle to finish school."

There was a pause while he stood, took a stretch, and thought about what he had suggested.

"Actually, don't say anything to Belle; Anna's not that much of a wimp, and likely wouldn't tolerate it. You might lose her friendship. Belle *might* work against us, but Anna may be quite upset with you if you say anything contrary to Belle."

27

Noel and Peter

The days reluctantly gave up some hours; breezes took the hint and sharpened and wafted about with fragrant hints of fall that caused a quickening in young and old. Crisp yellow, brown, and red leaves descended for children to kick around until a big person spoiled their fun and hauled the leaves into the woods. Although the Randalls employed a service each fall to rake and haul leaves away, before that event, Anna would raked up a pile for the children's play. A shame to waste the trees' largess. Melody hadn't called lately, and Anna gave no more attention to dancing. She had two paintings in progress, and that and the children kept her days full.

Robert had not been home in a week. Clients far out in Montauk wanted to discuss yacht plans. An agency in Manhattan wanted to go over a brochure that he had ordered. And always there was Melody, who would meet him in Manhattan for lunch or dinner. If anyone asked, he would call it a photo-shoot, and to prove it, he had his photographer take a day for capturing Melody on film. All of this took most of the week and Robert stayed in Manhattan. He would call and say hi, checking in with Anna and children. Other than that, he was hard to reach, keeping his phone off, he said, during the many meetings, then forgetting to turn it back on. Anna no longer bothered to try to reach him.

"While you were dancing, a couple appeared on the floor who were wonderful to watch," Stella said. "A striking couple, tall and slender. They moved completely as one and with interesting steps and flawless turns."

Stella had invited Anna out for another evening of music at Harbor House. They wouldn't have to dance with anyone, Stella said. Just have a drink, and watch and listen to the invigorating chords from the same band they had enjoyed last time. Back by popular demand; it was a stirring band—you would have to agree. Anna succumbed; Robert had been away too much, and she felt housebound. If that intolerable man who had insulted her was there, she'd give him her coldest shoulder. This time she would be prepared.

"Which couple?" asked Anna.

"Well, she has dark hair, poofed up, and he has gray hair...premature I'm sure, for his face is youthful, and they're slender and elegantly dressed. I wish you could have seen them dance."

Anna and Stella sat chatting, drinking wine, watching the dancers, and listening to the band flesh out rhythmic sounds. A few of the couples on the dance floor appeared to be in the freshness of love and eager to be close. A few looked tight and tired, perhaps asking themselves how they came to be there. Some of the men who leaned against the bar thought they couldn't dance, or were uncertain, didn't want to be seen out there. Some tried to dance with various configurations. Others wanted only to watch and drink, warm noses over their cold glasses. Nevertheless, the lively sounds coming from the musicians caused all the lounge dwellers to move in time with the rhythm. The energetic singer swayed and bobbed with the beat as she sang into her handheld mike.

"There's the couple I mentioned, moving to a table on the far side of the dance floor," Stella said.

"I see them. Oh, my...her eye makeup is awfully heavy. I can see it from here. I'm astonished that he can get around that."

They watched the man pull out a chair for his partner, then walk over to the bar to buy their drinks. They watched him fish for bills, which ones to take seemed to be a heavy decision. He paid, walked back to the table and set down the drinks. Then they stood again to dance. They moved gracefully with the quick Latin beat, bodies close, never breaking apart, looking the while into each other's eyes.

"He's what I need," said Stella, with a sigh. "Nice looking, dressed nicely, understands the beat. A wonderful dancer."

"And in love. Someone to love us. To show it in that way," said Anna.

Stella had noticed Robert's dismissive manner toward Anna. For a moment she felt sad for her; however, it wasn't a good idea to mention it. "I see what you mean about eye makeup," she said.

Anyone watching would have thought the romantic couple was in the first throws of love, completely self-contained. They danced every dance and knew they were the center of attention. They knew they looked good together, no world outside themselves.

"I'm in love with him," Stella teased. "He's such a beautiful, graceful dancer. Watch his feet." Stella knew the chances of finding such a man for herself, were indeed off the chart to the minus side. Was it pleasant, or purely frustrating, she wondered, to witness this devotion when it seemed to be so rare. She had had to adjust to life without a mate, and Anna's husband, spent too many evenings away. Keenly aware of what they were missing, they continued to watch the romantic couple.

"Do you think their bliss is all show?" asked Anna.

"No. He never looks at anyone else and his gaze at her is full of love...despite heavy eye makeup." Stella gave Anna one of her teasing smirks."

"You think so?"

"Yes. Notice how he holds her close...and he just kissed her on the cheek."

"I wonder whether she loves him as much. Notice that they never stop talking. All the time they are dancing, they are talking. Full time; they never stop. She's doing all the talking. When she faces this way, I see that her mouth never stops moving. She's continuously smiling for him, but maybe it's a *smug* smile."

They sipped wine and continued to watch the amorous couple.

"The more I watch, I realize we know her!" Anna said. "It's Noel, and that must be her fiancé, Peter. You know...she was Robert's nurse through his recovery. Must be all that make-up that camouflaged her."

"Now that you say that, I recognize her too. I wonder what she can be talking about constantly."

"They must be planning," Anna said. "What sort of home to have. How to arrange it. Where to go. What the glorious years ahead will hold. The vacations they'll take. He's a film producer. Has stars in and out all the time; so we've heard."

"Well, maybe all that makeup is a reaction to the stars she meets through him."

"I wonder whether she's only in it for money, or perhaps fame," Anna said.

Meanwhile the graceful couple was indeed planning their future. As they danced, Noel cast her bright smile on Peter and said, "No darling, we can't have Kyle move in with us. We need our privacy...for a while at least. We'll fix up a room for him to visit, but not for a few months. Let's get settled in first." Her head angled to one side, she said this in the most gracious manner.

Peter looked at her with longing. His love would not be deterred by this small setback. Although he had hoped to make a home for his son, he would be patient with Noel and her needs for privacy. She had been a sympathetic, understanding woman all through their brief courtship. He knew that her heart was compassionate and that after the wedding, she would soon invite Kyle into their new home. In his mid-twenties and divorced with child support to pay, Kyle had been thwarted by several low-paying jobs. Some people needed a bit of help now and then and Peter wanted to give him, not money, but a room and a few home-cooked meals. That way the young man could save on rent which would help pay child support. A hard working young man—he deserved a little help.

"And, darling, his kids will be noisy. I *do* love children, it's just for now; for while we're adjusting to our new lives. We'll visit them at their house, so they won't mess up ours." Noel continued to think aloud as they danced. "We'll need cleaning help. At first a woman to come in every day. Then, once I'm organized, I'll taper her off to...maybe two days a week. We'll always want her on Friday to get ready for entertaining on the weekend. And that reminds me, we'll need to line up caterers. We'll have many parties. And I love to dance with you so much that occasionally we'll hire a band like this one."

Peter listened. He loved her passionately. She looked terrific — slender, tall, lovely face, wonderful figure and a head full of shiny dark curls. Fit with him perfectly. He felt fortunate. Still, as they went forward, he would worry about expenses. A lot of money had gone out the door lately, and the plans Noel was describing would indeed stress his income; especially as she said she wanted to quit her job as per-diem nurse. With a large house to manage, she wouldn't have time to work, she had said. Well, he didn't have to think about all that right now. Gently and slowly, he would show her the impossibility of some of her plans. And the mansion she wanted ...well, that would be hard to pay for. Out of the question. Although he was a movie producer with a few hits to his credit, he had started from behind, and having enough money to fund future ventures wasn't necessarily a given. Movies were an uncertain source of income. Guaranteed, there would always be expensive flops in the mix.

When the band took a break, Peter stepped over to the bar and ordered another round of drinks. Anna and Stella watched while he again paused over the choice of bills to pull from his wallet. How lucky Noel is, Anna thought. Embarking on a new life with Peter who obviously adores her. And here I am with a restless husband. I never dreamed...did not see this coming.

A waiter leaned over to speak to Stella and Anna. "Not likely to find a desirable partner here tonight," he said.

"But, I'm already in love with *that* man," Stella said. She laughed and gestured toward Peter.

"Which man?"

"The one in the gray suit. The tall, slender one."

"Oh, that one. You don't want to love someone like that," he said.

"Why not?"

"I know him. He's cheap. You don't want to love someone who is cheap."

"How do you know he's cheap?"

"I can always tell. In this business you get to know people."

Stella guessed that the several times Peter had ordered drinks and paid for them at the bar, he had not tipped. No, she wouldn't want to love someone who was stingy. Not only was it not loving, it was the source of arguments; parsimony is not a romantic trait. She was better off without the attentions of a romantic man such as he. At least he seemed romantic. It could be that he was on guard now, fully realizing how expensive was Noel, and Noel looked to be unyielding.

The hours grew long, and Stella and Anna left the dance to go to their separate homes and their separate dreams. Anna left feeling as though she couldn't have romantic emotions of her own but must always be an observer. Stella left aware that watching the romantic couple had ignited within her a neglected flame.

My best friend, Alex Thompson...I've told you about him...and his wife are coming to visit," Peter said. "He called this morning; they'll be here late Wednesday, coming in from LA. He's going to be my Best Man." Then Peter went on to say how the guest room would work just fine for the Thompsons, and that they would probably swap stories reminiscing into the night. He looked forward to that. He pulled onto I-95 and headed the car north to the condominium he shared with Noel. "I haven't seen him in over two years. We helped each other out in Vietnam and I owe him a lot. I'm eager for him to meet you." Peter didn't want to deal with his movie connections for a while; keep them away, at least for a few months. Have peace from all that gossip, glamour, competition, and drugs; he was clean and wanted to stay that way.

During this time Noel had been silent—what Peter was saying bore some thinking. She merely smiled at him while she thought about how she could forestall his friends' visit. She had relatives and friends of her own to entertain first, as well as Peter's Hollywood crowd—they topped the list. She was already planning the party they would have when the decorators finished with the house that she knew she could talk Peter into buying.

As Noel returned from the dressing room where she had put on her silk lounging robe, she was aware that Peter, sitting on the edge of the bed, watched her movements. She sat down at the vanity to remove her makeup. Oh, if she could keep it on so she would look the same when Peter saw her in the morning. But that was impossible, for it would smear during the night. The false eyelashes had to come off also—they drove her nuts, and she couldn't sleep with them on. The hairpiece used to add some fullness to this thin hair had to come off or it would pull at her scalp during the night and be in disarray come morning. So, she removed the section of lush curls from her head, then opened a vanity drawer and set the hairpiece carefully inside. Then she gently peeled off her eyelashes and opening another drawer set them into a small case.

With this action Peter thought she was finally finished, but then, from another drawer, she selected a jar of cream and began to smear it over her face. He looked at her clean, bare face. He had seen it bare numerous times before, but not as he saw it now. He had been too much in love with her figure, her smile, and her dark hair—was that dyed? He thought he had noticed a tiny edge of white roots on occasion. But now—her face—was this starkly plain person the woman he would soon marry? He didn't wish to focus on it, but much of what he had seen as her charm, was gone. Did it depend on makeup? She didn't look like the same woman. Well, though quite pale, washed out, her skin did glow. Was that the cream? It could be that she was just tired. Maybe he would feel better about it in the morning.

"And Peter," she said, "please tell Alex that we won't be ready for a visit for a while. Ask him to come to visit closer to the wedding. We have to have your Hollywood colleagues in first, and that's a lot of people. I want to help you to promote those relationships and we can't have them all at once. We'll have the 'A' list first. Then the 'B' list, and so on down the line to eventually invite your accountants and support crowd. It's good for business." She loved the lists, that mostly she had drawn up, with occasionally a question to Peter, and at times, she shifted names around trying different arrangements. It was critically important, she thought, to have the right combinations.

She looked from Peter's reflection in the vanity mirror back to her own image while she spread the thick cream around her face. "I'll start lining up the caterers as soon as we're in the house. I'm so excited. I know you will want the house that I think is right for us. It has five bedrooms, six bathrooms, and a heated Olympic-size pool. We'll need those for entertaining. Let's look at it again and put in a bid quickly before it's gone," she pled.

They lay down and he pulled her close to him. He pushed all her ideas ahead. He knew they could work it all out, if she would only stop talking. He meant to ask her where she'd been the past few days, coming in late. He thought her work at the Randalls' had ended. Well, he would kick that can down the road. And in that can, he would put the discussion he would have with her about the small house they *could* buy. He needed to recoup some loses. He would hand it to her gently, that she was going on a tight budget. Had she always gone to bed with all that grease on her face?

28

Anna Was Not at the Cape

"See that man," said a woman standing next to Melody. "He's Monsieur Christian Boutin, a well-known French architect, and a good catch...if any woman can win him. He's the man who won the competition to build the new office complex in Westport."

"Oh, yes. I remember reading about him."

Melody had been sizing up the Harbor House choice of men with whom to dance; deciding whether it was worth her time to be here and pay for a sitter. Cass was working late as usual. She looked at Christian Boutin twice, three times, and afterward kept trying to get his attention. However, he seemed steadily unaware of her. Finally, she walked over to the bar where he stood watching the band, and as unobtrusively as she could manage, she leaned against the bar beside him, cocked her head, and swayed her torso in just such a gentle way that suggested she was absorbed in the music. Christian paid her no attention. It was as if she were not standing there. In a few minutes, Melody turned to him with a large smile.

"I think you should ask me to dance."

Although Christian was not as tall as Melody, he still appeared to look down his nose at her. "Sorry." He shot his cuff and checked his watch. "I'm about to leave. I won't be dancing this evening." He had been looking for Anna Randall. He came many nights, not to dance, but to look for Anna. "Where is your friend...the short one with dark curly hair?"

Thinking fast, Melody said, "She's gone to the cape for the summer." Where did that come from? She surprised herself.

"I see."

"She has a painting buddy and they went off together." No truth to that, either. Well, if it were later found out to be a fib, she would say she thought he was referring to someone else. She had many friends and couldn't keep up with them all. Maybe he would stop looking for Anna and dance with her. Later, she noticed that Christian had not hurried to leave.

After this conversation Christian worked longer days and after dinner stayed in his hotel suite. He had plenty of reading to do and architectural drawings to study. Anyway, he had to return to France for several days. But first there were a few things to check on here.

He walked around the nearly completed office complex, looking at shrubs, small trees, walkways, ponds, and benches that recently had been installed. He saw that the landscape gardener and her team were making adjustments, and he wanted to tell them how pleasing he found the arrangements to be. He walked over and introduced himself to the woman who, his foreman had said, was the landscape architect.

Stella, hidden behind hat and sunglasses, stood. She had been setting in an evergreen shrub, and holding out her dirt-covered gloves for Christian to see, apologized for not shaking hands. It took him a minute to realize where he had met her before. He recognized her as the friend of the woman who had stepped on him and whose fall he had stopped at Harbor House.

"I admire your design," he said. "It's organic. The way you've placed mounds and shrubs gives my buildings the appearance of emerging from the earth. It's exactly the effect I had pictured. And I know you have put in long hours."

"Thank you. It's labor of love," Stella said.

He stood quietly watching. He had more to say, or rather something to ask that he had to think about. Finally, as he watched Stella work, he felt emboldened, "Has your friend...the one you were with at Harbor House...returned from the cape?"

Anna? He must mean Anna, she thought, but Anna hadn't been to the cape. "You must mean Anna Randall. She hasn't been to the cape. She hasn't been anywhere." Stella laughed. "She does get to kindergarten a lot."

Christian grinned at her joke, then looked puzzled. He wouldn't be bold enough to ask more.

When Stella arrived home from work, she checked with Tess to see how her day had gone. Then she showered, put on fresh slacks and tee shirt, and went out to the kitchen to investigate the savory aroma wafting from there. She poured a glass of wine and then she looked in the oven to see a salmon and rice dinner that Tess had prepared; Tess was turning into an accomplished cook. Stella sat down, propped up her feet, and dialed Anna's number.

"Anna, I think you may have stepped on someone famous. Remember the man you fell over at Harbor House? We thought he was scruffy? Well, he's the French architect, M. Christian Boutin, who is responsible for the office complex that I'm landscaping. Imagine my surprise when today, he came over to where I was working, and praised my efforts. I hadn't met him before, because I had dealt with his foreman, and had only seen M. Boutin off at a distance. He recognized me and he—"

"How nice for you," Anna interrupted. "You never know, Stella, I hope I don't seem rude, but we're running late tonight and Belle is waiting for my list before she heads for the store. You know, sometimes she likes to go when the store isn't crowded. I'll talk to you later. Or better, come over for a meal tomorrow and bring Tess. You can tell me more then." After saying goodbye, she hung up.

Anna was interested, but only remotely. Her lingering sensations of falling on the paint-smeared Frenchman were mixed with the repelling dance partner who had slammed her car door. She handed Belle a list, turned to a painting, and picked up and dabbed on a wrong color. She wiped off that and applied the correct color. She'd rather not think about any of them.

She doesn't care who he is, thought Stella. So typical of Anna.

She laughed to herself. I was about to tell her that, for some reason, M. Boutin thought she was at the cape.

"One does meet the strangest people in these places," Melody said. She had seen Christian sitting at the counter in *Coffee An'*, bent over an architectural drawing. She sidled onto the stool next to him, and offered him her sweetest face.

"Oh. Ah...hi." Christian nodded to her. He had expected to sit there alone with his coffee and drawings, but Melody demanded his attention. He felt trapped. Well, he would make use of the encounter.

"Is your friend still at the cape?"

"Yes. She'll probably be there all fall." This lie was taking a chance that Christian wouldn't bump into Anna somewhere.

"Does she have children? And does she take them with her?" He had to stop this. His interest in Anna was way out of line.

Melody feigned interest in the menu and didn't answer—it was the wrong question. Finally she said, "I haven't seen you lately at Harbor House."

"I'm too busy now and often out of town."

"I've looked for you there. I'd love to dance with you." Though accustomed to flirting, Melody still flushed. This man's refinement was intimidating, uncommon among Melody's acquaintances. The way he was dressed, elegantly casual, or was it casually elegant? He wore chinos and loafers, and a light-weight blazer over an open-collared white shirt; not uncommon around town. Still, his appearance was different. Clearly, he stood apart. Someone for her to win.

Christian waved his arm in dismissal and said, "I don't think I'll have time to go there again." Without finishing his coffee, he put some bills on the counter, rolled up the drawings, stood, gave Melody a slight nod, and with a deep sigh, and leaving Melody sitting there staring after him, he walked out.

29

Foul Play at an Exhibition

"I've been asked to organize a fashion show for the good women of the Fairville Women's Club," Melody said over the phone to Anna. Her tone carried a sneer for the good women. "They have a perfect drawing room for the show, and they've asked the Fairville Art Society to organize a painting competition around the fashion show. And there will be a spread of food in an adjacent room. It'll be a large affair, well attended. Would you enter a painting or two? Tickets are $30.00 but artists get in free, and will be given name tags to wear at the show."

"Yes, of course. I would love to enter. Let me know when to drop them off and the size limit; some of my new work is quite large. Usually the limit on any side is thirty-six inches."

"I'll let you know. They don't have the prospectus printed yet, but I know they're restricting the entries at two per artist," said Melody. "It's a juried show and the judge is yet to be selected. I'm sure he or she won't reject *your* work. Actually, the word they use is 'declined'." She laughed. "That's supposed to make the rejection softer. A notice will run in the local papers, but why don't you hand your paintings to me and I'll drop them off. I'll be going there daily to organize the fashion end of the event."

How nice, Anna thought, for Melody to think of her when she must be so busy. She thought about what to enter, and decided on two paintings of dairy cows, painted in the field. It was a challenge to stand outside their fence and capture them moving around. In one field the cows were black and white, and in the field across the road, brown with white. She was pleased with these efforts. Painting moving cows meant that the head of one might wind up on the body of another, and tail on yet another. Only a plein aire artist would know the effort and magic involved, and both paintings had already won awards in previous shows.

So, on her way to the Women's Club, Melody came to pick up Anna's paintings. Anna asked her to stay for lunch and now they were upstairs in Anna's studio collecting the canvases.

"What an interesting collection of antique model cars," Melody said, selecting one from a fairly high shelf.

"Those are Robert's," Anna said. "He stored them up here to protect them from handling. That Mercedes is a model of one of the original cars made for the U.S. public. Robert had an old one when he was a kid, and he cherishes that model above all the others."

Melody lovingly fingered the little model. *Robert's old car*. She reluctantly set it back in its place on the shelf. As she and Anna carried the two cow paintings down to Melody's car, Melody thought that people would love these paintings, but this is one show Anna won't be juried into; Anna needs to be cut down a notch or two. She's married to the man who belongs to me, loves me, but she gets to live with him; has that show-place home, a full-time live-in housekeeper-babysitter, and two children who adore her. I don't know what the judge will like, but these paintings will never cross his path. She stored Anna's cow paintings safely in the trunk of her car. And that's where they stayed.

Melody was stoked when she learned that the Fairville Art Society had asked M. Boutin to judge and select the entries for the art show part of their fashion show. She would try to participate on selection day if they would let her. She had been to art school—no one need know that she had skipped most of it and hadn't painted since. This would be an opportunity to make a real connection to the man. She loved Robert (that thought would creep in between images of M. Boutin), but the attractions of fame seemed to have a stronger pull.

Alas however, on show submission day, the art committee held the selection process behind closed doors—locked in fact. Melody had tried the door.

On Friday, Melody carefully removed Anna's paintings from the trunk of her car, drew X's in the declined boxes, and returned them to Anna, apologizing that the judge had declined them. He had to be stupid, she said. But he was foreign, and being an architect, he probably only liked straight and parallel lines.

"Your cows are strong, expressive work. I'm absolutely floored that he didn't like them," she said her eyebrows knitted together as she emphasized the word 'like.' "Perhaps had you made your cows square, you know, architectural cows..."

Anna had not been too upset. "Rejections are part of it," she said. "To be expected. The next show will win another award for one of them and someone will buy it." But as she studied the two rejection slips, the X marks in the "declined" boxes glared at her.

30

The Hard Truth Needs a Breather

"Peter, dear. We need to get moving on buying our house," Noel urged. "Prices and mortgage rates are escalating. I know you've been in New York a lot, and haven't had time, but can you set aside this weekend to find our house? The last one I loved sold quickly."

Peter Lytton had been on location in New York for his new film, and up until now, he had put off telling Noel the fact that, due to two lean years, they would have to pull in financially. He had to recoup, he would say. They would have to settle for a small but beautiful cottage in a perfect location. And that actually—he would say—could be a lot of fun. And for a long time, the next year at least, there would be no entertaining except for family. Also, for a short while, a year or two, he intended to have a room for his son.

Therefore, to stage his persuasive talk, on a perfect Friday evening he took Noel out for a romantic dinner. When he gently but firmly explained their position, adding in the mix that she had wanted to quit work—thus they didn't have her income—she sat in silence and stared hard at him. Her food, the best one could find in Fairfield County at *Higgins's Gate North*, was going cold on her plate. Peter poured more wine for her while he waited for her reaction.

"Oh," she mouthed. She reached way inside. Was that why she

loved Peter? His money? His movie contacts? The large home? Was that the limit of her interest? Must be. Her disappointment was keen. She had pictured a large estate and a gay life with her at the center of attention, and suddenly in her mind it became a hovel, and a cloistered life of drudgery. No excitement. And with Peter's son to boot! Not wanting to ruin the evening, she tried to rise up out of her funk, but it was impossible. Her dreams were floating off into the cosmos, out of reach. She could almost see them growing smaller.

Neither could find more to say. Peter paid their tab, and in silence drove them home and to bed.

The next day, saying she needed a breather to think, Noel broke off their engagement, and called a broker to find an apartment for her. Then she called nursing agencies and said she was ready for work. Better to work, keeping her options open, than to sit cloistered in a cottage. And there was Robert Randall, her former client. She had had lunch with him a few times. An exciting, seductive man—he had hinted about a divorce—who appeared eager to flex a new-found freedom. Even with a divorce, she felt sure, he would be quite well off; she had worked in his home and had heard things. She picked up the phone and dialed the last number she would ever dial from the condominium she had shared with Peter.

31

Christian Has Another Go

Monsieur Christian Boutin toyed with his long-stemmed crystal glass, turning it about, watching light reflections cavort around the room. Ah..., Americans are dull, he thought. He took a sip, and had another thought...so are the French...but in a different way. U.S. chaps had more energy; showed up for work on time. The office-complex construction had gone well, right on schedule, and there were but a few remaining details to complete. Time to think about the next project waiting in France where, so far, he worked most of the time, as well as occasionally in the Far East. That thought held still for a moment while he pondered a new direction. Perhaps he would leave the next design for his father and brother, and bid on another for himself in the States. Unable to concentrate, he pushed aside the plans spread before him on the table. He continued to think about that silly, pushy woman who had said that her friend, the fetching one, who had stepped on his foot, was out of town—at the Cape. Weeks had gone by during which he thought there wasn't much chance of bumping into her again. And then, her landscaping friend told him that she hadn't gone anywhere. Anna, she had laughed, *did* get to go to kindergarten. He mulled that over. What could he do about it anyway? She had worn a wedding ring. And, he had no time or stomach for complications. And, so far, he usually worked in France.

Still, he wasn't sure why, but from a long list of lovely women, he felt compelled to think about this one; this one had some kind of hold over him. What was in the magic of being gouged by a falling woman's high heel? But he had had his arm around her, caught her perfume that he thought he could still detect. Felt her soft curls brush his chin. All because he had stopped her fall, and then stood by to watch her being harassed by the jerk who asked her to dance. Why should that cause a connection? He had watched and heard the man snarl abuse at her and slam her car door. Obviously, she had been trying to get away from him. The jerk! Never would a Frenchman—. He wanted to watch for her again at Harbor House. He could of course ask his landscaper for her phone number, but then he wouldn't feel free to call anyway. What would he say? Harbor House was it.

32

At Last Christian Finds Anna

"I've haunted this place looking for you. I hoped you would back into me again, but this is even better. I am Christian Boutin, catcher of fallen women...I mean 'falling' women. Sometimes my English..." he stuttered—then quickly, "May I have this dance?" His heart raced. He had come in, walked to the bar and ordered a glass of wine, turned around to lean against the bar and watch for Anna, when immediately he saw her. She appeared to be tentative about taking a seat. Perhaps she had just arrived. He hurried to ask her to dance before someone else did—never mind the glass of wine that he left on the bar—and with a purposeful step, he strode over to Anna.

Even without paint-spotted pants, Anna recognized him. And that accent. In that instant, she tried to sort out how she felt about him. He had a winning bright smile, almost boyish manner, something fetching—what?—about his dark, slightly unruly hair. Before he had been scruffy, covered with paint, or perhaps it was her distress that had influenced her so at the time. And now, could it be that he was in fact appealing? He looked—well—'crisp' was a good word. She couldn't help but note his crisp jeans and a crewneck sweater over an open white collar. And that clean aroma —was that cologne—men's? French perhaps? Take a deep breath before it's gone. Her feelings about him were undergoing adjustment.

"I'm Anna Randall. And yes, I'd love to dance."

Time was short. He had to be bold. "I've looked for you all over, Anna...hoping, in every store, to find you. You've interfered with my work," he said. "Sleepless nights. Coffee nerves. My project is falling down around me."

"All that just from having stopped my fall after I drilled into your foot?"

"It's true."

"Well, that's who I am. I step on gentlemen. Fall on them. Cause their projects to collapse."

"Have you applied to the CIA? You could be important to them as a secret weapon."

"Actually, I did, but they said I was too destructive. So I decided to raise children instead."

"Ah...good decision. Good qualifications." Christian couldn't believe he was holding Anna in his arms while they slowly moved around the dance floor. Could this be happening? He didn't know whether the band played something fast or slow. He didn't hear it. He heard only his heart beat above the music and wanted to keep his feet moving for as long as he could hold her.

"You may have to shout...my eardrums are beaten up from frequenting this place looking for you," he joked. "I was told that you were at the cape. I was ready to follow you to the cape, but when I looked at a map, I saw there were many capes. We would be too old by the time I found you. And I wasn't bold enough to ask which cape, after all, I saw that you were married...based on the wedding ring you wear."

He had to pause to think about the seriousness of what he wanted to do.

"It's true, I am married," said Anna.

He didn't reply.

"I wonder who told you that I was at the cape?"

"Some friend of yours. I don't know who she is." And after a second he said, "Then, I found out from our mutual acquaintance and landscaper, Stella Wilson, that you had never gone anywhere except to kindergarten. I pictured myself sitting in a kindergarten chair, knees up under my chin, in order to see you, the well-traveled woman."

Stella had urged Anna into trying another night out, and Anna had yielded. She had spent too many evenings at home alone. Robert wasn't home much lately, and who knew what he was doing. Anna couldn't think who would have said she was at the cape. This Monsieur Boutin must have her mixed up with someone else.

"You're not splattered with paint tonight."

"Eh?" He pretended to be deaf.

Anna grinned and whispered, "You're not covered with paint tonight."

"No, I purposely cleaned up my act in case you fell on me again. I thought you should know that I have another set of clothes."

Although Anna thought he was one of the restaurant's maintenance staff, she sensed an urbane bearing. Maintenance was all right, if he had some refinement and intelligence to go with it. The more she listened to him, the more she noticed his refinement. And, dancing with him, his holding her felt—good. She had to admit. She relaxed.

Though I know it's futile...you're married...." He had already covered that ground, but he hoped she would say her husband had died, or had taken off with a hooker, and she just hadn't removed her wedding band yet. She didn't.

"Right." She would not lead him on.

"I'm not married," he offered. "Up until now I've yielded to the demands of my work."

As he slowly led their steps, he held her as close as a man—who didn't know the woman, and felt she was a fragile flower, which if he wasn't careful he would crush—could. He hadn't noticed that around them people were twisting to a fast beat. It wouldn't have mattered.

"You must have developed artful techniques to keep the women away." Anna could be playful, if not encouraging.

"That's true. You know those lances that knights used in

tournaments. Well, in France, I have to carry one around with me to fend them off. Fend off women, that is, not knights. People stay out of my way when they see my little car coming with a lance sticking out the window, and pity those hapless pedestrians who don't pay attention. I've nicked a few, and then I get out to survey the mess and have to call a cab for them. Dirty my handkerchief."

"How inconvenient. You live in France?"

"Yes."

"Do they have knights in France?" She looked up at him. He wasn't all that tall, neither tall nor short, but he was taller than she was. And his arms were strong. She kept thinking about that.

"Yes. Surprisingly, France has modernized. It's a well-kept secret, but each day, we have a night."

"Each day, a night! Is that confusing? I think you just triggered my gag-threshold." She found the smile he fixed on her to be the warmest she had felt in years. "And, do you have a moon, also? Like ours?"

"Yes. I've noticed it is similar. Much the same, in fact. Installed last year. They accommodated me and hung it right in view of my cottage."

"It's definitely a different moon then, for ours hangs quite near our house. Are you working here at the restaurant?" Anna asked, on a more serious note.

"No, I'm an architect and I'm working locally on a project that is finished now, actually only a few last details to see to. My family has an architectural design company in France and my design won a competition to build an office complex here in Westport. I grew up in the business. Bent my first nail at age three." She was so cool: not attempting to attract him, trap him, entice him, win him—that he felt a need to elevate his status in her eyes. Otherwise he would never have so openly discussed his achievements. "I'll be wrapping it up in about a month. I hope. I have other contracts waiting in France." He had not yet cemented his idea for staying in America.

Then Anna realized that he must be the man about whom Stella had called. She had read about him and his project in the local paper, and now had to order up a new impression of Christian Boutin. She had thought *scruffy*. Well, *scruffy* is looking up. "When you came in spotted with paint, I thought you were a house painter. Not that I have anything against them, but they've been too much at my house lately, and I don't want to see another soon."

"I'm not usually involved with painting, but I had to demonstrate a finishing technique that is widely used in France." He wanted to tie up a connection to her—whatever that could be. "I hope we can meet and dance again before I leave."

Still trying to sort out this twist, Anna had no reply.

They continued to dance. He would dance with her all night if there were a way.

"What do you like to do, Anna?"

"I raise two children and keep a home. I go to art school part-time, paint, study." She stopped. He wouldn't be interested in more of her history.

"What do you paint?"

"Landscapes. Still-Lifes. I've had some success with awards and sales. Even nationally," she added, lest he think, as Robert did, that her work wasn't noteworthy. She didn't add that her paintings commanded high prices — at least in her opinion the prices were high.

Ah—a perfect excuse to see her again, he thought. "I'd like to see your paintings. Would you bring a couple that you want to sell to my hotel, The New Englander, in Westport?" He wished he could frame the astonished look Anna gave him. "Saturday would be perfect," he went on rapidly trying to sell her on this idea, build trust. "Saturday at 5:00. Another artist is coming then with some of his work. I hope to select a few for the new offices. A few of my clients like for me to source paintings for them and I take works from several artists over to their homes, or offices, and often they buy. They've come to rely on my taste. I don't take a profit. I like to see works hanging that please me; especially in my buildings." Then he realized that he would be embarrassed if he didn't like Anna's paintings. On second thought, he knew, were that to be the case, he would buy them anyway. Anna would never know. He would ship them off to France if he had to, the French would buy anything.

This sounded wonderful to Anna, but she held back her excitement and simply said, "Thank you. I'd love to. That couldn't be easier. I live in Westport."

Christian thought his angels must have smiled on him again. What good luck. Tonight he had been presented with another opportunity to see her, and yet another to come when she would drop off her paintings. There has to be a reason she lost her balance and found his feelings. It's getting better and better, he thought. However, she's married. Why is she always alone? His sense of decorum wouldn't allow him to ask.

They arranged for Anna to deliver her paintings on Saturday to Christian's suite at The New Englander. Meanwhile, he made sure no one else danced with her, and somehow she didn't mind. His arms gave her a feeling that had gone missing for years.

While waiting for spackle to dry enough so that she could paint over it, Melody took a break from house repairs to stop by Anna's. Belle opened the door for her, and barely spoke before directing her up to the atelier. Melody found Anna wrapped in a paint smeared smock, putting the finishing touches on a canvas that she had painted at the Duck River Cemetery. Anna was bubbling over with good news.

"Something exciting has happened, Melody. You'll be so pleased to hear my news!" Anna scraped old paint off her palette, while she waited for Melody's response. Melody looked at her with wide-eyed eager interest. "Remember the man I told you about?" Anna continued, "The one I stepped on at Harbor House, and whose pants were covered with paint? Well, it turns out, he isn't one of the workers there, but is a French architect working in Westport. His name is Christian Boutin and his design is that new complex we've been reading about in the paper."

Wow was the only word Melody could think of in her astonishment, and so she said it, "Wow!"

"He had been helping his crew the day I fell on him," Anna said, "which explains the paint. He's a hands-on-boss, the best kind. The great news is that he asked me to dance last night, and when he asked me what I liked to do, I told him about painting. He wants to see some of my work, perhaps to sell to his clients." Because Anna had splashed a couple drops of turpentine on the palette and had begun to wipe it clean, she hadn't noticed the frown creasing Melody's brow.

Melody pensively fingered the little car models that were lined up on the shelf. Then, "How nice for you, Melody. When are you going to show them to him?"

"Another artist is delivering paintings to him Saturday, late afternoon, at The New Englander where he is staying," Anna said as she scrubbed. "And he invited me to bring over a few at the same time. Maybe he'll buy one. It's always wonderful to sell a painting; an affirmation."

Melody's thoughts had nothing to do with Anna's paintings. Her first thought went more on the lines of—this was the man who hadn't wanted to dance with her. Her second thought was more crucial: this is working as Robert and she had planned. She now had a new piece of the plan to tell him, and she could hardly wait. Everything moved toward seeing Robert more. Although, he hadn't been around much lately. While thinking what all this meant—what the outcome could be, Melody fingered the little Mercedes model. Then she found her resolve.

"Anna, that's great news! An excellent opportunity! I'm so happy for you." Oops! Melody had told M. Christian Boutin that Anna had gone to the cape. Should Anna ask Melody about it, she would have an answer ready. She would say she thought M. Boutin had someone else in mind.

With the little brook, marsh grasses and stone bridge, the water-lily pond, and of course the trees, the Duck River Cemetery was a favorite plein aire painting site. Different colors each season, each month. A New England landscape painter's dream all in one spot. And safe. There, one could feel safe painting alone. With wide trails winding through ornamental bushes and wild flowers, it was a favorite shady place in summer, or sunny place in winter for runners, walkers, and dog-walkers; so there were always people around. And, among Anna's canvases were several that she had painted among those lights and shadows, and now she looked through those that were finished and varnished, to select two to take to Christian. She decided on a vertical format, with yellow-flecked grass and background trees, and on another, a horizontal format with three silver-gray trees standing in a row like sentries, their tops flaming-red, fall colors. A vertical format for tension, and a horizontal format for peace. Both canvases measured twenty by twenty-four, were framed with gold leaf, and both had been accepted to recent statewide-juried shows. Maybe Christian Boutin would like one of these; although, was he the juror who rejected her two cow paintings? She thought perhaps he was. She stacked the paintings into her hatchback; told Belle she was off to see if a local architect wanted to buy them for his clients, and she would be back in a few hours. Wish her luck.

As Belle watched Anna drive off she waved good-luck wishes from the door. She did wish Anna good luck. Heaven knows Anna didn't have much of a life; Mr. Robert rarely home. Well, the children were a joy; that was good luck in itself. A little something outside to jazz up Anna's day wouldn't hurt though. Anna always brightened when she sold a painting, or won an award.

Belle went inside, heated water for a cup of tea, then sat at the kitchen table with the children while they picked out letters and words in the book before them. Their soft chatter and the warm sweet tea were lulling, and Belle didn't need to stir herself for a while since she had already prepared dinner; it had only to heat through. She had time to think. She thought about how easy the children were with their gentle dispositions. She had been in friends' homes where the kids fought and screamed, but these two girls, a year apart in age, played well together—always laughing. She thought about how Anna and she had met back before the children were born. At a time when Belle was homeless, Anna had volunteered to serve lunches at a soup kitchen in Bridgeport. By choice, Belle had moved away from a toxic home situation in which her stepfather was beginning to put moves on her. Then, when she moved into her friend's house, the friend's brother broke into her room one night and tried to assault her. That ended that; she moved out the next day, and there was no one else who could take her in. At the shelter, she had a place to sleep and two good meals a day and was grateful for them. The people there were good-hearted, and no one bothered her.

After a few months of working two days a week at the shelter, Anna, ready to take a break, had seen Belle, now a familiar face, sitting by herself and had gone over to join her. While serving lunches, she had watched Belle, had studied her intelligent face, watched how she treated those around her, and thought Belle was someone she would like to know better. When Anna was there, lunch together became a regular occurrence. Anna hadn't pried, but in time Belle told her about the situation that had landed her in the shelter. She would find a job soon, she said, but looking for one wasn't easy with no home and no phone and no wardrobe. And she had one more semester of high school to finish; schooling had been interrupted by her having to leave home.

Anna talked it over with Robert, and one day while eating with Belle at the shelter, Anna sprang a proposal: would Belle be a housekeeper for them? She had hesitated to ask, not knowing whether Belle could see herself as a housekeeper. She would have a salary, regular hours, time to herself, and time off to finish school. She would have a room and her own bath in their home. It could be open-ended—Belle could leave any time, Anna had said.

Belle mused about how she had stared at Anna while she tried to process this. Was this real? She hadn't been able to get words out —her life had looked hopeless for so long. She had to be dreaming. Anna's words were unreal enough that Belle had had trouble hearing them.

Anna, fearing that she had insulted Belle, explained that Robert and she needed help. He had bought a house that was too large for their family, and they were going to have a child before the year was out. Maybe Belle could help them while helping herself. That's how Anna had put it.

Belle had recovered her senses enough to say congratulations. She didn't know what else to say. She felt she had sunk so low, was she worthy of this opportunity? She had begun to think of Anna as a friend, but their different stations in life made her wary.

"Give it a try, Belle," Anna had urged.

Belle had given Anna a weak yes, but she was scared. She believed that she trusted Anna, and Anna had said that Mr. Randall was all for the idea, but she hadn't met Mr. Randall. What was she getting into?

It had turned out to be a wonderful situation, Belle thought, as she listened to the children softly naming A, B, C's. She must have had a slew of angels watching over her. She had now lived with the Randalls for five years, during which time she had learned enough about cooking that Anna had raised her salary many times and she had been able to put away a nice financial cushion. And now because of Anna's encouragement, she had finished high school, and had almost completed two years at community college. Try it, Anna had said. Anna had believed she was that smart. Imagine! Best of all, she knew that the Randalls were her friends. She would be loyal to them to the grave.

33

Something Dark Lurks Nearby

A nna carried the paintings, one hanging from each hand, through the hotel lobby to the elevators. In the past, she had been there for dinner and vaguely knew the hotel's layout. Christian had said to come straight to the second floor, Room 202. He would expect her and another artist from five o'clock to five-thirty. She aimed for five-fifteen. She didn't notice the photographer in the lobby, the one who paid special attention to her and took several pictures.

With a welcoming and expectant smile, Christian opened the door and greeted Anna. She was as lovely to him in daytime as she had been in the low lights of Harbor House. What would he do if he couldn't bear her paintings? He would not let on. Would assure her of his admiration. Would ship her paintings to France if he had to. Then what would he do if she supplied him with many awful paintings? He would just have to fill the French waste bins with them. Anyway she was a married woman and he had no right to expectations for involvement with her.

"Come in. Come in, he said. "I'm pleased to see you." He thought she was a bit shy, perhaps uncertain whether he would like her work. He took her two paintings and placed them against the sitting room wall where light fell on them. Then he introduced Anna to Gary Porter, who had also brought two landscapes. And when

Christian dared to look at Anna's paintings, he saw that his fears had been wasted energy—her paintings 'worked'. What a relief, he thought. Beautiful colors and energetic angles in one, and beautiful colors and a soothing wooded scene in the other; neither one overworked. France's trash bins were spared. He nodded his admiration. Anna and Gary were silent while Christian stood back, hand to chin, to study and carefully examine the four canvases.

"Lovely," he said. "All four paintings work well. Neo Impressionism...a favorite genre. What are your prices?"

They quoted figures.

"I'll buy all four. I have no doubt that I can place them with my contacts. Probably in the new buildings." Christian was delighted, for he hadn't known what to expect of Anna's work. From the recommendation of a reliable source, he knew Gary's would be most acceptable and of a style he favored. True, Anna had said that she had won awards and sold paintings, but that meant little—people would buy anything. And he set about writing checks to cover the sales.

When he handed Anna her check she said, "I'm so pleased that you do like these, for I suspect you were the judge for the Fairville Women's Club art show recently, where you didn't accept two of my paintings."

"I didn't? I'm surprised. You obviously have extensive training, and your fresh style works...really works for me."

"Yes. Two paintings, both of cows in the field."

"I don't remember cows." As he squeezed his brow into a question, his face showed the truth of this. "The show received more than a hundred submissions that I had to cut down to fifty; always a sensitive, challenging task. Nevertheless, I would remember cows. I grew up with cows. I love cows. They live all around me in France. My first word was 'Moo.' In French, of course." His generous laugh filled the room.

"It's true," said Melody. "Right back to me with big declined check-marks." But, she believed him, that he hadn't seen her cows.

This was serious. "I'd like to see those paintings, see whether they trigger my memory. I don't believe they made it into the selection committee. I know, seeing your work today that I would not forget your cows, and I do not remember paintings with cows. And I certainly want to buy your two landscapes." He took a moment to look at Anna, and to feel his attraction to her. She wore scrubbed jeans and a plain white cotton shirt, long sleeved with cuffs turned back. Her curls were brushed back off her face and tucked behind her ears. She wore light make-up and still had a clean-scrubbed look. She looked pleased. And he wanted to please her, and it seemed so easy.

"Let's celebrate." He broke his fascination with her face, with having her close again, and said, "I have a nice chilled Pouilly-Fuissé." He opened the small refrigerator and removed the wine. "French, of course." He gave them a pretend smug look. "And the sun has gone over the yardarm. If you can stay a bit, I'll order up a tray of hors d'oeuvres. It's my pleasure...if you don't have to leave right away." He hoped, in particular that he could have a chance to talk with Anna without loud music filling the room, as at Harbor House.

"Thank you, I would enjoy a glass of wine," she said. "I don't have to be home right away."

Gary concurred, "That'll give me an opportunity to ask you, Anna, where you painted these." He gestured toward her landscapes. "Our styles are similar, and I would love to see those sites. Maybe you would allow me to go painting there with you; always nice to have another artist nearby."

"That's the Duck River Cemetery," she said. "In Old Lyme. I would be happy to introduce you to that site. Quite peaceful there."

That drew a laugh. "We could have guessed, Anna, that you would like to have peace and quiet when you were out painting, but we didn't know that you would go to that extreme," Christian said.

"The residents are not likely to bother one," Anna said. What joy! Two new light-hearted friends, she thought. "Seriously, Duck River Cemetery has acres and acres of wide open areas, fields, ponds, as well as woods."

Christian placed a call for room service and asked that they bring up the usual. While they waited for room service, he poured wine, and they drank a toast to the four sales. No stranger to good wines, it was still perhaps the best Anna had tasted. As Christian and Gary discussed France and places there where Gary had painted, Anna sipped wine and looked around the suite. There were three rooms: an entry hall, the front sitting room with a TV lounge adjacent, and in a mirror, she could see behind her, an open doorway that must lead to a bedroom and bath. The furnishings looked fit for royalty, nineteenth-century traditional walnut woods, beautifully polished. Christian must have been living here for months, definitely not on a house painter's income. What Anna mainly thought about though, was that he seemed acceptable in every way. As they sipped wine, she tried not to look him over, but she liked what she saw, and he had that fresh, clean aroma around him that made her breathe deeply. He wore crisp khakis, a tucked-in black shirt, and topsiders. No socks. He looked to be toned, poised, self-assured, and his eyes were kind.

He answered the knock at the door and stepped aside to let the waiter wheel in the table of food. It was a feast. Plates of bite-sized canapés including caviar, smoked salmon, stuffed mushrooms, crunchy cheese puffs, and what all. The hotel restaurant knew what Christian wanted served. Except for murmurs of appreciation, conversation stopped while they savored the spread before them. They would not need dinner.

"Can't we do this everyday," asked Gary. "I tell you what...I'll bring you a canvas or two every day and you supply wine and hors d'oeuvres. I'm sure I can talk Anna into joining me for this." In between bites he looked up at Christian, and then to Anna for approval.

"Exactly," Anna said. "We'll make it a condition of sale."

For a second, thinking that having Anna there every day would be worth all those sales, Christian couldn't reply. He had to re-focus. "Well, if you continue to supply me with this quality, I'll do it. Though I may have to open a gallery, and also a restaurant."

While they continued to enjoy the carefully prepared cuisine, Anna listened to Christian and Gary setting a date to see Gary's

French canvases. Then Gary turned to Anna and asked whether they could plan to paint together at the Duck River Cemetery, and they agreed on a day during the following week. Gary might become a good painting partner, Anna thought. Obviously he painted rather similarly to her which meant he understood the challenges, and the time required to work up an outdoor, a la prima painting. Nice to have such a companion. She usually painted alone, for she had avoided getting involved with painters who talked the whole time. And some painters wanted her to drive them, which was okay except for their different timing—times they would want to leave early, other times she would have to wait for them to finish up. It could get complicated. She would give Gary a try.

Without seeming to, while they talked, Christian studied Anna. He had one sensory perception on his dialogue with Gary, and another sensory perception on Anna. He had not been wrong in his original attraction to her. Her character was open and honest, and not of a sort that advertised itself. Her aura said I'm worthwhile knowing, if you are perceptive to see that. He liked her quiet manner and her soft voice, easy to listen to over the test of time. Again, he wondered about her marriage. Somehow she appeared to be unmarried. She probably didn't know that, he thought. Well, well.

They had stayed long enough. Anna and Gary thanked Christian for the opportunity, and for the delicious food and wine. As they stood to leave Christian yearned to ask Anna whether he could see her again, but he wouldn't ask in front of Gary. If nothing else, he wanted to have lunch with her one day. If he asked now, he would have to include Gary. Didn't fit. He liked Gary, but at this time had no reason to have lunch with him. Perhaps he could phone Anna later, another day. Gary walked Anna out through the lobby and to her car. They did not notice the photographers at the end of the hallway, in the lobby, and in the parking lot.

After Christian saw them out, he sat for a while in the semi-dark, thinking about Anna. Her appeal definitely grew the more he knew her. He needed to see her, and yet it made no sense. She was married, and he was wanted at work back in France. He felt that he had looked at her as looking at a building where he yearned to dwell. But, perhaps he was just overdue—he had postponed emotional contacts too long. Women usually gave up on him. He would be gone here, gone there for weeks at a time, and so many women didn't seem to have lives of their own; needed him to stick around, make their lives whole. His heart had been broken more than once by a lovely woman who wouldn't wait for him.

With a cocky grin, Anna flashed Christian's check for Belle to see. Belle eagerly listened to her good luck selling two paintings.

"What an honor. You've sold many paintings, but to this French architect...that's above any honor I can imagine."

"And, I have a new painting friend, Gary. He was there with two of his landscapes...stunning paintings. I hope he can paint without needing to chat. You've heard me say it before, that I can't concentrate if another painter is bending my ear all the time. Frustrating. Gary produces serious work, though. Thus, it's unlikely that he will be an annoying painting partner. What's strange, Belle, is that M. Christian Boutin was the judge for the Fairville Women's' Club juried show, where I entered the two oil paintings of cows. I mentioned them to Christian, and he said he didn't remember cow canvasses. And he assured me that he loved cows, grew up around them, out in the fields, of course," Anna laughed, "and was certain he would have remembered landscapes with a cow theme."

Belle looked at Anna. She held Anna's gaze a few seconds deciding what to say, how much to say. Finally, she ventured. "Aren't those the two that Mrs. Clarke delivered for you?" Then Belle broke the gaze and continued chopping vegetables for soup.

Anna had no quick reply. She formed a scowl while thinking back. Yes, Melody did deliver those to the show. "Surely..." was all she could bring forth.

"Well...I'm pleased, Anna, that that Frenchman loved and bought your landscapes." Belle was happy to have a topic at hand to prevent her thinking about whom she had seen shopping and laughing together that very morning at Trader Joe's, arms around each other: Robert and Noel.

34

An Exploratory Visit

B en didn't know what to expect on this visit to Judy; he had something of great interest to tell her. As he drove from Connecticut to Virginia, he thought over the past, his history with her. He had adored her. But after six months of dating, when they learned that she was pregnant, she had surprised him by saying she loved the boy back home and intended to go back there and marry him; no one would know she had had Ben's child. That just hadn't worked out for them.

Ever since, he had sent her money; he didn't need it and she did, and there was still a small place for her in his heart. Fascination for Melody had shown him the intimacy he missed; for many years he had paved over that need. Yes, there were endless women he could have, but they were all too eager. Too pushy. He couldn't get interested. Would he still feel some of the old spark he had felt for Judy? Probably not, but anyway that was not his reason for this visit to her.

Copsey Lane. If he took the next right, Copsey should appear on the left. Judy Lassiter expected him. The years had softened his pain from fifteen years ago when she had let Leon Sample, M. D. place their child for adoption. Softened his frustration with her refusal to marry him. He was merely someone in her past whom she had cared about for a time, but not enough to commit. Even though he had not seen her during the past fifteen years, he had been half and more supporting her since their son was born. The rest of her income came from a small inheritance that Ben hoped she had managed well. He had written to her, and then had called three days ago to ask whether he could drive down for a visit. He had something to tell her. Of course, she said yes.

Judy had to hustle around. Straighten up. Pick up a bit of clutter. How could one person make such a mess, she laughed to herself. Collect so much? Oh, well! She had too much to do, and sometimes she didn't have the energy. Too much to think about. And anyway, it was organized clutter. Oh, and how she wished she had had the plumber come to fix the toilet. Many times, she had planned to do that, but then the money wasn't there. At least she had painted the bathroom, and it was clean and tidy; people could wash up. She didn't mind using the old outhouse, but her guests might. She had maintained it over the years by dumping lime down the hole, and painting its outside with a mural of trees so that it blended in with the forest. She had even decorated it with beads where buds would be. The fanciest outhouse in the world. Getting out there in winter could be misery though! Sometimes, in a hurry, she had actually trudged out there with bare feet. In snow.

And it was an ongoing struggle to organize Elmer, her friend from church, to finish the tree house; an ongoing struggle to tear him away from the various women who clung to him. Shameless. She longed to live in the tree house; be close to nature. And even though the tiny dwelling would be complete with electricity that she needed for music, she would burn candles. There would be a window to open, a bed, and a small skylight that would just peek through the branches to let in a patch of heaven. Ah, to lie up there at night with a breeze coursing through, and gaze at stars.

She looked around, wondering how her home would look to Ben. There were long strands of colorful beads hanging in doorways and windows. She thought they made the cottage inviting and cozy, but how would it look to Ben? She didn't know him anymore. It had taken years to work all those beads and crystals, and they reflected light and color, made the rooms seem to dance. And sometimes when breezes rolled in, the beads ticked and clicked together like something alive and welcoming. Although moving in and out through the strands had been a nuisance at first, she had adjusted to slipping through them.

She had time to shampoo her hair, but it still hang in strings. Needed a good cut. Oh, well, it would have to do, no time to get it cut now. Surely Ben wouldn't stop sending money because of stringy hair. If he did, she would scarce have enough to get by. Don't think about that now. Just hope he doesn't expect to stay here. But —this bulk—she patted her stomach and hips, no time to take off fifteen pounds.

She pulled on a long skirt with a leopard print and elastic waist. The skirt hung nearly down to her ankles, hide those knees. Over the skirt, she wore a loose, beige-cotton kaftan with three-quarter sleeves, hide those arms, and a fringed-fabric tie belt. Her typical garb. She layered two strands of various beads around her neck and drew several bracelets up her wrists. Her fingers already displayed four rings. She wore beaded sandals, of course; even in this chilly weather her pudgy toes needed the freedom. She dressed this way when she played drums and crystal bowls over at The Meeting House. The Meeting House attendees loved her act. She had found a place to belong.

In her mind, she tried to form a picture of Ben whom she hadn't seen in at least fifteen years. He had not shown a romantic interest in her since she left to marry the boy back home. Ben heard that she hadn't married, was abandoned in Virginia, and sent her money. And he had never stopped sending it. Judy didn't understand his motivation, but she relied on that income. She didn't ask questions, but each year at Christmas she wrote to him a thank-you note.

With waist-high weeds brushing his car, Ben pulled into Judy's dusty, dirt driveway that led up to the side of the house. He parked, pocketed the keys, and looked at the ramshackle cottage. Well, it had a charm about it. And lots of greenery. And privacy. From the side he could see the on-going construction of a large tree house, and in back, a beautifully painted outhouse. *My. Oh my.*

"It's great to see you, Ben." Judy stepped out of the door and came down the steps to welcome him. She reached out a hand.

"Hello, Judy. You're looking good," he said, taking her hand. Well, that was true. Her face was smooth, unlined, still pretty, and her hair had maintained its soft and natural gold color. He could see the old Judy Lassiter. She looked healthy enough if you could see passed all the drapes and beads on her. And, my! There was a bit more of her to see.

"Come on in and have a seat while I make us some coffee." She led him up the front steps, then she disappeared into the kitchen.

Ben settled into a comfortable stuffed chair about his size, propped one leg over the other, and settled back listening to homey noise coming from the kitchen. So far, so good. Fascinated by the order about, as well as mild disorder, he looked around at her collections. She has a system he thought. Across the ceiling were rough-hewn beams with hanging baskets full of undefinable stuff. Uneven walls supported miscellany, and there were nooks with little tables, each table stacked with this and that. On one table lay a flute, and across the room stood a spinet piano. Though old, it appeared to be polished and well cared for. Several pieces of sheet music on the piano's stand looked challenging enough to Ben.

Judy returned with a tray and two fragrant coffees. "If you need to wash up, the bathroom's down that hallway on the left. If you want other facilities you must use the outhouse in the back." She hoped he had no such needs. He looked elegant sitting there calmly, one leg crossed over the other. A little too preppy for her taste, he wore pressed jeans with an open collared blue shirt tucked into a thin brown leather belt with a gold buckle, and what she thought were boating shoes. No socks. She couldn't picture him using the outhouse. He clearly had aged well the last fifteen years. She flushed that she herself hadn't been too concerned about appearances. What would he think? And would he recognize that her home was her castle?

He sipped the excellent coffee, thinking it a special blend. "Thank you for this delicious coffee, Judy. Have you been well?" His face wore true concern.

"Yes." She said quickly. "I have thrived in this part of the world. It's peaceful and there are no extremes of weather. No hurricanes, floods, earthquakes, or tornados." She hoped that truth didn't stop the money; perhaps he would think he had sent enough. "How about you?" she asked.

"I'm doing quite well. My practice is substantial, and I'm happy with it." He looked around, not sure what to say next. For a while the only sound breaking the room's stillness was the clinking of cups on saucers as they sipped coffee, or of a bead or two tapping its mate. "Tell me about the flute."

"Oh, I practice. You'd be surprised what five minutes a day can do. I pick it up when I pass through the room and blow away at it. Good for my lungs."

"And the piano?"

"I practice that as well. Wednesday nights, I play for prayer meetings down the road at the Meeting House. I'm pretty lousy at the piano, but they appreciate my efforts, and I'm the only one willing to make the effort.

Ben absorbed that information for a moment. He drummed his fingers on the chair arm while he looked around, not with nosiness, but with a need to be occupied. He needed the exact right moment to tell her why he had come. Somehow at the perfect space he must slide into it; meanwhile small-talk would suffice. "Tell me about your tree house. It looks quite extensive."

"Yes, it will be. It's not finished. I plan to read and listen to music up there. It will be known as 'The Tea House,' or maybe the 'Tree Tea House,' " she smiled, "that way, if I have a run-in with someone and they come to make peace, I can refer to it as the 'Treaty House'."

"Enough!" He laughed. "I get the picture." He could relax: she was still youthful and capable of being silly.

She pushed some of the dangling threads of hair back over her shoulder and said, "Elmer, a carpenter I know from the Meeting House, is building it for me. He's temperamental and I can't push him. It's nearly complete with a shelf, a bed, a table and chair,

159

electricity, a lamp, and a window that opens. Also a small skylight that will open. He insulated it for me. No plumbing though. Maybe that will be an add-on down the road."

"My...that will be something. Down the road? Isn't that kind of far?"

Judy's eyes rolled to the ceiling and back down to Ben. "Really!" Now, what else could she say? "I'd love to show it to you but I can't because there're no stairs. It's already beautiful inside. Elmer uses a ladder that he hauls back and forth. I hope he finally gets around to making stairs. Sometimes I picture a rope ladder that I can pull up; then no one can bother me."

Ben hoped the stairs or rope would be substantial to hold that extra weight he could see bulging through the folds. "How's the tree doing?"

"That sycamore tree has thrived...seems to enjoy the additional attention and company. It has accommodated me by spreading, creating more shade."

There was a pause now, everything appeared to have been said, and for a few minutes, they were relieved not to make conversation. "I'd like to take you out to dinner," he said. Have a glass of wine, then tell her about David, he thought. "Is there a good restaurant nearby?"

"Yes. There's a nice hotel not far. I would love to eat there, and I think you'll enjoy it. People come all the way from D.C. just to have dinner there. I'll call and reserve a table, for it's quite popular."

This visit was a struggle, not something Ben would want to do often; at least he could look forward to a fine dinner. He stood to stretch and take a turn about the room to look over Judy's busy collection of interesting things. He wasn't being nosy, just interested; she was an unusual and interesting woman. In a little sitting room off to the side, he spotted a drum set. "Tell me about the drums."

"I play drums on meditation nights at our Meeting House. First, I drum softly and then I play crystal bowls. It's quite spiritual. They love it, and a few bring little hand drums to join in. Some relax so much they fall asleep. I have to compete with snoring."

Ben did not want to picture that. "Well, I'm pleased that you have found a peaceful place to be."

"I do love my life." Again, she hoped her honesty and forthrightness didn't stop his checks, but she could hardly mention it.

Ben had worked his way over to a window and stood looking out wondering how they were going to fill the hour they had to wait for dinner. "I see that you have quite a large garden, and perhaps some nice ornamentals," he said. "Come out and show me what you like to grow. I'd love to have a garden...even if only to grow tomatoes.

Relieved by his suggestion, herself wondering how they would fill the hour, Judy led the way to the garden. She could name each bush and tree and had planted most of them, and on one side was a plot for vegetables, now tucking in for its winter rest.

At the right time, Ben drove them to dinner.

Seated in the softly lighted hotel dining room while they savored wine from long-stemmed crystal glasses, they talked about the old days. Ben told her about changes that had taken place, and about his medical practice. Slightly anxious, Judy listened, wondering when he would get to the reason for his visit. She didn't think it was to tell her about his practice.

Finally, she broke in, "Ben, your letter said you had something to tell me." She buttered a roll while she watched his face.

He paused. He wasn't even sure he wanted to tell her. Nevertheless, she had a right to know. She had the innate intelligence that he had admired long ago, she could handle the news.

"Judy...I've found our son."

Her knife dropped with a clang onto her plate. That was a sucker-punch. She plunged down deep for a feeling, for what to think. She had never had trouble knowing how to act, what to think, what expression to put on her face, but this was beyond absurd. The wind was sucked out of her.

"Oh. I'd almost forgotten I had one." She said nothing more. What did Ben want from her? If he thought she was going to express guilt now, well, he didn't know her. At the time, she had done what she had to do, and she had made peace with that. The family, her fiancé, all, had put pressure on her to come home and get married. Next to that, her attachment to Ben had seemed only to be a fling. Moreover, had any of them known about the pregnancy, they would have disowned her. Right now she felt that maybe her back was up against Ben.

He kept quiet, waiting for her to arrive at some comfort level with his astounding revelation. He saw confusion in her face. "I'm not expecting you to do anything, Judy." He wanted to assure her, let her relax. "But, I've always needed to know about him and his welfare. Once I gained influence as a physician, I applied pressure to Dr. Sample, the doctor who black-marketed him; pressure that I could not apply when I was a poor and unknown medical student, pressure to reveal the adoptive parents. Threats...you might say."

Judy stared off around the room. Her thoughts soared looking for a corner in which to rest, seeking shelter somewhere. She felt paranoia that each person in the restaurant was in on Ben's and her conversation, and knew all about her past mistake.

"It's a good thing I tried to find him when I did," Ben continued, "for over a year ago his adoptive parents were killed in an accident. Although he was in the car, he was spared, receiving but a few contusions. He's been living with his adoptive grandparents, whom he loves, but they're too elderly to adjust. And, he hasn't been happy since the accident; you can imagine. They need whatever I can do for them."

Ben waited. He wanted to let Judy have time to hear what he had said. "His name is David...David Marlow. And I believe that he's had a good education so far, and he's athletic...captain of his soccer team." Ben's face glowed with the pride he felt saying those words. He thought about that—his new source of pride, a powerful blessing. "I've been watching his games, and he's a beautiful, strong young man." He had to stop his story to think about what to say next.

Judy remained silent, a hand up twisting the beads at her neck, her face calmer now; perhaps she had nothing to fear, and she opened her heart to absorb Ben's story.

"But after the accident, he began to slip. He started missing classes and soccer practice. Coach had to remove him from the team for a while. Sometimes his grandparents didn't know where he was."

They took a minute to think of the possible implications.

"He seems to like me, Judy...really pays attention to what I say. I think he looks up to me. I think I can get him back on track. Coach recently put him back on the team and when I'm at the game, I see him look over to where I'm sitting to be sure I'm watching. You can appreciate that his adoptive grandparents are grateful for my interest and help. They're regular people and I enjoy visiting with them as well. We talk constantly about David. They show me pictures and tell me about his childhood." Ben didn't add that he wished he could have seen the lad growing up. He wasn't sure how to continue; the sensitiveness of what he wanted to say was making his eyes moist. He took a gulp of wine.

Judy found her voice. "It sounds as though you have formed a good connection with them."

"I have. They welcome and accept me. I've also visited his school. He had already been asking about us, Judy. And, this is my good news...David is willing to transition gradually to living with me. He'll have me *and* his adoptive grandparents. Best of all...I'll have him. I can see that he continues in sports, if he wants to, that is. Take him skiing. See him through college." Ben had to stop for a new supply of air.

"I didn't mean to hand you a burden, Judy. I know your life has been somewhat hard and it seems that you have worked into a measure of peace. I just thought you should know. If you think this over for a while and decide you'd like to meet him, I'll drive him down during a vacation. I haven't told him that I know where you are, but, knowing the kind of lad he is...sensitive and thoughtful...I believe he would like to meet you. It's up to you. Meeting him, having a meal with us at this same hotel should not confer pressure on you or him."

Judy's hand trembled slightly as she lifted her wine glass. A reprieve: she had feared that she might be called on to make a home for the lad, and she knew that would not be a good situation for either of them. "I understand. Let me think. It's been a long time. A lifetime. I'm a different person now, although I never did see myself as a mother." All seemed to go quiet for a moment as if time itself paused to listen. She had a split second's thought—what would she have said had the boy been a really bad apple whom they must try to save? Fortunately that wasn't an issue.

"I think...I would like to meet him."

"You don't have to be a mother. You can be a friend. Kids need all the good and real friends they can get." Then Ben delivered the final jolt. "He has your coloring, Judy, blond hair, green eyes. The instant I saw him, I noticed his resemblance to the young you whom I remembered."

Before leaving the hotel Ben reserved a room for himself for that evening. Then he took Judy home and showed her in the door. He wouldn't come in, he said. He wanted to turn in early and drive back to Connecticut the next day. He'd be in touch.

After a good breakfast the next morning, he drove straight home. Judy seemed content with her life, and he would have to seek that unknowable something to complete his; it wouldn't be with Judy. Maybe it was but a moonbeam that hit some, and not others. The tiny fragments of love that he had carried all those years for Judy were flat-lined. Actually, he'd never had a thought that he and Judy would again join up as a couple, but he also had not been able to discard that last mote of expectation; the one that he had stayed busy ignoring while building his career. Judy had told him years ago she wouldn't marry him, was going to marry another. Years ago he had almost expunged his mind of her, but finding David had made him wonder. Clearly now, he thought, as he drove north, she had not been his type. It's as if, as we mature, we shape into some preconceived form not visible or expected in our youth. And his form, the one he had grown into, was quite different from the one

Judy had grown into. He had sometimes wondered about women who hung too much jewelry and things on themselves; as though they were only certain that they existed if they could be adorned with enough stuff. And beads! He would dream about being attacked by beads.

He looked forward to seeing Melody, gorgeous, simple, and classic Melody. She was taken, but who knew what the future held? He had vaguely carried the torch for someone all these years; he could carry it a few more for someone else. Moreover, he had young David in his life. David would continue to live in Noroton with his grandparents until the semester ended, but he and David would be getting together on weekends after soccer practice. At some point soon he would tell his good friends about finding David, and at the right time he would tell David about his mother.

Before he reached home, if it weren't too late, he would stop by the Clarke's house. If Cass's Rover was in the driveway, he'd pass on by. If not he would stop in to say hello to Melody. But what he did not expect on arrival at the Clarkes' was Robert's *Porsche* in the driveway. Again. Ben drove on.

35

Trouble Lurking in Photographs

"I'm stoked! My photographer got exactly what I need." Robert congratulated Melody. "You did well. He has wonderful, clear shots of Anna and a man leaving The New Englander together. He has pictures of them exiting a room, coming off the elevator, going through the lobby together, and more in the parking lot. I don't recognize the man." Robert's pleasure over this success was almost palpable over the phone. "He photographed Anna going in with several paintings and emerging with a guy, without paintings, two hours later. No one needs to know this except you and me. Photos are already in my lawyer's office, and are just what I need to keep the divorce ball in my court. And I'm house hunting. I hate to do this, but life is short. I had a wake-up call with that accident."

Melody waited for him to mention getting together to celebrate. He didn't. A long pause hung in the air. She wouldn't say anything —wasn't wise to apply pressure. She had faint flickers of guilt about her role in the photographs but not enough guilt to ruin her happiness. She had merely related to Robert that Anna would take paintings on a certain day, at a certain time, to sell to a stranger who stayed at The New Englander. No need to mention that Anna had the attentions of a famous Frenchman.

"I'll catch you later," Robert said. "I have a lot going on right now." He pressed the phone hook, released it, and dialed another number. "Hi," he said into the phone. "Are you free for dinner?"

36

Help Arrives

Christian was elated that he had a valid reason to call Anna. Actually, he had several reasons; however, he had to prime his nerve for a moment. Then he dialed the number on the card Anna had left with him.

"Anna," Belle said, handing her the phone, "it's a man with an accent."

"This must be Christian," Anna said into the phone. "The only man *I* know who can't pronounce proper English, lives with cows, and drives around with a lance thrust out the window."

Belle made a face; hearing Anna's cheerfulness these days was a small miracle.

"The same. I work on my English, have impaled only a few pedestrians with the lance, and cows love me; they think my English is perfect." He paused to switch into a more serious tone. "I want to tell you how much my clients admire your paintings. I could place more if you want to sell more."

"That's nice to hear, Christian. Especially at this blue time: something horrid has happened, although I should have seen it coming." She hesitated waiting for courage to continue. "My husband is suing me for divorce, and would you believe...my attorney called me in to see the photos that he's using for evidence of adultery. He has photos of Gary and me leaving The New

Englander together when we left our paintings with you. That's the only reason I'm mentioning this sordid situation to you. I know you will be surprised."

Seconds of silence bore witness to Christian's disbelief. "That's an outrage. I'm sorry to hear that. Can I help in some way? I can witness that both you and Gary, whom you had not met before, were bringing paintings for me to sell."

"Thank you, Christian. Although I'm loathed to expose you to that indignity, it might help my case. I won't fight Robert, but I do want to defend myself against such absurd accusation. I'll tell my lawyer. If he likes the idea, I'll tell him where to reach you, if that's okay with you."

"Please do. I want to help you in any way I can." It was not a good time for small talk and Christian wisely said goodbye, please call when you can to let me know how it goes."

Anna hung up thinking that it was helpful just to know him. He had been reaching out to her, and the strange thing was, he had been reaching out at a time when she, though she had been drawn to him, and had had no idea that she could respond. And now, she found that he was someone with whom she needed to talk.

37

More Than Boxes Gets Unpacked

"For how long is your lease?" Melody asked.

Robert's move into the cottage he had rented in Weston was finally complete and he had called her over to help unpack boxes. She pulled a silver bowl from its wrapping, and, giving it a wipe with a soft cloth, she placed it on the sideboard. She loved silver and took a second to see her reflection in its bright mirror-like surface. The silver returned the pale yellow of her hair. It reminded her of a lesson from a painting class years back, that the color of silver was the color of whatever it reflected.

Robert paused, reluctant to answer. He didn't like to be quizzed. "The lease is for one year with the option to rent month-to-month after that. That should give me plenty of time to find exactly what I want to buy, update it if needed, and move."

Melody caught the parts of his answer that said "me" and "I," instead of "us" and "we." She would slowly teach him to remember "us" and "we." Can't come down too suddenly, she thought, these things take time.

"Well, I love looking," she said. I hope *we* find a home large enough for me to have an atelier. I have had some art training and it's an interest I'd like to pick up again. Give me something to do when I'm not working. And I can teach the twins when they're home on snow days...of course your children as well. That trip with Anna through the Metropolitan renewed my interest. I didn't agree with Anna's critiques, so it stirred me to develop my own ideas. I have a lot to offer."

She took another package from the box and removed its wrapping. "And I want to grow tomatoes. My garden isn't sunny enough for tomatoes."

"Hmm," Robert's jaw tightened—*We*? As he worked nearby unpacking prints of marine designs, he was struck with a desire to reinforce his "I" and "my," and while not entirely certain why, he said with emphasis, "I'll be able to find a substantial place...thanks partly to your efforts. My first requirement is an acre or two with plenty of trees. That should be easy. I hope to find something north of Westport; a nice old house that doesn't need too much work. I can spare a man from the plant for a day now and then to build cabinetry and hang shelving. Make repairs as needed. Sam will be perfect for that. He's an artist with wood."

"I'm surprised you bothered to pack this thing," Melody said as she unpacked a long, pale-blue, boat hull. Why is it cut in half?" She flung it onto a couch.

He turned to see what she meant. When he saw the blue hull that she had carelessly cast aside, he met her eyes with a glare. He said nothing but stopped unwrapping, and in two strides, stepped over and picked up the hull. He carried it over to a wall where he had hung framed prints, and laid it down while he measured. He then picked up a hammer and two small nails, and drove the nails into the wall. He gently polished the hull and mounted it on the nails. He stood back and gazed at it lovingly. But his anger was heard through the speech he hammered out.

"She's an *Elvstrom 35*. My favorite sailboat. Made in Denmark. This is a perfect to scale fiberglass model of the hull. A beautiful seaworthy ship. My father had her brought over and we spent many vacations on her sailing up and down the East coast. I wish he had kept her." He reached into the box, pulled out another package, and gently removed its wrappings.

"Huh." During these minutes, Melody was frozen in place, watching Robert's movements. His anger that seemed to fly in suddenly had surprised her. He hadn't shown this anger to her before. And, she knew nothing about boats—that stupid blue thing looked like a messed-up piece of plastic—but she would learn; he had given her a book about the basics of sailing. Although his company built humongous yachts that were practically hotels, he had said his heart was in sailing a boat he could manage alone; truly work with wind and sea. Challenge nature a bit. Challenge himself. In fact, it was high time he joined the yacht club, he had said. Get the kids into a sailing program. That would also include her twins, she felt sure. Inside her mind she had built a complete life with Robert. Would it trouble her, after he and she were married, to bump into Anna at the yacht club? Well, why should it? Anna had no idea about their collusion in Robert's getting his divorce, and anyway, Anna had an understanding nature. Melody knew that she herself would be happier with Robert, and Anna would be happier without him. In time Anna would come to see that.

"The men you had unpack certainly left a lot of boxes for us to open," Melody said, as she unwrapped a silver candlestick.

"Oh, I purposely left some boxes for us. I wanted to unpack certain things myself. These silver pieces were my mother's ... very old. Treasured. And the hulls...others often don't appreciate their value. And my antique car models should be in here somewhere."

"There's no more silver to unpack," Melody said. "And I haven't found the large repoussé silver bowl. Didn't you bring it?"

"No. It isn't mine. That's Anna's family's from generations back."

"Couldn't you have slipped it into one of the large boxes anyway?" She looked at him with a pout. "Don't they say possession is nine-tenths of the law? Or something like that...take it and it's yours. I'll miss it. It's a stunning piece and looks wonderful on your piano. I fell in love with you all over again when I saw that bowl. And Anna probably would never have missed it."

For the second time that day Robert turned toward Melody, swallowed hard, firmed his mouth, and gave her a wilting stare that she missed. With her head turned down looking into another box, his stare passed through her like a dart through air. He turned to empty the box that held his model cars. He arranged them carefully along the sideboard. But where was the Mercedes? The most treasured of all, his first car. He stopped unpacking, grabbed the phone, and dialed a number.

"Hello, Belle. I hope this isn't a bother."

"No, Mr. Randall. What can I help you with?" Belle was appalled that he had left his family and divorced Anna, but he had always been good to her, and she still had a measure, though diminishing, of respect for him. And, maybe he would change his mind and come back. She knew Anna expected that he would. In the past, she had called him, "Mr. Rob," going forward she would call him "Mr. Randall," unable to call him that which easily came to mind, like "shit-head." Or worse.

"I've finished unpacking my model cars, and the Mercedes is missing. I don't remember seeing it when I packed, but I was in a hurry. Please watch for it, and if you see it, put it aside for me. I know the kids wouldn't touch it. They never have. They know better."

"I will," Belle said. "I'm sure it will turn up, and I'll save it. It's valuable, isn't it?"

"Yes. It's the first Mercedes made for the U. S. public. My first car. I bought it used and I wish I had kept it. And the little model is an antique."

Melody stood by, listening.

When Robert put down the phone, he saw her calculating look. "What?"

"Well..." She carefully phrased her reply. "You are asking Belle. Maybe *she* took the car. With all the confusion of your moving, perhaps she thought that you wouldn't miss it. I understand it has some value."

"Not a chance. Belle is an untouchable miracle. Wish I could get her to follow me wherever I move." He could hardly avoid sensing Melody's smugness. "Frankly, even though it's a treasure of mine, had Belle a need for it, she would be more than welcome."

"Gosh, you love Belle so much, maybe more than you love me. I didn't realize I had to measure up to Belle." She waited for him to tell her that she was tops.

Rather, he squared his fingers into a frame and peered at Melody through the frame, taking her measure. "Hmm," his only reply. Then he looked around the room to judge their progress. "That's all we're going to unpack for now. Think I'll do a bit of arranging."

"Why are you taking down those prints?" Melody asked. She had looked up in time to see him removing two marine prints from the wall.

"Oh, they don't go here. Noel helped me unpack yesterday and she hung them there while I was on the phone."

"Noel's been here?" Her voice swooped up into a lift of sound.

Instead of satisfying Melody with a soothing reply, Robert checked his watch, then moved around looking in boxes yet to be unpacked, sizing up what remained, planning. Meanwhile, the sun had tracked across the rug pulling in its lights; daylight had begun to recede announcing the approach of evening. He switched on a lamp. "I should see you to your car now," he said. "Cass and the twins will be wondering where you are."

"No, my sitter is staying, and I warned her that I would be in late."

Nevertheless, he went to the closet for Melody's coat and began to help her into it.

Melody frowned. "This isn't my jacket."

"Oh. I guess I must have accidentally packed one of Anna's."

Melody didn't comment, but she couldn't remember seeing Anna wearing that jacket. She went to the closet and stood a moment examining its contents. Then she removed the jacket that was hers. He helped her put it on.

I'm sorry, but I realize that I have to go over some accounts tonight," he said, "and can't make dinner with you." He opened the door for her. Saw her look of disappointment. "But, shortly, when I find my way around this kitchen, we'll cook up a feast together." He managed a smile.

He walked with her to the car and planted a quick kiss on her cheek. She drew the keys from her purse and opened the door of her BMW. (The old Rover had been satisfactory when she and Cass lived in Manhattan where it was garaged most of the time, but after their move Melody had insisted on a proper image for herself. After all, in Connecticut one could hardly go anywhere without a car.)

Robert gave her a cheerful wave as she drove off. She didn't look back or wave.

When Belle hung up from talking with Robert, she told Anna about his call.

"Huh," Anna said. "That's weird. He packed those models himself. They were always on that shelf, as you know. Antiques. We wanted to keep them out of the way so they wouldn't be a temptation for the children. Robert planned to have a showcase built for them."

38

Rage and Sorrow

The long awaited ghastly court date arrived for the Randalls' divorce hearing. As though to show their sympathy, the heavens wept with torrents of rain, and blustering winds pushed things about, breaking umbrellas, bringing down branches; let all below beware—the earth feels rage.

Within minutes of each other—both with heavy hearts—Robert and Anna arrived at court. Divorce had never figured on Anna's horizon, and for days she had thought of herself as a stick figure moving through a frame with a will not her own.

And Robert—though he'd wanted it, planned it even—had an unpleasant feeling in his gut. He tried to think this over one more time. He recalled how instantly he had been drawn to Melody, and had thrived within her response. But he had been restive before he met her, it just hadn't surfaced. Nothing was clear. It was doubtful that Anna was having an affair, and he had a tinge of guilt for using those contrived photos, but Anna, and spending the rest of his life with her, wouldn't somehow come into focus. He couldn't quiet his expectation of more, more challenges, more excitement, a renewed flush of feeling. But would he find that? After his boating accident, some undefinable force had propelled him down this rutted path. He couldn't back out, for once this whirling procedure had been started, it was as if he were being sucked into its vortex.

Christian drove Anna to the hearing, and stayed to witness that she had been delivering paintings, not having an assignation. Belle attended the hearing to vouch for Anna's character, and to swear that Anna was not the kind of woman or wife to have an extra-marital affair.

But the photos Robert had acquired for his case carried weight. The one that showed Anna and another man leaving the hotel room together offered a suggestion for adultery. Robert didn't care whether her adultery was a fact, he needed an argument to prevent the settlement's bankrupting him. He didn't intend to deprive Anna and the kids; just wanted their assets to be divided equitably. Still, with all the negotiations back and forth, both he and Anna were exhausted by now. He would get *this*; Anna would get *that*, and so on. They were both easy: Robert didn't have a strong case, and Anna loathed fighting him. Besides, it was clear that he wanted the girls and her to be well cared for.

After the court scene, Christian invited Anna—urged her in fact—to stop off for a glass of wine before he took her home; help her better to accept the situation by talking off some of the tension, and they now sat across from each other in a cocktail lounge. Anna looked a little shaky; pleased for the diversion and pleased for the low light, she wanted to hide from the day's unreality. And although grateful for the moment's peace, and Christian's calm support, she had to pull deep within to be social, to show her appreciation, to say the right thing—if there were such. Only banal obvious constructs came to mind.

"Thank you again, Christian, for going to court to witness for me. I'm sure it was humiliating for you, and I apologize. You know that I wish it hadn't been necessary, but your testimony was a big help, and I hope it won't make the French slander rags." As she said this, her body slumped, unable to find the energy needed to hold itself erect, and she folded her hands around her drink, as if it were life-support. She looked up at Christian's kind face. "I can see the headlines now," she said. 'Well-known French architect caught in divorce scandal'."

"Don't worry," he said. "They won't slander me. They've seen me coming down the street with my lance! Besides, the French love a good scandal, perks up their day. I would be famous. Good for business." He sipped his drink while he dredged up another line. "New contracts would pour into our company." He managed to bring a smile to Anna's tired face. "Speaking up for you was the least I could do. I was happy to stand the discomfort on your behalf."

He had offered to drive her to court and be a support for her, and she had accepted. His presence was a comfort in her otherwise cold and distraught world. He was a warm fire on a cold, dreary day, but more than that, his magnetism was pulling her toward him.

"I can't imagine why Robert thought I was having an affair; so unlike me. Not that I wouldn't have enjoyed intimacy with you." Their eyes locked onto each other. She now considered Christian to be someone special to her in a personal way. "But I thought I still had a marriage. Thin stuff though it was, the past year. And an affair with Gary...not a chance. We only paint together. We say 'Hello. How's it going?' Paint. 'Goodbye, see you next week.' I wouldn't have contested our divorce. Robert's actions the past year showed that his mind was elsewhere...not on our marriage or home, and I wouldn't have fought him. I would have hung in and tried to improve the situation between us...not easy to do, as he was home so little as it was. I guess he felt threatened somehow and needed the photos to make sure he wasn't fleeced. After all these years, he didn't know me."

Christian nodded in sympathy. They sat in silence for a while each wondering what was ahead.

"Now...though I know it's not a happy event for you," he said, "and not something that you desired...you are free. And I want to spend open, honest time with you. I've held you while dancing..." He stopped; he was going too fast, but his thoughts and hopes fluttered about like prayer flags. He understood that Anna needed time. She must first adjust to her new unwelcome status, and to the strain she's been through. He took her hand—he had wanted to hold her hand for, it seemed, all his life. "I can wait," Christian said.

For a moment, Anna's confusion prevented a reply. She hadn't wanted to be unmarried. She had had to go through a divorce she had not wanted, but through it, this man before her had been a support, an appealing and considerate support. He was a gentleman of the first order. If only she could get her mind more clearly around these changes.

"I'm grateful that the photos didn't implicate *you*," she said. "At least Gary isn't a public figure, and he isn't married, so he hasn't a wife to be hurt." Anna had known for a while—from the way Christian often took her hand, and from the way he looked at her, showed respect, listened to what she said—that he was hers. Even so he had never pushed himself on her; that was important. And, her feelings for him had come on so slowly, so gently, in such an organic manner, that she had not recognized their approach. This could be painful, for he would be returning to France where his clients waited. She avoided the topic.

Without Anna's knowledge, Christian had extended his stateside stay to help her. When he heard that Robert wanted a divorce and had moved out, he stayed to offer support through her ordeal, and to witness that she had merely been delivering paintings. In court he had said that Mrs. Randall was a trained and accomplished artist, and anyone could see her paintings in the new office building on Wilton Road. He stated in court that the man in the photographs with Anna was another artist who had also delivered paintings.

Christian couldn't explain it, but out of all the women available to him, he had connected to Anna: he was caught in Anna's sphere. He had felt an unexpected comfort and warmth within her quiet, unassuming manner. She held her sparkle in the background, but it was always there when appropriate, often surprising him. He could not imagine how this would work out. His career had occupied him for too long and he was quite shaken over Anna's effect on him. But, he usually resolved events as he wished.

39

Something Worrying Down the Street

S tella, never one much to go on about herself or her personal life, was now more than quiet on the topic of Ryan. After she said no to dating him, she received in the mail an erotic pamphlet that advertised porno flicks. There had been no name or return address, but the postmark was Westchester, New York. Ryan lived in Armonk, New York. If Ryan sent the mailing, it was further proof that he was a man to avoid. She thought over the unsettling incidences that had occurred: both his laughing about a shady nightspot, as well as offering her a stolen computer. And, most disturbing, recently she had passed him sitting in his car down the street. Just sitting. Probably he had sent her this inappropriate mailing. She called for an appointment with her attorney, Allan Turner.

He arranged to see her right away, and now she faced Allan across his immense walnut desk.

"I'm worried about a man I dated for less than a month until he turned out to be creepy," she said. "After he revealed his shady side in several instances, I refused to see him again, but he kept calling, and soon I got hang-up calls. Recently, I received this porn literature in the mail from an unknown source, postmarked New York."

She pushed the pamphlet across the desk to Allan, and paused while he thumbed through it. When Allan looked up for more information, Stella said, "But, this is what I'm really worried about

...the man lives and works in New York State, and yet, on a few occasions when I've passed, he's sitting in his car down the block...the route that Tess, my daughter, takes walking home from school. Once, Tess said, he rolled down his window and asked whether he could drive her home. Of course, she said no. She knows I consider him bad news."

"Mailing this type of literature across state lines is a federal crime," Turner said, "and maybe I should call the local FBI agent."

They discussed this option. Stella said no. At least not yet. "It's happened only once. I'm more concerned about his sitting, waiting in his car. Tess will be walking a different route for a while."

"A positive step, Stella, will be to get a detective to tail him. Make it obvious. Pass by slowly. Stare into the car at him. Another intimidating trick is to keep dialing his number and hanging up. He'll realize someone's watching him. I know a good man for the job, if you agree. It's a starting point, and if you're still bothered we'll take a look at what to do next."

"That sounds like a plan," Stella agreed. "He lives in Armonk, as I said, and his name is Ryan Black, but I don't have his phone number."

"The detective will find that."

40

Another Kind of Slow Burn

R obert had a rare day off and had asked Melody to meet him at *Bretagne* and Melody had now waited twenty minutes. When she waited for someone—someone important, that is—and Robert was important all right, twenty minutes was her wait-limit. And Robert was never late. Today, though, he was late. Even if she wanted to walk out now, she couldn't because she had asked to be seated, and had ordered a bottle of wine. She first ordered a half-bottle of a crisp, dry chardonnay that she knew Robert liked, but it looked so small in the cooler that before the sommelier opened it, she exchanged it to a liter. Then, thinking that Robert would arrive any minute, she let the waiter open it. She sat sipping wine and mulling over her situation. In throes of elation to see him (it had been seven days since they had been together) she had taken special care with her appearance: had a manicure and pedicure, eyelash extensions, penciled a touch to her pale eyebrows, And had been to Phillip Bruce's hair salon to have his magic applied to her flowing locks. She was reordering her life for Robert. The princess waited.

After she had waited half-an-hour, certain that he would walk in the door soon and might be in a rush, she went ahead and ordered *coq au vin* for two. If he couldn't make it, she would have one hell of an expensive lunch. She could have avoided this by not taking a table. How was she to know? By now she had phoned him twice, but he wasn't picking up. It looked as though she would be out above eighty dollars. More than two dollars per minute wait time. He was now forty minutes late, eighty dollars late. Melody was not used to drinking this much; three times now, the waiter had filled her glass. The *coq au vin* was excellent, though it appeared to contain canned mushrooms. She grew tired of sitting there, and sitting and sitting. the only diner eating alone. She looked around. Actually, she was the only woman, and men stared at her. She felt like a fish in a fishbowl. Nothing beat the indignity of being stood up.

She signaled the waiter for her check. She gave him some excuse for her companion's absence, and, leaving some of that expensive wine behind, she paid the tab and left. Driving home, the blue humiliations wafted over her. How could this be? She knew that with all his recent changes, his new status, he faced new challenges for his time. Even so, she hadn't seen him in a week, and when he phoned to make the lunch date, he said he was dying to see her, that he'd been busy, but he would make up for it. No doubt, he would be embarrassed when he realized he had forgotten lunch with her. Well, she would make it easy for him; she would understand. Still, she had to work at cooling this slow burn.

41

An Offer of Help from an Unexpected Source

Not suspecting Melody's part in her divorce, Anna continued to see Melody and Cass socially. On occasion, the Clarkes would join Ben, and Stella for dinner at Anna's. Sometimes Melody had to fight back the urge to confess to Anna her role in the divorce. But mulling over the social benefits conferred by Anna's friendship, Melody pulled the cloak of innocence tighter and wore it proudly.

Ben was eager to attend Anna's dinners because of Melody. Melody attended to keep Ben's attention energize. She didn't take him seriously, but needed the attachment he had for her, wanted to keep that alive. Cass leaned with the wind. Stella looked forward to seeing Ben.

And then there was Christian Boutin; only he knew that he had invented reasons to stay in town. However, Anna did not include Christian in these dinners. Though her friends knew that he had been a witness in court, that he had merely received Anna's paintings, only Belle knew that he and Anna were seeing each other in a personal way. Anna was slow about these changes in her life. Too much happening too fast. She wasn't ready to discuss this special feeling growing for Christian. No need to rush. She hadn't yet become used to her divorce. Christian would be gone soon, and that would be the end of it. No one need know. Still, he would always number among her cherished friends.

Ben did *like* Stella, but was unaware of her growing affection for him. He thought her pretty, and paid more attention to her than he had in the past. Funny, how intelligent and grounded she was these days; something he hadn't noticed before. If he wanted to provoke an intelligent comment, he turned to Stella. But around Melody intelligence was not usually his first thought. Melody still fascinated him, and so he gave Stella a thought, but hardly two. Stella left each of these dinners feeling a bit empty. Melody went home with Cass. Ben went home alone. Anna had the children and Belle; they were good company.

"We thought you would have introduced us to Ryan by now," Anna said to Stella during one of these dinners. "You've been holding out on us."

"It's a long story, Anna, but, I don't see him anymore. And, after I started avoiding him and not taking his calls, I started getting mysterious hang-up calls. Also, twice now, I saw him sitting in his car, a block away, on the route that Tess takes home from school. Creepy."

"Oh. Sorry to hear that. That *is* creepy. Well, I won't ask again."

Stella wouldn't mention other negatives about Ryan, at least not at this time, so she said no more. She was grateful for sensible friends who, she knew, would not pry.

"If you have any fear...," Ben's frown revealed genuine concern, "you call me and I'll come right over. We'll let him think he has competition...my car in your driveway. I'll catch a nap on your couch if you'll let me." He pulled a card from his wallet, and on it he wrote his private telephone number, and handed it to Stella. She looked at it and then quietly looked up at Ben. Her eyes and her appreciative look gave him an unusual feeling; not a feeling to which he was accustomed. Something wistful in her face that held him.

"How thoughtful you are, Ben." Melody said tilting her head to the side. "You can sleep on my couch any time," She looked at him with one eye, as a fall of hair had covered the other. She had seen that Ben was caught on Stella's face. Pull him back. Don't let him forget where his attention belongs. "Maybe I can find a man staking out my street," she said with a sarcastic tone.

Cass smiled happily as though the idea of Ben sleeping on their couch was a commonplace, uneventful occurrence.

Ben turned to Melody, but the flush he normally had for her was now ploughed under in a strange land for a few seconds. He did not recognize his confusion for what it was.

42

Evil Tactics

In woodworking class, Tess had learned to make quite tidy small wooden pagodas for gardens, and she had been able to sell a few. So throughout the summer she continued the class, gaining new skills. It was but a short walk to school, and in case Ryan found it worthwhile to continue to sit in his car, Stella mapped out a new route for Tess. Tess, of course, could have done this without help, but Stella needed the security of knowing where Tess would be. On the first day of Tess's class, using the new route, Stella walked with her. Now this was the third day that Tess had walked home the new way. There were two extra blocks, but her satchel was light, she was strong, and the route seemed free of problems—no Ryan to be seen waiting anywhere. Tess relaxed.

Today, a white van was parked up ahead by the curb. It wasn't Ryan's car and Tess was all set to ignore it. But as she continued on toward it, before she had time to think that something was amiss, the van's passenger-side door flung open, Ryan jumped out, grabbed her, and pulled her inside the van, satchel and all. Tess caught a fleeting glance at the driver, a grim-faced brute she had not seen before. He kept his eyes straight ahead; he did not look at Tess. He locked the doors immediately and gunned the van before Tess had time to get her bearings and fight off Ryan.

"You idiot!" she yelled. "Let me out! You must be mad!" She tried to open the door. She would jump out of the moving van if she could open the door. But she could not.

"If you're sweet to me, everything will go easy. Will be okay. I'm not going to hurt you," Ryan said. He leered at Tess.

"You're nuts! You're a crazy idiot!" And with her free arm, she slugged him across the face. Before he could react, she flailed her feet about, kicking wildly. Kicking anything, she managed to give the steering wheel a kick, and stomp on the driver's knee. The van jerked around crazily. Tess became a wild woman. Her teeth drilled into Ryan's arm.

"You bitch! You're a bitch just like your mother! You're bad news! Unlock the door," he yelled in a rage to the driver. Then he reached across Tess and pushed open the door. She forced her teeth deeper into his flesh. He shoved her out of the van.

Her head hit the curb, and for a while, she couldn't know what had happened. The van sped off. She lay there. She thought about her mother, would she ever see her again? She could barely make out footsteps that seemed to be rushing toward her. She prayed that it wasn't Ryan.

"Tess has multiple contusions, lacerations, and a mild concussion. You can see her, but she's sedated, and I want her to rest. A police detective has been in to speak to her, and her mother is with her now."

Dr. Tanner, the neurosurgeon who treated Tess, spoke to Anna and Ben who, it seemed for hours, had sat waiting expectantly. When Ben received the call from Anna to tell him that Stella needed his help, he had rushed to confer with Tanner, and to lend any support he could.

"I found her I.D. and emergency numbers in the satchel that the ambulance EMT turned in," Dr. Tanner said. "Then I called her mother. Tess will be much better tomorrow, and I don't expect her to have any lasting problems. I think the worst she's suffered is the psychological trauma. Still, she'll have to be watched. You can talk to her tomorrow. Today, I'd rather keep her quiet."

"Yes, Doctor. Absolutely. We're so relieved to hear that she'll be okay." Anna said. "We don't know what happened." Anna's pained expression begged for answers. "Stella called me and said Tess was in the hospital and she didn't know why, and she quickly hung up."

"There were witnesses who saw her fall from a moving van," Dr. Tanner said. "She appeared to have been pushed out of the vehicle. They called 911 and waited with Tess until the ambulance arrived. They think the satchel may have softened her fall."

Ben and Anna could only stare, unable to express their disbelief.

"When she goes home, I want her to rest thoroughly for two weeks. Symptoms of something more serious can show later, but I'm not expecting that in Tess's case."

"Did anyone get the license plate number?" Anna asked.

"I don't know about the number; however, I was told that witnesses have come forward to identify the van from which Tess fell, or was pushed. I understand the police have a man in custody...the owner of the van...and that he has identified the man who was with him, and who allegedly drug Tess into the vehicle, and who also threw her out apparently, after she kicked and bit him."

"Well, thank God for that," Anna said.

"Tess should be able to tell you in a few days, but don't press her until she's ready to talk about it. If she wants to discuss what happened, a hospital counselor will be in to see her tomorrow," Dr. Tanner said. "It helps sometimes to drain pent-up fear and emotion."

Engulfed in worry, Stella sat near Tess's bed, watching her breathe; looking for any sign that Tess was okay. This was the worst event she and Tess had ever endured. That cretin, Ryan, could not have found a better way to hurt her, than through her daughter—Tess, who had never lifted a finger against a soul, who helped others every chance she had, who helped Stella around the house, and sometimes went to work with her. Tess, a wonderful *old* soul.

Stella was dealing with pressing feelings of guilt. She thought over the events that involved Ryan. At first she was attracted to him, thought he had good qualities, but as soon as his true nature began to surface, she had dropped him like hot ashes. She couldn't have done better than that. It didn't help to console herself that it could have been worse—not at all. That man was pure evil. She felt that surely, if she saw him, she would kill him with her own hands. Thank the gods that Dr. Tanner and the members of his team assured her that Tess would heal soon. There would be psychological scars, and they'd deal with those after Tess came home. And thanks be that Tess had the courage to fight Ryan—bit the hell out of him—they said, in fact left teeth imprints on his arm. Tess was tough. Her bold actions would serve her self-confidence. Stella could hope that Tess had infected him with a lethal bacterium the gods had conjured up just for that one instance.

She put her mind to picturing Tess's getting well enough to be out doors again; able to come to work with her on weekends when her homework load was light. She could sit and read and watch Stella work. She had been grooming Tess for landscape design so that if Tess had to make her way alone, that skill would serve her well. And, there was a mysterious letter waiting for Tess that she would give to her when she was up. Whew! Stella had to stop thinking for a minute. She hadn't suffered so since she and Tess were on their way to bury their beloved husband and father.

Dinners were now glum affairs, but still Anna wanted to know that Stella ate something. Stella was spending all day at the hospital, going home late only to rest for the next day. Anna was able to convince her to look in long enough to eat before going home. When Tess had recovered enough to enjoy a good meal, Anna packed up Belle's good cooking, and everyone: Anna, Ben, and Stella, crowded into the room to have dinner with Tess. Tess would smile now. Stella thought she herself might actually survive the horror.

Often, Ben was at the hospital and he would make it a point to confer with Dr. Tanner, check on Tess's recovery, and visit with

Tess and Stella for a half-hour or so. The news was good, and mother and daughter were easy to be around; they always had something to say noteworthy, funny, or thought provoking, that Ben enjoyed hearing. He in turn, made them laugh.

On the second morning in the hospital, Tess opened the letter that Stella had saved for her. "It's been waiting two days for you. From someone named David."

"Hi, Tess,

> I have good news. I found my biological father; rather he found me. And you're not going to believe this, so sit down! He lives in Westport where he is a physician. My grandparents and I like him very much, and he wants to make a home for me with him. Do you realize what this means? Next semester I'll be back in high school and can witness all the mistakes you make in shop!

> My father may bring me to Westport for visits.

> Your friend in havoc,
> David Marlow"

"The news is good, judging from your flush and grin," Stella said.

"Well, I don't know if it's good news. The twerp is coming back to bother me in shop." She stretched a wide grin and flung the letter down on the bed.

"Ah ha! *That* twerp," Stella said.

On the second afternoon in the hospital, Tess heard a timid knock at the door. That's strange, she thought. When she said, "Come in," the door opened slowly a crack, and one eyeball stared at her. A range of emotions alternated for Tess: fear? humor? Then the crack opened a little more and Tess dreamed she saw David's smile.

It was not a dream; the twerp was here.

"They told me that a wild girl, who should be in a zoo, occupied this room," David said. "Bites! I thought maybe I could subdue her with candy, but I don't know whether I should venture in."

"Nerd! Keep your distance and you'll be safe."

David Marlow stepped in preceded by a box of Godiva chocolates and a chess set, and right on his tails was his new-found father, Ben. "I would have brought flowers, but I was afraid you'd eat them during one of your fits."

"Tess, have I been on another planet?" Ben asked. "I just learned that you and David know each other." As Tess nodded, she kept a sly face on David. "When I said that I wanted to look in on the daughter of a friend, 'Tess,' David said he knew a 'Tess' in Westport. Pinch me and tell me this isn't *The Twilight Zone*."

David rolled his eyes in collusion with Tess, as he nodded toward Ben.

"I'm ashamed to admit that I know this dork," said Tess. "Looks like he's come back to pester me."

That evening Tess was able to play a demanding game of chess, and had found a devil of a challenger in her old friend from school, Ben's newfound son. When Ben could drive him to the hospital, David visited. If Tess were napping, David would sit quietly and read. Otherwise, he and Tess would furiously go at each other with knights and bishops, shamelessly capturing queens and hurling invectives. Watching them, Ben thought that both were happier, and he would report this to Stella, who had returned to work to finish her contract; after all, bills still had to be paid. Usually Ben was able to step in to Tess's room late in the day when Stella was there. He found that he looked forward to catching her up on Tess's progress. He would say something like, "Aside from her giving all the staff a hard time, making them all resign until I had to hold a meeting, raise their salaries astronomically, beg them to stay, tell them this imp will soon be gone...Tess is doing quite well."

"Well, that's not what I heard," Tess countered with a smug grin. "The nurses were talking in the hall about what a dangerous doctor you are, and that you shouldn't be let into patients' rooms. So I asked Dr. Tanner to be sure and protect me."

"See what I mean," he said, "bothering the staff."

"She's always been a problem," Stella said. "I need to find a good shrink for her. Know any good ones?"

"Unfortunately, no. It's hopeless. The good ones ran when I broached the subject of Tess, and Tess would quickly turn those not-so-good into quaking imbeciles."

The banter went on in this way, with all concerned washed in the grace of well-being.

On the forth hospital day, Dr. Tanner wanted them all out, and so he sent Tess home. This was something of a problem for Stella, for she had to complete the office complex landscaping before winter set in. She hired a nurse to come daily and stay with Tess for four hours, but that wasn't enough. Tess was getting around—in and out of the kitchen, and to the bathroom.

As soon as she knew that Tess was settled at home, Anna called.

"Although Tess seems to be quite steady," Stella said, "nevertheless I'm worried about her falling."

"Stella, I'll be there a couple hours each day," Anna said. "And I spoke to Ben and he said he'll drop in on Tess each day at lunch time, and will bring David to visit for more chess games. David has also arranged to pick up any schoolwork that might be waiting for her. She's not even going to be allowed to get behind in shop."

"I can't thank all of you enough," Stella said. "You and Ben are the reason I can feel some comfort and peace through this. A few weeks from now, Tess must go to court to identify Ryan. Sadly, I introduced him into my little family, and when I stopped seeing him, he had to take his vicious revenge. Now, Tess must continue to pay the price."

"I haven't wanted to ask, Stella. Can you talk about it?"

"It's horrible," Stella said, and she related the entire story to Anna, beginning with the offer of a stolen computer. "Thank God for witnesses, so it doesn't have to be solely Tess's word."

Anna waited to let Stella's painful news reach out; it was sometimes a comfort to talk about it. Seemed to drain off the negative energy for a time, until the unbelievable memory invaded again.

"You never know who is out there," Stella said. "When I met Ryan, and learned that he was an English professor at a community college in Westchester, I thought he had to be a clean and trouble-free, respectable man. But not so it turns out. My attorney has learned that it takes time for colleges to search a teacher's background—get in all the facts in time for classes to start. Now they know that Ryan is a felon."

"Well, he's in more trouble now," Anna said, and as though Stella could see her—fist to chin she had been moving her head from side to side trying to help Stella repel her dire news.

"I hope so. With a prior record, good on-the-spot witnesses, and Tess's identification...that should get Ryan stopped. At least for a while."

43

An Uh-Oh! Encounter

It was a perfect Saturday for Ben to take David shopping and for lunch, and the Darien Sport Shop was one of the finest enterprises in southern Connecticut for sports equipment and sportswear. They were on a spending spree, Ben pleased to have reasons to lavish something on David. David had not been deprived of life's necessities, but Ben, had been deprived since David was born for giving to him, providing for him. Ben's purpose today was providing for David—anything he saw, but of course Ben waited, holding back his enthusiasm. Perhaps they would decide on archery —Ben's fenced rear yard had sufficient room, or they could install a basketball hoop. All kinds of ideas sprouted. Anyway, whatever he and David decided, any growing young man could use another pair or two of shorts, tee shirts, and sneakers in the current style. So Ben stood around while David selected.

"Ben!" The voice from across the aisles of clothing slammed hard against Ben's face. Everyone turned to the source and stared. "How nice to see you today. What are you up to? The hospital actually gave you a day off?"

This question came from a large grin and voice Ben recognized, one he dreaded to hear. It came on firmly, no holding back. Valerie strode across the room. Ben finally turned around to see her marching toward him.

"Valerie. Nice to see you." He hoped he could escape having to say more and turned back away from her, trying to appear busy looking through men's shirts.

But intrepid Valerie had made it across the aisles now and had Ben by the arm. He had managed to avoid her for weeks it seemed, and hadn't returned a phone message, and she was not about to waste an opportunity and relinquish him now; miss the chance to invite him to something, anything, perhaps lunch.

"Ah, Valerie," he said, caught in her clutch. How to find the place to keep her at a stand-off, and yet not offend an important hospital board member; he could scarcely do that.

Valerie was about to say, Ben, how about lunch? We can go next door to Maxi's, but David had stepped over and waited, looking from Ben to Valerie.

"Valerie, I'd like for you to meet my son, David. David, this is Mrs. Llewis. Mrs. Llewis is a hospital board member. I think she's personally responsible for keeping the hospital propped up."

Valerie's little lunch speech stuck in her craw, moved farther back in fact, until it was submerged in disbelief and disappointment. *Ben had a son?* This had to be a joke. Ben was single, unattached, free. Wasn't he? He had a relative who was still growing? Who could be a wise kid? At that smart-aleck age? Trouble. Still, she extended her hand to David and they exchanged greetings—David's open and friendly—Valerie's stiff with caution; this would have to be explained. She looked around for a woman, any woman, to come up and claim this boy. Then she decided that indeed Ben and David must be together.

"Where have you been hiding a son?" she asked Ben. "Lo these many years. And why? Surely your old friends deserved to know about him." She hid behind a smile; after all, it was too soon to condemn Ben, and surely this would turn out to be a prank.

"He's been an undercover agent for the CIA." Ben didn't have to see David's assumed serious face, he could feel it. "But his mission is down now, and they're releasing him to get some public school experience. You know...putting him into *real* danger."

Valerie's quizzical expression was well worth the joke. She clearly couldn't decide whether Ben's story was true. Neither Ben nor David were about to give her more information. She would just have to guess. After she got back to the hospital with this information, all the staff would have to guess. Still, Valerie would eventually find glory, Ben knew, in being the first to hear about his having a son.

"Valerie, I'm sorry to rush, but we're on a mission today to get some gear for David, and our time is limited. I'll see you back at the hospital." And Ben turned David away and toward sports equipment in the showroom's rear.

Valerie wanted to run around shouting, *The sky is falling*! *The sky is falling*! for she could think of no greater let down. Ben with a son! She didn't like children, and boys were children until about age forty, or even older in most cases. Where had Ben been hiding this one? Well, certainly she didn't want to have lunch with the two of them; not her idea of a good time. This was bad; she would have to find out more.

44

Ben Learns an Unexpected Truth

For the past week Melody had not seen or heard from Robert. She subtly tried to pump information from everyone but no one had heard from him. He had called Anna once to say he would take the children the weekend after. However, Anna did not pry into his activities or whereabouts. Melody consoled herself that he needed time to clear his head following the divorce, and would soon be in touch. A divorce proceeding was stressful whether you were the one who wanted out. She expected he would soon say it was time for her to separate from Cass because he needed her for himself. The agonized wait. Powerless. When she called his cottage several times, there was no answer. Driving by didn't help—his car could be in the garage. She could not drive into his plant without a pass card. Once she dared to zip through the gate close behind another car, but a guard wouldn't let her into the plant. She angrily ordered that he call Robert to let her in, that she was a special friend, and she knew he would want her to visit. The guard made the call but after a long wait, Robert's secretary came back on the phone and said Mr. Randall wasn't available. Wasn't available, period. No other message. Melody's embarrassment prevented a repeat of that pursuit. She was trapped in stress tighter than an Iron Maiden, and almost ready to bite those expensively manicured nails. She decided to leave a message on his service, to the effect that she understood, and was available when he was free. In her mind this would be a calm, unpressured message, but when she tried his number again, and his machine picked up, she said tensely, "It's imperative that I see you. Call me right away. I'll be home alone and Cass is out of town." (This wasn't true, but she would say anything to encourage Robert to call.) She waited all day by the phone. He didn't call. Late afternoon she left another message. Disappointed, crushed, she could barely urge her body forward to cook dinner. She couldn't sleep. Several times, she drove by his cottage, and when once she saw a light, she pulled into his driveway, rang the doorbell, and waited, but no one came to the door. On another, similar occasion, she thought she heard voices and then quiet.

The following days offered her no relief. Her anxiety level prevented her applying herself to any task for longer than five minutes. She had reasoned long enough; had long enough told herself to be understanding, be patient. Her frustration built until she had to talk to someone—find a sympathetic ear.

Ben would be a good person to consult, she thought. After all, as a physician, he was used to hearing problems. And he was a friend. Actually, she thought he would do anything for her. She left a message for him asking would he please come over as soon as he could; she would be home all day. She tried to compose herself; Ben would probably come over at 5:00 or so, perhaps she could get herself together by then. She filled and emptied several ashtrays and while she smoked another cigarette, she sat with ice packs to reduce eye swelling from frequent tears. With a stern and loud voice, she told the twins that she was expecting a visitor, and they would have to stay in the family room and be quiet.

When Ben rang the doorbell, she called out for him to let himself in. He stepped in and saw that she was a nervous mess, hair splayed in all directions. She slouched over a glass of what looked to be whiskey, her slippered feet propped up on a hassock. Somehow, she was still beautiful; even more so, for he felt pity tugging at his heart.

"Please make yourself a drink and have a seat. Everything is over on the liquor caddy." She gestured, pointing with her cigarette." She did not get up, or smile.

The house reeked of stale tobacco. Ben stood in the entryway not sure what to do. He could hear the children quietly playing in the family room, and to his sensitive ears, the sounds of their play had a sad quality. He saw that until he did make a drink and sit, Melody wasn't going to explain her problem. Hardly aware of his actions, he reached for a glass on the liquor caddy, looked around for the scotch —what was left of it, poured a shot, looked for ice, and seeing none, took a seat facing Melody. He wanted to hug her, tell her everything would be okay, but his instinct was to wait. First, listen.

"For nearly a year now, Robert and I have been involved. Closely involved."

There was a pause; the air hardly moved, the room itself afraid to breathe.

Melody focused enough to think about what she had just revealed. "That's putting it mildly," she said stoically, eyes narrowing as if she might be dozing off. "We are talking about marriage. It's the motive for his wanting his divorce, and I know he expects me to leave Cass now."

Ben thought he hadn't heard right. For an instant, he thought Melody was making up something: some fascinating fiction, a test, something to confound him, get his attention. But then, he saw her red eyes, saw the slight trembling when she lifted her glass, and in the following quiet he heard again, ringing in his head, exactly what she had said. He churned. His gut churned. Surely she was kidding; playing to see whether he cared. But the reality hung in the room: Melody continued to look serious and pained. Without a show of surprise he listened to the story Melody unfolded about her involvement with Robert, his promise of marriage, and their love for each other. Ben slouched into the chair as if pressed down under the weight of her speech. Disappointed thoughts flip-flopped from the way Melody had gently led him on, to the underhanded conniving in which she and Robert must have been engaging all along—perhaps since they met. When Ben did not sympathize, Melody's tone became defensive.

"I don't feel bad for Anna's sake," she said, "because she and

Robert are incompatible, at odds, a shell of a marriage. Though Robert confided this to me, he didn't have to...it was obvious. Surely you noticed." She looked at Ben with a pleading face, seeking confirmation.

Ben had fallen mute. Searching for a hidden reality, he listened, his face immobile. If he had had a desire to confirm Melody's conviction about Anna and Robert, he would certainly have withheld it; not engaged in that gossip.

Melody told it all, except her role in the plot to help Robert with his divorce. "Besides, I think Anna was having an affair," she said, looking down at the overfull ashtray as she pressed out her cigarette. She did not see Ben shaking his head *No*. "And now, I haven't heard from Robert for over a week, and I'm beside myself. Do you have any suggestions? Do you know what he's up to? I've tried many times to reach him. Even dropped him a note. I know that he wants me. He and I have solid history together. And I know that he'll want me to be one of the demonstrators on his yacht during the New York boat show. I'm a big-ticket model now and have to arrange my calendar way in advance." An exaggeration; she offered this as an explanation for her anxiousness and anxiety.

For long minutes, Ben couldn't look at her; her face would look like stone instead of porcelain. There was nothing he could say. Nothing. Silenced by this *coup de foudre*, he sat quietly twirling his drink. He rubbed the back of his neck; it had stiffened and was painful.

Melody mistook his silence for pondering a way to offer help with her dilemma. She talked on and the more she talked, the more Ben's suspicions grew. He had thought it strange and unlikely, the way Robert and Anna's divorce had come about that quickly. And where did those photographs come from that Anna said Robert's lawyer presented in court? Who took those? When Anna had only been delivering paintings? He would never have suspected that Anna would have an affair. But then, he had never dreamed about Melody and Robert either. He had been aware that Robert could have shown more concern for Anna, but they always seemed to get along with each other. Who would have thought that Robert was restive? And Melody? There had always been something disquieting about Melody that he had overlooked and now it fell exposed. Was that his own heart he heard screaming? The outer silence grew until he had to say something.

"Ah." He stood—it seemed to take every one of his cells pulling together to lift himself from the chair—and went over to the liquor caddy to add a splash to his drink. He had to do something. Had to concentrate on what was important. He asked whether he could add to her drink.

She held out a shaky glass. "Thanks." She took a deep breath and tried to relax. Ben would help her.

Although, if Ben would err—he would not err with his professionalism, and actually the situation between Robert and Melody wasn't his business. And he soon realized what he should say.

"Melody. In any relationship, still in early stages—"

"It's not in early stages."

Silenced, Ben stood looking around the room, hearing again the children, then finally looking at Melody's pained face. He would subdue his own feelings and continue to respond to her as he would a patient. He was a better man now, could gather the strength to step aside, not feel anything and so he said, "It's better for the woman not to pursue the man with letters and phone calls." He spoke as though she had not interrupted. "That may push him away. Men are pursuers, testosterone driven. I don't think you have a choice except to get busy with your activities. You'll feel better soon and who knows what Robert will do. I haven't seen him or heard anything about him in several weeks. He's probably lying low because of the divorce."

"Noooo!" she wailed. "I want to see him! I need to ask what's going on; why he hasn't call. I'm sure he'll want me for the boat show. Can you try to reach him for me? I've been unable to." A tear moved down her face.

"No." He let that word have time to carry. It hung there between them. "You'll have to wait this out. If he feels as you say, you will hear from him. If you don't...do not pursue him. He knows where you are."

He wanted to change the subject. "Have you heard about Tess? Stella's daughter, and her accident?"

Confused, her thoughts and feelings in astonishing disarray, it took Melody several seconds to hear the change and reluctantly to shift into it. "Yes I have. It's too bad." Her distracted tone did not ring with conviction.

Ben fixed her with a solemn stare while he appraised what little feeling she had for the change of topic. Then he took his glass to the sink, and placed it among other dishes piled up there. "I have to go, Melody. I'm on call tonight, and I have my son at the house. He's expecting me to stop for pizza on my way home."

"Oh, don't leave now," her voice carried a plea. "I heard about your son. Couldn't he call for a pizza delivery? It's not like he's a child."

Ben did not reply.

"I hope you're up to the challenges of a teenager," she added, saying to herself that Ben had not *had* to invite the boy to live with him.

"I think you'll feel better soon." Ben walked out and pulled the door shut behind him.

Although he could not immediately shut down his feelings for Melody, Ben saw how fooled he had been with the three "Misses" of human folly: *mis*information, *mis*led, and *mis*taken. He felt hot, seared with a molten poker. Chagrinned. Embarrassed. He had to get out of there, and for the first time he was happy to get away from Melody. And as well, he would be disquieted for a long time by his flawed judgment. As he drove off, he put down the window to let the breeze blow away his storms of regret.

45

Parents are Popping up All Over

Now, for a while, only Anna, Stella, and Ben met for occasional meals. When she wasn't buried in homework assignments, Tess joined as well. Anna knew why she had no partner. Stella knew why she had no partner. Ben figured he would never have a partner, but he was delighted to include his son. David enjoyed this and fit in easily. Ben would proudly tease, "Not only have I gained a son, but I've gained a soccer captain."

"Ah, the twists and turns of life," Anna said. "The gods are always vigilant, watching, ready to punish or reward. If we become too complacent...whack: they fling at us the very arrow to most shake us up. And sometimes, as long as we remain innocent, as you are, Ben, they shoot us with an arrow for reward. Yours had a name on it: 'David'."

Anna perceived that David might be a bit embarrassed with the focus on himself, and so she quickly changed the topic. "I keep asking the Clarkes to join us, but Melody always has a reason why they can't. She says she's busy in the city most days and exhausted at night. I've also called Noel and Peter, but no one answers. I wonder how their wedding plans are progressing."

While serving desert, Belle overheard this. She had had a suspicion about a rift between Noel and Peter, especially after seeing Noel and Robert together at Trader Joe's. *Arm in arm*. It might amount to nothing; Belle had always stayed apart from family gossip, and so she hadn't mentioned it to Anna earlier, and now it was too late.

Only Ben suspected why Melody and Cass were avoiding them. Not because Melody felt guilt, he supposed, but because she was distraught, and feared revealing the facts in an emotional outburst to Anna. He suspected Melody was embarrassed, as well, because she thought he had not understood. He hadn't in fact—understood—her character.

With holidays ahead, the lighter, brighter moods of the season infected everyone, weaving in expectant hopes and amusement. Stella's brow relaxed into a smoother, less worried aspect. Tess had mended quickly and wanted to join the fun. Even so, sometimes she looked to be locked somewhere behind a dark wall. Everyone thought she would rest easier once Ryan was put away, they hoped for good.

Although the topic of the trial was somewhat avoided around Tess—everyone wanting to keep things light for her benefit—it was otherwise seriously discussed among themselves: how the trial was going forward with a date on the court's calendar; faith in Dr. Tanner who would be describing Tess's injuries as consistent with her being thrown with force and hitting the curb; how Stella's attorney, Alan Turner, had faith in the evidence and in Tess's testimony, and faith in the issue of Ryan's former felony conviction; and that their witnesses were strong, competent witnesses who were eager to testify that they had seen Tess grabbed against her will, pulled into the van, and afterward, several hundred feet down the street, as they gaped in disbelief, had seen her expelled from the moving van. Ryan's free days would soon be over.

Tonight, around Anna's table, Ben had his own heavy, but exciting topic to bring forth. He had pondered how and when to tell David that his biological mother lived and thrived down in Virginia, and that he had called on her recently. He wanted to tell David about Judy, and he wanted to tell David that she knew their son was an outstanding young man. He wanted to offer David a chance to drive down to meet her. No pressure. He thought Anna's dinner parties, among safe friends would be a perfect time to broach the subject, keep it light; it had to be done. Although he had doubts, in the end, he couldn't resist.

"It's not just anyone who can pull out extra parents," Ben placed a meaningful look on David. "*Two*, David."

"Two?"

"Yes." *Plunge in.*

"You have a biological mother in Virginia, and although until last week I had not seen her since you were adopted, I visited her recently."

Silence around the table while everyone digested more than they had expected to. Brows rose. Eyes widened.

Ben had already told David about the heavy censure that caused Judy to give him up at birth, and now he waited for this new thunder to roll. David's chin perked up and his eyes rounded out like coasters. Tess gave David a look that told it all: *how great is that*!

"She's a nice woman. She lives in a tree house," Ben said, going for hyperbole.

"Ah ha! That confirms that you're descended from apes," Tess said.

"Apes don't live in tree houses," David said.

"Your mother has a branch of her own," Ben said.

"We can't call her my mother, for I had a dear mother who was killed."

"You're absolutely right, David. Good thinking. Thoughtless of me. Actually, I'm sure she would be pleased to have you think of her as a friend, and call her, 'Judy', for that is her name."

The others around the table had quietly taken in this startling exchange, surprised that in public Ben would spring this sensitive news. However, Ben had thought it through and had decided that in front of their close friends, his announcement, making somewhat light of it, would work. It wasn't as though David had to acknowledge Judy. He didn't have to if he didn't want to. But if he should agree to meet her, he would see himself in her. That wouldn't be at all bad. Ben expected that Anna and Stella would concur.

"Judy's a little different," Ben said.

"What do you mean? How different?" David asked, wariness in his voice.

"As I said, she lives in a tree house for which she has no ladder." Not true, of course—Judy wasn't living there, but this was a good situation for light drama.

"You aren't serious." David hedged his feelings although he was reassured by the unmistakable spark in Ben's eyes.

"I am. When I saw her, the builder of the tree house was still using his ladder that he carted off on his truck. She said she'd be happy with a rope ladder that she could pull up for complete privacy. And beads...if you ever get to meet her, take beads. She's nuts for beads." Then Ben looked at Tess and said, "If David decides to meet her, you can take him shopping for beads." Ben kept the tone light. David should feel no pressure.

"I'm happy you are here, Tess," David said. "I need a nerd to help me interpret this craziness, and a crazy person to help me absorb it. You qualify for both."

"Get over it, David," Tess said. "Some people need more than two parents to keep them on the straight and level."

David flicked a pea at her.

Ben didn't mentioned to anyone that he had, with Judy's permission, contracted with a plumber to fix Judy's bathroom. He didn't want to think about Judy's having to slush through snow and ice, maybe in the middle of the night, to the outhouse. Of course, if Judy needed to go when she was in her tree house—that was her problem. She would just be up a tree, he laughed to himself. He wouldn't put a john in a tree house. *Oh...wait until David sees it...if he will.*

"She's quite interesting, David."

"Just how is she interesting?"

"Lets just say that more than most people, she has ways of enjoying life.

With such an intriguing mother, David felt his genetic stock rising. And after some thought about that, and the long pause it took for him to say the words—everyone waiting, expectance perfuming the air, Mrs. Randall nodding her head as if to say "go for it, David," he said, "I think I'd like to meet her."

"It's all set then for she'd like to meet you. As long as you're comfortable with the idea, we'll leave on Friday for Judy's. She's ready for our visit, and knows that we'll be taking her out to dinner and staying at the hotel one night, and then driving back the next day. I know she's looking forward to meeting you. You do not have to be more than friends."

"What a wonderful surprise for you, David," said Stella. "I wish I were going with you to meet this interesting woman."

"Just get a tree ready," said Tess, "in case he comes home in a swinging mood."

David seemed relaxed about the trip prospect; he gave Tess a wink.

On Friday, Ben stopped by the Marlows' to collect David for the trip to Judy's. David came down the steps lugging a large misshapen bag that clunked and rattled as he descended the stairs. His grin seemed to fill all the space between him and his father.

"Is that going with us?"

"Yup." David didn't explain.

"It must be a secret."

"Exactly."

"Okay. I'm ready, if you are."

As they drove, David thought about all the twists and turns on the path of his life. It was certainly an adventure. Much had closed —losing his parents—and much had opened, gaining a father. He looked forward to new opportunities, but felt the sadness of one door closing for another to open. At least it seemed so. And imagine, moving back to Westport and helping his friend, Tess. As for his biological mother, he had been warned that she was "different," but nice. Harmless. And he didn't need to embrace her. She had not been able to keep him, and maybe he could learn to understand that. Learn the pressures and judgments that had controlled her.

Watching fields, trees, and traffic move by, Ben thought about his past actions. His new connection to his long missed son, David, was the best event in his life. One of the best for David, also, he hoped. Still, Ben couldn't guess whether introducing David to his natural, but slightly eccentric, mother was a positive thing to do. Nevertheless, on a scale of one to ten, he thought it rank about a nine. He had thought about it for a long time; went to sleep nights with it on his mind. Dreamed it. His best instincts said do it. How could it be other than positive? Judy was a cheerful, positive, unthreatening force. And now they were on their way. What was the mysterious rattily package David brought? A secret. David wouldn't let him touch it. Ben noted how comfortable they were riding along together, neither feeling they had to keep a conversation going.

In the meantime, Judy could barely stand the tension as she waited for them. They were due within the hour and she was ready —had been ready since 7:00 a.m. Although she had been cleaning and organizing all week, she spent the morning on extra touches. She had bought a vacuum, something she had lived without all her life. It was certainly quicker than the old broom. She tied back some of the hanging beads to make it easier to get in and out. She was used to them, the ropes of beads, but couldn't expect her guests to manage getting through them easily.

She heard the car drive up and went out to greet them. Ben emerged from the car wearing a broad smile and came forward to shake Judy's hand. Judy watched while a tall and gangly young man stepped out of the car, reached in the back seat and hauled out a large bundle. Maybe he was as nervous as she was, but he eagerly came forward to shake her hand. At this point, shaking hands was the most sensible action, she thought, and he probably thought so as well. After they said their hellos, David handed Judy the heavy bag and suggested she open it outside.

She opened the bag, and started pulling out lengths of thick, smooth rope attached to pieces of highly polished wooden rungs.

"A rope ladder!" she almost shouted.

"I made it in shop,"

For a moment Judy had to search for a reply and a thank you—so much all at once. "Perfect. And it's heavy-duty, strong and beautiful." She beamed with delighted surprise. "I love it. Now I won't have to wait for that laggard, Elmer, to build the stairs. He's chased by too many women. They find projects that make it hard for him to get here. She patted the ladder as though it were already an old friend, "Do you mind if I wrap beads around it...decorate it?"

"It's yours and you are to treat it as you like, and you can haul it up when you wish. It should last a while, and is completely adjustable." David relaxed. This was going to be easy. He already liked this woman even though he couldn't think of her as his mother. He looked around. "Ah. You have a clever hobbit-house. I like it."

Just wait until he sees all the stuff and beads inside, Ben thought.

"And look at that!" David said. "I almost missed it. An outhouse painted to blend right in with the trees. Outhouses are so practical. We need one in Connecticut with all the power failures due to ice storms. When our power fails, the well pump won't run, and we have no water. Can't flush the toilets."

Not much will go wrong, Ben thought. I believe we all are passing this test.

46

Christian Does What?

It was time, Anna felt, to ask Christian to join her and her friends for dinner. He was in her life more and more and the children and Belle enjoyed having him around; he intrigued them. By evening's end, Stella wished she could back into someone like M. Christian Boutin, and said so.

"Christian, do you have a brother, or cousin...single, of course?" Stella asked. "Somewhere in the age range of, say, between thirty and sixty?" Her grin stretched over and touched Christian. "And in need of an American widow? A cool guy? One I can back up to and step on? With stiletto heels? and thereby win his heart?"

"Well, not exactly in your age range, Stella, but I have a six-year-old nephew, and an eighty-five-year-old widowed grandfather."

"Christian you're useless. It's true: Frenchmen are totally unreliable. What does Anna see in you? And what's your secret, Anna? How did you know when to fall on him?"

"In her defense," he said, "I had to arrange to be there behind her at that exact moment, in order that she would back up on me, crush my foot and fall into my arms. It took some conniving. Even though I had never seen her before, I knew she was a woman about whom I needed to know something...what made her crooked smile, what made her 'tick,' as Americans say." Christian beamed. He looked at Anna's happy face and reached for her hand. "That's hard to arrange. Takes practice. I could not walk for a month. My business suffered; without my supervision walls went up crooked. The doctor said thirty-six bones were broken in my foot," he frowned. "I'm still limping. I just hide it well."

"How you do jest, Monsieur Boutin," Tess said. "You only have about twenty-six bones in your foot."

"You must know about the French, though," Christian gave Tess a mock serious look, "they have to be one up."

"Yeah...in your case, ten-up," Tess countered.

Stella was hard put to suppress the joy she felt in Tess's continuing to lighten up, join in the repartee—and now a new jokester had joined the group. Anna and Stella had gone through major adjustments in their opinion of Christian.

Ben had not met him before, and had no opinion adjustment to make. Pleased that Anna had Christian for a good friend, Ben also suspected that they were forming a deeper connection than just friendship. He didn't think that he wanted Stella to meet a Frenchman though. Not sure why. He found himself studying Stella. He noted her glossy dark hair, and her features—classic. It was as though he hadn't seen her before. Well, well, he thought, situations can change in a hurry.

"Stella, let's go have a night cap," he said to her after one of these dinners. "I know how to dance, too. I think."

"We could give it a try," Stella said. "But, leave your scalpel at home."

"Right. Glad you reminded me. I always have one handy in my pocket just in case. I wouldn't want to stick you in the ribs," he said as he goosed her ribs. She jumped. He had been holding her coat for her, and at that moment as she turned to insert her arm, she stepped backward on to his foot. He steadied and held her for a second. "Nice perfume," he said.

"See, mom," said Tess. "Not to worry: you have the same talents as Mrs. Randall."

Although her marriage to Robert had been more frustrating than satisfying in later years—Anna never quite sure what was wrong, lonely even with the children and Belle around, that feeling after you examine the parts of yourself and find a cog missing, and your gears don't seem to mesh, aloneness you had when your partner was away much of the time—she still felt remorse for the end of the marriage. And joining her light-hearted and amusing friends over a meal always had the effect of lightening her mood. She knew they enjoyed Belle's cooking and Belle seemed to thrive on entertaining. Anna made sure to give Belle a hearty bonus when company came to dinner to compensate for the extra work. And yet, Belle would have done the work for nothing if it brought Anna a smile.

Anna tried again to have the Clarkes join the group. She phoned them. "Melody, I hope you and Cass will come to dinner Saturday."

"Thank you for asking, but I'm afraid we can't. Cass will be traveling to a seminar, and I'm working a fashion show, and taking a late train home. In too late." Quick thinking. She didn't want to see Anna, or Ben, or be in the Randalls' home. Though she wasn't entirely ready to let the friendship drop, Melody was bitter toward Anna for the guilt Anna unknowingly and innocently had bestowed on her: her unacknowledged but well-earned guilt.

"What have you been up to, Anna? Did that architect buy a painting?" Melody knew he had. She had heard from Robert all about Christian's testimony in court; his avowal that Anna was in the hotel simply to sell paintings. And no one but Robert knew that Melody had helped him obtain evidence; manipulated Anna until the divorce was a fact.

"Indeed he did...two. It was a kick."

"Have you seen him since?" A nosy question; her bitterness pushed; she wanted news of Christian.

"Yes, I have. I've had dinner with him." Many times, Anna thought. She didn't want to broadcast this, but she could feel Melody pulling. Anyway, if Melody came to dinner, she would meet Christian, so there was no reason to hide him. Images of cow paintings suddenly rose in her mind. Christian, when he asked to see them, had firmly vowed that he had not seen them before, and would not have rejected them from the show. He wished they had been included, he said. What could Melody say about this? Anna wondered. She probably left the paintings off at the show and they had not made it to Christian's view; perhaps waylaid off in a corner. But then, who would have marked them as rejected?

"Well, don't count on him. He's taken. I occasionally see him with a stunning, sophisticated woman...often dancing or eating together. Holding hands." Melody's story grew with the fertilizer of bitterness. She couldn't stop inventing. She had such a capacity for it. In the ensuing silence she read the effect of her announcement.

"Christian? M. Boutin, the French architect? Are we talking about the same man?"

"Yes, Anna. I met him during the art show. He stopped by after it was hung to see how well the paintings worked together. He sat for a while to watch the fashion show. French accent. Dark curly hair. Not tall, but solid."

Anna's essence seemed to drain out, paralyzed by snake venom, not recognizing the snake. Love builds esteem, confidence and hopes for a future, then takes it all away; cuts that scaffold away with one whack.

"Oh. He's only an acquaintance." Anna meant to cool her emotions. "Besides, he'll return to France soon."

"Well, I did want to warn you, Anna. He's a man about town; he even asked *me* to join him for dinner. You've been through a great strain lately. I would hate to see you hurt again."

For a few seconds, silence continued.

"Point taken. I'll try you again in a few weeks," Anna said. No one would know her disappointment. "We all miss seeing the two of you." She hung up.

Melody and Cass were lucky to have each other, Anna thought —such as it was. So much for Christian; good thing she hadn't fallen for him. Didn't she still have her heart? Although the heart place in her chest felt hollow, a flimsy, empty thing. In a nearby mirror, she saw her sad face, and forced a smile.

"Belle, if it sounds like M. Boutin, or is M. Boutin on the phone, please tell him I'm not at home. I'm not sure what is going on with him, but Melody has seen him out with a woman with whom she says he is obviously intimate. So I want to stop any further contact with him."

"And you take Melody at her word...?"

Anna thought about that. Why shouldn't she?

47

Melody's Interference Unlimited

Though It had been a painful transition now that her divorce from Robert was final, and the loss of Christian's companionship was a required adjustment anyway, for he would return to France, Anna didn't object as much to go dancing at Harbor House. Stella had made an effort to get her out—to be around people who weren't grieving, hear a band, soak up that energy—and Stella was always certain to be humorous; Anna would have to laugh in spite of herself. And the band Stella had in mind was tops. The second time the topic came up, Stella had said that if Anna didn't go with her, she would bring all the band and dancers to Anna's house, and that would be a mess for Anna. And also damned expensive. Anna agreed to go. She would learn to filter unwanted dance partners.

So, on this night, she entered Harbor House cautiously, like a cat in a strange place. She and Stella found seats and ordered drinks, then looked through the throng of dancers. There was Melody engaged with several men around her as usual giving her the old stake out. Anna had expected perhaps to see her, but the obnoxious man, the one who had slammed her car door, was the one she dreaded to see, and so far, his face was not in the crowd. She pictured herself ramming his butt against the wall.

Soon Melody saw Stella and Anna, and leaving her entourage of admirers in glowing mid-sentences, she joined the women.

"Isn't this a wonderful time to be here?" Melody asked, looking around at the assemblage of handsome people. "I've met *really* interesting guys...newcomers. I'll introduce you to them." And she waved them over. This was safe, she could share, for she had no particular interest in these men. With wide eager smiles, three men walked over, happy to know that Melody hadn't forgotten or forsaken them. There were hellos all around, and two and three-way conversations started up.

Then Anna saw Christian leaning back against the bar. He must have just arrived. He was alone. Though Anna tried to look away quickly, their eyes met for a brief instant.

He looked hard at Anna, a question forming. He needed to understand why she had refused his calls. He had been certain that she shared his feelings. He didn't know whether to approach her. His hurt welled up. He decided he had better make a move to get clarification, difficult though it would be. There was no reason Anna should avoid him; he had a logical need to hear from her what was wrong between them. Whatever it was, couldn't he and she correct it? He wanted to say how much he missed her. But he should wait until he could catch her without so many people around.

From what Melody said, Christian's assurances were not to be trusted, and Anna intended to hide her disappointment. She had merely missed all the clues; he had been a beacon of possibility that dimmed. Her tears were close to the surface now. Maybe if she walked to the restroom she could get control. She told Stella that she was going to the ladies' room. "Please guard my drink," she said, and turned toward the restroom. She didn't want to discuss why it was hard to breathe, why she felt so dismal.

However, the gods of complications arranged, at the same instant that Christian thought he must make his move, for him not to see through the crowd, that Anna had walked off, and by the time he reached the group, in her place sat Melody. Melody saw him approaching and offered up her come-on smile. It was too late to turn back; he continued toward her, surprised to see that Anna was not there.

"Did Mrs. Randall leave?" he asked. He had come there that night, as on other nights, to look for Anna and had no thought of hiding his imploring look.

"Yes." Melody said with her cloying smile as she looked up at Christian. "She left." If she couldn't have M. Boutin, neither could Anna. If caught in her fib, she could always say that she thought Anna had left.

That must be the end for Anna and him, Christian thought. She was so irritated with him that she had to leave, and he didn't know why. She wouldn't take his calls, and ran from him. He felt his face flush. He had to get out of there. Get some air. Let his system think about something else. He mumbled good evening to Melody and left. He had come there only to find Anna. In his distress, he couldn't remember where he had left his car, and when he finally found it and took a seat, he remained immobile for a while. Clouds passing before the bright moon made it look like the moon was winking at him. I know—folly, he thought, I'm wasting my time with folly.

Anna came out of the restroom, her feelings better under control, and took a quick glance around for Christian; she couldn't help it, he had become a magnet for her. She had hoped to talk to him. Feared to talk to him. Wouldn't talk to him if she could help it. Where was he? There was that knowing look of Melody's again.

"You just missed Christian." Melody said. "He came by to say hello, but he had to leave. The sweetest guy...he asked me to have lunch with him, but I'm too busy this week." She said this to Anna as though the event were the most natural thing in the universe. Then she casually looked around with a nonplussed expression as if the idea wasn't worth further consideration.

In your dreams, Stella thought. Over the music and chatter, she hadn't heard Christian's conversation with Melody, but she heard this one. And she didn't know about Christian's calls to Anna, that Anna wouldn't take. Nor did she know about Melody's scheming tales. Yet, she sensed that Melody's words were not to be taken seriously.

Later, when they were seated in the car, Stella said: "I can't see that dignified Frenchman with Melody. I thought he was your special friend."

"I thought so too, but according to Melody, he has other special friends, and his words aren't reliable."

"Humph! Whose words aren't reliable?"

"Christian's not what he seems to be. Recently, when I called to invite Melody and Cass to dinner, Melody told me that she has several times now seen him with another woman. Close to the other woman."

"Huh," Stella used her wise and knowing look, but Anna didn't see it. Stella waited. Anna had more to say.

"Melody said that Christian also asks her out. My problem is that I thought he had real feeling for me. I certainly did for him. I...."

This hesitation was left hanging.

48

A Welcome Clarification

The holidays came and, as is their want, left so quickly it seemed sneaky of them to leave everyone not quite fulfilled. Christian had previously mentioned to Anna that he would be in France to spend Christmas with his mother and father. The children were back in school and things were quiet—a good time for Anna to concentrate on painting. Her class had started again, and Gary wanted to meet for outdoor painting while the children were in school. Belle said someone kept calling who would not leave a name. Belle thought for sure it sounded like M. Boutin, but maybe it would be better not to say so. Anna paid little attention, for though he had moved out, Robert still received an occasional business call at the house. One night when Christian called, Anna picked up the phone. She had just come in from painting, hungry and tired. He asked her to join him for dinner; he had decided that he must confront her.

"Not tonight, Christian." *Why bother*? But Anna found that she cared more than her good sense wanted to.

"Would Tuesday work for you then?" he persisted. Until he received a yes, he would ask for each night of the month as long as he had her on the phone. He had to wait an eternity for her answer.

"Okay," Anna said. "Thank you. I can make that." No enthusiasm. Soft touch again. But she knew how to guard her heart now. Eating with him would be okay. Not that it would matter, but perhaps she could find out what motivated him.

After laboring with his appearance—making certain he was as appealing as he could manage, wishing that he could be exactly the man to appeal to Anna (a tiny touch of E*au Sauvage*), having his shoes shined, the rental car waxed, collecting her on the dot at seven, saying hello to Belle, who greeted him so warmly that he knew she was on his side—now, in the most romantic restaurant he knew of, Christian sat across from Anna. He reached for her hand and pressed it hard. He would not lose this opportunity.

He started: "I've struggled to find you. I fear I've given you reason to avoid me and I don't know what it could be. The last time I saw you at Harbor House, I wanted so much to talk to you, but you disappeared. Your friend said you had left. I've grown to know that I cannot...not possibly...not even think of leaving without knowing what's wrong. Being abroad for a week, thinking about you every second...well, maybe every tenth second," he wanted to get a smile from Anna, "taught me that." He had to take a long, deep breath for the next words. "And I must be in France again for at least a week. And before I leave, and I know, I know this is sudden, but I've waited and hoped, it is not sudden for me, that we, you and I, have a lasting connecting...one with a future." He wasn't sure how to read the surprise on Anna's face. He paused to take a deep breath.

"You must think about this and tell me why you have avoided me."

Anna politely listened through all his urgent plea; first forming a large NO, then slowly letting the NO slide away to be replaced by something uncertain, and softer.

"But, Christian. I thought you were involved with someone. Melody said so. I wanted to avoid you. I didn't want to get hurt." She gave him a serious frown.

"Anna!" He hardly knew what to think. "I've had no one. No one at all. I'm always alone. I thought perhaps you and Gary had something going; I knew the two of you were painting together. I had to find out. I can't think what your friend had in mind." He paused. "And it was she who said you were at the cape. That caused me to pull back; lose time with you. Are you certain she's a friend?"

Anna yielded; doors she had tried to close were springing wide open exposing her again, although she believed this earnest man whom she had dearly missed. She thought she would melt into her chair. She reached across the table and touched Christian's face—how could this be?

"Anna, you must honor me. I think I knew this moment would come, knew my feelings the night you fell on me, smashing my foot, making me an invalid." He smiled; he felt emboldened. She offered no objection. "You must make retribution.... I've needed a nurse-maid ever since, and you must make amends." Afraid he had perhaps gone too far with his teasing, he backed off, releasing her hand. "Seriously, Anna, you know I don't want a nurse-maid." Trying to assess whether she believed him, he stopped talking. He wanted her to believe him. Then he filled the silence with his whispered words: "I have never said these words to another." Anna had not spoken. He wouldn't let her. He knew all the objections and didn't want to hear them. But the moisture he saw welling in her eyes told him the truth—that she did not want him to leave her alone. "I know the problems," he continued. "I have to be in France part of the year, and I want you to come with me when you can. You will love it! Endless painting sites and gallery connections. Anna, you must agree, if not for me, for France." He crossed his heart in jest. "France needs your landscapes, and I'm forbidden by a complex and ancient French law from carting them over there without the artist's company."

There was a pause while he further processed whether he needed to lighten up.

"Moreover, I can have all the work here I want and I plan to buy a cottage here." He wanted to continue saying, "with your approval in hopes that it will be yours as well," but thought perhaps he had said enough for now.

Anna, relieved to learn that her feelings for him had not been misplaced, struggled to hold back tears. Christian pushed back his chair, rose, and pulled her to her feet. She hugged him as tightly as she could. That was her answer. And when they kissed, applause swelled from around them. Christian, surprised, nearly forgetting where he was, turned and saw three of his employees at a table across the dining room. He gave them a slight, embarrassed, but proud bow.

"Just mending employee relations."

"Yeah, just don't ever pull that on us," came the reply.

"Let's get out of here," Christian said, feeling complete to be able to take Anna's arm.

49

A Threatening Fork

Why hadn't he noticed before the way Noel worked over her food? The manner with which she used her fork like a weapon ready to lunge, or as a baton-waving cheerleader? Had he not noticed this before? Did two legs in casts make him that vulnerable? Or was it that he had been confounded by her perfect legs? Robert watched Noel as she sat across the breakfast table from him. She talked a marathon of words; obligatory sentences following a rush of hyphenated thoughts never seeming to reach the finish line. And in between bites she propped her elbow on the table, fork in raised hand, food for the next bite on fork, then she popped it into her gaping mouth, and fork went back up in the air, and sat there on her raised arm until impaling the next bite. Never did she lay down her arm or fork; rather in between her spiel, she twirled the fork, flipped it, and sometimes she reminded him of a conductor about to lead an unseen orchestra. When he took her out for dinner, had she waved her fork around? My God, he hoped not. Love must truly be blind if he had overlooked that.

When he was confined and helpless after the accident and Noel had taken charge, she was eye candy, and he had thought her a soothing angel. A vision. A woman to win. Now clearly, if she didn't watch it, she was in the process of taking a back seat to Melody and Anna. *Anna*. Something he could not have thought would happen. Dignified Anna. Anna who didn't rattle on so, or guffaw loudly in public. When was it that he thought Anna talked too much? He couldn't remember. In his recall, now, Anna seemed to leave him space. Solid, sensible, even pretty, Anna. He and she had made a good home together.

Should he tell Noel? No, she's apt to knock him down. He wanted to whack her arm out from under that raised fork. He needed distance, quiet time to think. And Noel had quit her job and wanted to hang around his plant. During work hours. Disaster.

After Peter Lytton had plugged the channel for cash and spending, Noel had wisely, in her opinion, taken a dive out of that engagement. She had learned that marriage to a movie mogul didn't necessarily equate with an up-market life—too many short ups and long downs. Expenses were wild, and money always had to be put aside and hoarded for the unexpected flops. (Actors couldn't seem to get into character or cooperate if they weren't paid on time.) Now, however, she firmly expected to have a proper lifestyle with Robert Randall; one in the exact image that, for her, constituted the good life. Hadn't she loved Peter, a friend had asked. Well, yes she had. Still did. But you know love needs an injection when discretionary spending develops anemia, she had answered. Besides, she also loved Robert. One can love many men. Don't men love many women?

She was talking again. "I'm glad dear, that you haven't yet put a binder on a house," Noel said, in between chewing. We're going to entertain often...your customers, and the plant engineers. We'll need a spacy home...open spaces, glass sliders to a pool with a wrap-around deck. Heated pool, so we'll have a longer season." Her eyes rounded large with excitement. "I have the perfect house in mind, and it's a wee bit larger than the one you were thinking about."

He knew the house she meant. A palace. "Noel, money is tighter now than it was before my divorce. I'm paying alimony and child support, and you seem to have quit work...no income there."

Noel gave him her type of understanding smile: half smirk, head tilted sideways. He spoke nonsense.

"I've had to pull back production a bit, due to losing the Bauter sales," he said. "And there are the expenses of closing one plant to consolidate. I don't have that building sold yet, and there are taxes, insurance, maintenance, and security to pay until it sells. And there's the expense of upgrading my computer system; quite necessary and in the long time that will pay for itself. But the initial outlay comes first. All of that comes first." He thought he had already covered these facts with her. Had she listened?

"But, dear, our new home will help with sales. A place to entertain clients. A good marketing plan. My heart is set on it."

"I'll go according to *my* financial plan, and what there is to spend," he said coolly.

Noel ignored his scowl.

"I'm not in the habit of going into unnecessary debt, or of exceeding my income. I sit down twice a month with the accountants and review exactly where my company and I are financially."

"But, dear, you're not looking at the long view."

He wouldn't argue. He had long ago learned the power of not needing to be right. He got up from the table, leaving her to finish eating alone. He went to the sink and silently washed up food-encrusted dishes left there from the night before when, each thinking the other would do the washing-up, they had watched TV for a few hours before going to bed. Noel had said she wasn't used to the new routine yet, but she would get used to doing the work in time. He realized this was different from when she nursed him at his former home, for Belle was there to do the cleanup. Now Noel drank more at night, and didn't show her puffy face in the morning before 11:00. How hard could it be to get used to not having a job, he wondered. Being home all day? These days he put together a bowl of cereal for his early breakfast and then headed to the plant to be there by 7:00 when the men arrived.

Then all too often Noel would arrive at noon and ask him to take her to lunch. The first few times he had found it amusing, a nice distraction, but it had begun to wear. Then, even though he would decline, saying that he had been leaving the plant too often—that he must stick with his men; his workload did not break for lunch—Noel would hang around, interrupting his concentration and his drive. He would sense the disaffection under her skin. When he wouldn't give her attention, she would select one of the workers and, with a flirty manner, drill him about his project. The men couldn't work that way. Robert began to want her out of the plant. Forever out of the plant. She didn't understand a plant and its workflow, and didn't really want to hear about it.

So at dinner one night, after what seemed like a full week of this problem, Robert's suppressed irritation flared when he saw Noel's fork suspended in air. It seemed to be a trigger pointed at him.

"Noel, we have to change something." He wanted to tell her to bring down her fork, and keep it down, stop waving it around, but couldn't bring himself to treat her like an untrained child. Even so, his anger and frustration spilled out into other areas and forced him to speak. "I apologize if this is hurtful for you, but I don't want you to come to the plant again." Her puzzled look stopped him, but only for a second. He had to do this now. "It's distracting for me, and it's disaster for my men while they struggle for perfection. The other day when you quizzed Tom Banks while he applied fiberglass, he botched the job and it had to be redone. A costly waste of time and material. Held up production. He didn't blamed his mess on you, but I saw what happened."

Frown lines divided Noel's brow. Did she hear right? "But, I'll miss you during the long days," she said. "And I find the plant interesting, and I had hoped we could have more lunches together."

How did the beautiful, leggy nurse, self-aware, seemingly comfortable in her cocoon, become so demanding and whiny, Robert wondered.

"Noel, I rarely stop for lunch during work days. My men do, but as owner, I don't have that luxury."

"But that's six days a week, and on occasion, seven. You used to love having lunch with me." She pushed her lips up into a pout, and raked food around on her plate like an impatient child.

"That's true, but I was negligent, and it cost my men too much wasted time when they needed me for questions. Our luxury yachts are complicated to build and demanding of all our skills. Nearly each piece is hand crafted, welded, caulked, painted or stained and varnished. Not something that can be fabricated quickly; not kindergarten blocks." He sighed and took a deep breath to allow his speech to carry its weight. "Each boat's interior is different and as demanding as putting together an intricate puzzle, and my men are skilled craftsmen, highly paid, but I'm the naval architect. And, anyway, usually you and I have Sundays together. And we have down-time at the plant twice a year, a week each, I can take time off then."

"Terrific! Two weeks a year!"

He wasn't happy with her sulk. It appeared the woman had no will at all to understand. Just like a blocked, spoiled child. "This is the way it has to be until I recoup from the changes. Surely you're not insensitive to the economy moves I've made. I traded in the Porsche for a utility pickup, and sold the Cessna. That drastically lowered expenses. I help you with cleaning and cooking so we can do without a housekeeper. I've even dropped a few memberships for the time being. And we can still eat out a couple times a week."

The pout Noel passed to him annoyed him further. "And as for a larger house, it's out of the question. You go ahead and watch TV, I'll do the washing-up and then I'm going for a walk." He rose from the table and carried his dishes to the sink. He did not look back at Noel.

50

The Unreliable Appearance of Things

"**D**ad was funny, Mom. He didn't know how to fry eggs."
"Uh-huh. I can believe that without a stretch," Belle said. She flashed a grin to Anna.

"Yeah, he made us lead him through it. We had to tell him to put a little butter in the pan and break in eggs. We had to show him how to break eggs; how to turn them over, which pan to use." The children looked for Anna's and Belle's reaction to the strange ways their father had; at how handicapped he had become. "He got way behind and we had to make the toast. He couldn't remember anything about making breakfast. He thought pepperoni was breakfast sausage. We had a lot of fun. We *laughed* at him!"

Had the universe just flip-flopped? Anna's policy was never to quiz the children after their visits to Robert and Noel. She didn't want to turn the children into little reporters. But on this occasion, the idea of Robert's cooking breakfast, *or cooking anything*, was too much, and curiosity won over discretion.

"Where was Noel?"

"Oh, Noel was in bed. She doesn't get up until 11:00."

Belle and Anna couldn't deny the amused looks they exchanged. Ah. Belle thought, all those years with both of them waiting on Robert, and now he's having a wake-up call; probably wishing he could give Noel a wake-up call. *Chuckle, chuckle*, He's being tested. He will not for long put up with a woman who sleeps until 11:00. If Belle could say anything good about Robert, he was hard working and expected everyone else to be as well.

The next morning, as he drove to the plant, Robert thought about the fleeting days, and the swiftly approaching boat show in Manhattan. His company was in good shape; another yacht order had come in that he would sign during the show, with options for more. That would set up the rest of the year. He looked forward to that, he throve on his work; he had made good business decisions. He thought about his private life; he had made some mistakes, a few whoppers. Of course he wasn't invited to the usual New Year's Eve party that Anna and he had always hosted; those were wonderful. A nice crowd. Even though she wasn't particularly sociable when it came to large groups, Anna, with Belle and the caterers, went all out. He would miss that. He wondered whether Melody and Cass would be there. Cass came around to the plant now and then to follow up on system performance. Strange guy, Cass: sleepwalking through life had turned his drive into drivel. Cass had no idea that he and Melody had been involved with each other. If he did know, Robert thought—he didn't care.

He thought about his lack of sleep; stressful dreams kept waking him; dreams wherein he was desperately seeking Anna, never finding her. In one dream he was in a multi-storied building going from floor to floor, in and out of stairwells, up and down, and finally yelling, "Anna." Someone shouted back that Anna was on the sixth floor. But the floors weren't marked, and no one could tell him which one was the sixth. And so he went up and down hunting the sixth and never finding it. And then, when he went outside in the extremely dark night, he could see Anna inside a brightly lighted window. And he couldn't get back in. He thought about Anna going around with some Frenchman. A *frog*. Isn't that what the Brits called the French? Frogs? And the frog spending time with his children, while he himself had begun to feel that he was missing out on knowing and growing with his children. Something he hadn't noticed before.

He thought about the boat show. Would Melody be working it again? He had grown fatigued with her, and Noel had turned his head so, that he had decided not to ask Melody to help at the January boat show; might stir up too much dust. What happened to move Noel into his life instead of Melody, he wondered. Could it be only that Noel wasn't married and Melody was? And Noel had no kids. He had heard how cut up Melody had been when she learned that he and Noel had married. Big mistake, it turns out. Noel's care after the accident had blinded him. Blind-sided? Didn't they say that many men fell for their nurses? And those legs! Right now, he would swap them for a pair that were up and walking around before 11:00, and standing before the sink to do dishes. He thought about Noel's dropping her nursing contracts, while at the same time wanting him to spend a bucket. More than he had. She would break him if he let her. He thought about trying to reach Melody. No need for her to fall out of his life altogether. Because the modeling work he had given her had boosted her career, she might not be working the show at all. Working the boat show might well be beneath her now. He would give her a call.

51

Surfacing

For three days Melody had shrouded herself in a trunk in their damp cellar, refusing to ingest anything but water, and little of that. Cass didn't know what to do. When he asked her if he could do anything, call anyone, she would moan a pathetic no. When he suggested calling Ben, as a friend, she almost screamed no. Had his own actions brought this about, Cass wondered, or was it something not related to himself? Although he had discouraged Joselyn some weeks back—as usual, it was the same-ol', same-ol', her clinginess had turned novelty into nausea—he still felt guilt.

Had his philandering habits led Melody to this? What caused her to go berserk so? He had had no warning. He knew he had been gone a lot, had done pretty much what he wanted, mistresses and such. But they had always lived that way, and anyway, Melody occasionally had her flings. Although he always thought he could have done better in marriage, it had worked out to be calm and convenient, easy on the nerves; handy for him, as he saw himself enfeebled much of his life, allowing pretty women to chase him. He could not resist. He and Melody hadn't had excess money to spend on each other. Not many vacations. And yet, he would spend on his secretaries and various flings he had going at the office, and Melody would buy jewels for herself, generally when their finances were at their worst. Once, the day after he told her that he had been laid off, she went straight out and bought herself a ruby they could not afford. At some point, he would feel contrite about his affairs, and would confess to Melody, would promise to remain faithful to her from that point on. He always meant it. She was always hurt, but not too hurt, he thought. And she never suggested leaving him, or getting a divorce. He didn't want a divorce after all—too much trouble. And another wife might not put up with his flings and lackadaisical work attitude—not bringing in a high salary. He had been laid off a few times for not being an aggressive salesman, and Melody put up with that. After each affair, it would only be a matter of time, two months at the most, before he would notice a new set of pretty legs at work, smile at their owner, and get her to fall for him. He couldn't help it. He was as handsome, laid back and vulnerable, as any man could be. That long-established routine could hardly be the cause of Melody's withdrawing into the cellar trunk. The twins' pleading had no effect. A couple times a day they would beseech her to come upstairs. She would reach out and hold their hands, but she couldn't reply to them.

He would go down and try again. She must be starved. He would cook something special for her—perhaps tempt her that way to stop this silly acting out.

What day is it? Though there were issues right below the surface begging for attention, Melody couldn't think. What year is it? Why didn't this damp hellhole of a trunk womb help her? What were those images she saw wafting through the dark? Two happy people in an old photo? It's she and the man she had just married, Cass; they had finished the marriage ceremony just a moment before the picture was taken. Married. Her fate sealed. There she stood in a white, short skirt, looking pleased as punch, her arm in Cass's. She could easily fake those smiles. But in fact, she did put her heart into the marriage, at least for a while. Did Cass look slightly worried? His image seemed to drift down from the cobwebs above her. Melody tried to make it out, but the light was dim, her vision clouded, and the weave of her body so frail. She remembered: she had met Cass at a concert. During intermission he came up to her and introduced himself. Two tall, blonde-haired, mirror images. That's how they must have looked to others. Later on, she asked *him* to marry *her*—didn't she? They would make beautiful children; she remembered saying that. Why not, he had said. He could not find a better combination than his genes with hers, and besides, he was rather weak willed; it felt comfortable to let her make those decisions. He said yes.

It was out of focus, but she thought their marriage of convenience began that way. Afterward, neither of them could stop looking around for other mates; Cass aware on some deep level that he had not pursued her; Melody aware that she had not been pursued. They felt the stirring of that unfulfilled need. Oh how, all those years, she had missed being pursued. Her brain was clearer now, but she had no strength.

Then the twins were born, killing any potential career for herself. Fortunately, the twins had inherited Cass's laid-back disposition and didn't present many challenges. She thought that was how it went. Life was easy. Nonetheless, the effort of living n a less-than-fulfilling marriage, took energy. Often they struggled to cope.

Though groggy from depression and the enervating effects of three days in a trunk in a damp cellar, the images were stronger now.

"It's unusual for us to consider walk-ins," the woman at the Ford Modeling Agency had said. Melody had braved up to walk in. She clearly remembered that. "But we'll give you a try. Modeling is not easy. You can look absolutely perfect, but not have traits necessary to please the camera. Some models look perfect to the eye, but flawed to the camera. Some flaws actually help, but others are fatal to the camera's eye."

Didn't it happen that way? That day, when she left the agency, she had a modeling assignment. A start-up. Soon she received more assignments. Cass rocked along in sales, neither excelling, nor disappointing.

Another vision: a face she had hated to see, never wanted to see again, *longed* to see. She focused on that compelling face, that silvery white hair, those searching eyes. She couldn't forget. She had made the large mistake of thinking that Robert, powerful, sexual, was all hers. He was sexual in ways her marriage had not provided, and she believed that she had completely filled his needs, and he would in turn fulfill hers. Mistakeful thinking. He was simply another flawed but, interesting, powerful man whom the Universe would forgive for his flaws. And she had had a role in his divorce from Anna! But marrying Noel? She had never seen that coming! Had never before felt such pain. If she ever got out of this trunk, she would take a flight somewhere. First class. If she could get out of here, she would hug the twins and then fly off. First-class. They would all go together: Cass and the twins. She needed to see Cass and the twins.

The dank, raw cellar air had soaked through her sweater and had coated her chest with scum. She had trouble breathing. Her hair was sticky. She tried to focus on the next image in the dark before her—looking down at her. The image grew closer.

"Won't you come up? Cass asked. "You've been here three days, and you must be starved. I've made chili...your favorite with three kinds of peppers and filet."

Melody struggled to focus. This *was* Cass. Worried Cass. Unusual for him to worry about her. She yearned to touch his face but her hands were heavy. How could she lift her hands?

"Where are the twins?" she whispered.

"Louise has taken them to playschool for me. I've worked hard to keep them occupied so their young hearts had minutes of freedom from worry."

"I want a banana split." Another whisper.

"Anything, anything," Cass said. "Let me help you out and I'll go make one."

"I'm cold," she said. "I want to brush my teeth."

"Yes. Yes. I'm sure you must," he comforted.

"I want to shave my legs. Comb my hair. Yes, help me up." A thin layer of damp dust had settled on her. "I want to soak in a tub of hot water. Wash my hair. Blow it dry. Dry. Dry. Anything dry. Put on a warm, dry robe."

Cass took her arms and began to pull her up. He thought that her joints and muscles would hurt from being limp for three days, so he got his arms around her waist and raised her as gently as he could until she firmly planted one leg over the trunk's side. He supported her weight while she raised the other leg over. Then she rested on the trunk's edge.

"Let me put down the lid and you can rest here more comfortably," he said.

She allowed him to pull her to a standing position and support her while he lowered the trunk's lid. Then he lowered Melody down onto the lid to rest. He thought that maybe she should have the banana split before she tried to make the stairs into the kitchen.

"Sit here a minute, Melody, while I make your banana split. I'll be right back. You need to sit a bit before you try to take the stairs." She was shaky, but he had little choice and he waited a minute to watch her. She seemed steady enough to sit while he rushed up to the kitchen, but her ashen color terrified him.

With Cass upstairs, Melody's eyes began to adjust to the light from the kitchen door. Sitting upright for the first time in three days she felt dizzy, had to firmly press down her hands on the trunk for support. Has it been three days? It seemed like three minutes; time had stood still. Though her mind was clearer now, she had no sense of the lost time. She really missed the twins and needed to get her arms around them. If she could get upstairs, she could do that. She had a dim feeling that they had been begging her to come up. She sat and gently rocked her body forward and back, eyes closed. Her crushing thought—how could she continue?

It seemed but an instant until Cass returned with the banana split. She slowly nibbled at it while he sat on the trunk with her and watched. Then, with a wavering hand, and not looking at him, she gestured toward him with the ice cream dish, which he took, setting it down on the floor. Finally her eyes turn to him with a plea to help her up the stairs.

52

Stranger Than We Could Have Known

In time, and at the right and proper time, Christian asked Anna to be his wife. And in time, and at the right and proper time, Anna said yes. All those nights of patiently, or perhaps impatiently hanging out at Harbor House had caused the Universe to smile on him. Sometimes, remembering, he would look with that particular French gleam of his at Anna, and remind her that he had spent his evenings at Harbor House to keep a lookout—ward off short guy—should he bother her.

"And I never knew," Anna said, "always thinking you to be home happily sharpening your lance." Then they would laugh at each trying to out-corny the other. And they would talk about where they would live. And what about Belle? They must have a room for Belle.

"Sorry I haven't called in a while, Stella. We're on the go full time; there's always more to do. Christian's been busy arranging for his cottage here to be leased."

"What's it like, Anna? What's his cottage like?"

"It's a cottage you might expect of an architect: added to and added to in interesting ways. Christian calls it a cottage, but there are four bedrooms and five bathrooms, and it's in a park setting surrounded by beautiful woods. I've put photos in the mail for you. And already I have two paintings in a gallery. And Stella, we haven't been able to reach Melody."

"We heard from Cass that she finally came out of the trunk," Stella said, "and when she did emerge, Cass said, tears rolled down her face, and she hugged and kissed them all as though her life depended on them. Cass is cooking good meals for her, now that she will eat something. None of us can figure out what happened to her. And she's never available."

Of course Ben knew, but that track—he would professionally block at the gate.

"I wonder what's behind that. I guess Melody is stranger than we could have known," Anna said. "And you know about her telling me that Christian was involved with a woman, and about her telling him I was at the cape. And then, when I finally had a chance to ask her about that, she mumbled apology and said, truly, she thought he was speaking of another friend of hers. As well, she said a few times that he had asked her out, and when I teased him about that, he said, 'Madam, warts will grow on my face if I'm not telling you the truth. I have never thought of any such idea'."

"Well, we've tried to keep them the loop," Stella said, "but she makes it hard. We can't get them to join us for anything. And, Anna, listen to this: Ben and I went over one day to help Cass when their sitter had cancelled, and Melody was not functioning, and there, smashed against the fireplace bricks, was that porcelain dish you gave her for a house gift. Pieces lying all over the place. And when I pulled out a cereal box, I found...what do you think...? Robert's little model Mercedes. It had been tucked in back behind cereal boxes."

"What could Melody have wanted with the little model?" Anna asked

"Well, I know it didn't drive there; gas tank's too small."

They laughed.

"I'm won't mention it to anyone but you...not even Cass; he has enough to worry about, but I pocketed the little car to save for Robert. Although, I'm not sure he's worth the effort."

"What strange goings on. Must be hard on the twins. I hope Melody continues to recover," Anna said.

"Her malaise seems to have something to do with Robert's marrying Noel; although we aren't sure why."

Stella could hardly contain her new information. "Ben and I will keep trying to look out for her, but we've been busy ourselves, Anna. We would both love to see you. How would you like to put us up for part of our honeymoon? There'll be a crowd...we want to bring Tess and David. Some honeymoon, huh!"

53

That Wasn't So Bad, Let's Do It Again

"It's so nice to hear your voice, Melody."

"Robert! Where are you?"

"In Manhattan. I've been thinking ahead to the boat show, and that triggered many wonderful memories, and I found myself thinking about you and wondering whether you would be working the show."

"No, I won't be. I've had some success lately with contracts that bring in much more money. They don't leave me with time to work the show, but I'll be around to visit. I've missed you. You can sell me a hundred-meter." She twittered that silly laugh again that he had always found annoying. Now it was welcome. "How have you been?" she asked. "Of course, I heard that you and Noel married...that was a surprise. I must say, it threw me for a while. I had no idea." It was easier for Melody now to speak about it lightly.

"Well, I've made some mistakes. We can talk about them if you would like to get together for a meal when you're in the city. I'll be working the show again, as you know. I'd like to talk. I can stay over any time. I'm at your disposal. Why wait? How about tonight?" He laughed. "I need your help with a problem."

"I'd enjoy that," Melody said. "We had good times together. I'll have to check with my sitter...Cass is out of town. I'll meet you at the show." She said bye and set down the phone. As she looked into her wardrobe for the right costume, she brushed up that knowing smile.

www.ingramcontent.com/pod-product-compliance
Lightning Source LLC
Chambersburg PA
CBHW050926120626
46552CB00001B/56